# Libya Story

James Ward

COOL MILLENNIUM BOOKS

3

This edition published 2021.

A CIP catalogue record for this book is available from the British Library.

ISBN: 978-1-913851-09-5

*Cover picture taken by the author shows Nelson's Column.*



This novel was produced in the UK and uses British-English language conventions ('authorise' instead of 'authorize', 'The government are' instead of 'the government is', etc.)

To my wife

## Chapter 1: A Mini Trilogy

*Episode 1: Present day. Islington, London*

John Mordred had been having the same dream for over a month now. It always began in the *Station Hauptbahnhof* in Berlin with him displaying Mabel's picture to passers-by. "Have you seen this lady?" he asked. (The quaint way he used 'lady', as if it was the nineteenth century.) "Have you seen the lady in this photo?" The few people he managed to speak to – the majority were always unreachable - seemed to fly by in the opposite direction. *No. No. No.* Like ghosts on a mission. Down through Germany he went, then Austria, Hungary, Serbia, village after village, town after town, country after country, until he arrived in Turkey. As he traversed the Anatolian peninsula, the crowds became slower, denser, more indifferent. They were totally focussed on their goal now, heads down, ploughing grimly against him towards that incredibly distant railway station in Berlin. By the time he reached the frontier with Syria, no one was interested in his inane little enquiry any more, much less the photo. It was always at this point that he had the same terrible realisation. He'd gone the wrong way. He should be in Italy. And because of that, it was almost certainly too late.

He awoke with a start.

He rubbed his eyes and swung his feet over the side of the bed. A nice sunny Tuesday morning. Ten minutes till his alarm went off, but he wouldn't need that any more, he was already full of adrenalin. He stood up and stretched.

Today was going to be different. Apart from anything else, today was *resignation day*. He picked up the single piece of junk mail from his front door, tossed it onto the sofa and went into the bathroom, showered, shaved, and combed his blond curly hair, stooping slightly, as usual, so he could see in the mirror. He ate two Weetabix in front of the television – *Good Morning Britain* was on, and the woman with the fez and the golden armlet had been longlisted for yet another literary prize – and surveyed his surroundings. Nothing worth remembering, really. All anonymous. And this was the last thing he'd ever do here: eat a bog-standard TV breakfast with a couple of newsreaders. Afterwards, when he was at a safe distance from Britain, he'd ring his mum. Ask her to put his things in storage for him, please. Or bin them. Mostly they weren't worth keeping, not even for sentimental reasons.

Anyway, he was only thirty-one. Plenty of time to accrue new rubbish if he wanted it. Better rubbish, even. The best.

He positioned himself about a metre from the window where he couldn't be seen and looked cautiously down into the street. Yes, there he was. About forty, Caucasian, big overcoat, slight paunch. Mitchell, he was called, apparently. One of twenty men and women who took turns to watch him or his flat. None of them was much good. He'd made the first nearly a fortnight ago. Six days later, he knew all their names.

And of course, that's why it would be safest to escape when he got to work. It'd be what they were least expecting.

Which didn't mean they weren't expecting it at all, oh no. They'd budgeted for every possibility, even the unlikeliest.

He put the kettle on and had two strong cups of tea, then donned his best suit – go out in style, that was his motto – and a pair of brown brogues, and he was ready. Time to head for the proverbial office.

He thought he'd be able to walk straight outside without feeling anything, but a sticky web of memories caught him just as he was about to open the door. It wasn't a big flat, so everything of note had happened just behind him, here in his living room. He took one last look: dim echoes of occasional visits by colleagues and family. Nothing outwardly interesting, but each one – because of what he did for a living, the fact that people didn't usually get across his threshold without excellent reasons – imbued with a special, unique significance.

And Phyllis. Ah, dear, yes. His heart turned over slightly and he exhaled a sigh. She'd been here. More than anyone else. She'd be at work now. His workplace. Their shared workplace, till today.

He probably wouldn't see her, though. She tended to avoid him now.

Good or bad? He didn't know.

If things had been different, he'd have fought back. Told her he loved her and so on. Flowers, texts, entreaties, public self-debasements, the works. But that wasn't possible any more. Not given Mabel.

He grabbed himself by the inner scruff of the neck, walked out onto the landing and locked the door behind him. Then downstairs and out of the building. He caught the usual bus to Lambeth Bridge, sat in his usual seat and used his phone to read his usual newspaper surrounded by the usual commuters in their usual clothes wearing their usual sour expressions. Somewhere rural, they'd probably have been his friends: after all, they'd been travelling to work together every day for the last four years. But this was London. No one did 'nice to see you again' here, not without cast-iron sureties. It usually ended in a stabbing, or that's what they thought. For all he knew, they might even be right.

Two seats behind him, Cordelia, a young black woman in a suit, sat pretending to read a novel. Another of his dear shadows. Oh, how he'd miss them.

He - and she - got off at the river embankment and walked briskly along Millbank. When he entered Thames House by its large gothic front door, she kept going. Doubtless she'd find her way inside later, maybe even by a different entrance. Meanwhile, Colin, the receptionist, was dealing with what looked like a group of policemen in plain clothes.

How did Mordred know they were policemen? Experience, partly: you learned to recognise types in this job. But also because, when he thought about it, he knew why they were here. They were here for him. They were going to arrest him.

In the normal course of things, he was expected to check in. But Colin knew him by sight, and this was his last day. What could anyone do? The police certainly wouldn't come after him, not on his way in. No, it was getting out again that would likely pose the problem.

He exchanged greetings with junior colleagues on his way to Ruby Parker's office. *Hello John, morning Steph; morning John, good to see you Guy; Hi John nice suit, hi Suki thank you; morning, morning; hello, morning, good morning.*

And then he was there. He knocked. Ruby Parker called 'enter'. He went inside.

A small black woman, probably in her mid- to late-fifties, probably in a skirt-suit although he couldn't see her bottom half since she was sitting behind her desk and didn't dignify his entry by standing. She looked as happy to see him as the people on the bus on the way in, but probably even less so on the inside. If she felt as she'd recently told him she did, she was doing an excellent job of hiding her antipathy.

"Good morning, John," she said.

"Just came to tell you I'm on my way now," he replied.

"You're adamant?" Spoken as if even she didn't know whether it was a question.

"Unless you've had a change of heart."

"Absolutely not. What I meant was, you're aware that this is almost certainly a one-way street?"

"We've had this discussion. What would you do in my position?"

She smiled thinly. "You're right. We *have* had this discussion. Good bye then, John. I won't wish you luck, for obvious reasons."

He closed the door behind him. Now it was just a case of getting out of here. Past the Annabels and the Alecs, in the first instance. Then the police.

Easy peasy.

*Episode 2: Six weeks before the present day. The Mediterranean Sea, 200 miles off the Libyan coast.*

10pm and the Odyssey was bustling. In Room OR2 another surgical operation was nearing a successful conclusion and 23-year-old Mabel Mordred and her 30-year-old colleague and lover, Jean-Marc Bouchet, were ordered to take a quick tea-break in the ship's mess. On a busy day, like today, everyone took it in turns to eat and grab an hour or two's sleep. No one had yet turned in for bed – *Médecins Sans Frontières* personnel were used to long shifts - but food was easier to procure, and just as important for concentration.

Cheese and tomato rolls and coffee. The two ate and drank in silence for the first minute because they were very hungry. Mabel had a pale complexion, black hair tied up in a bun, large eyes and thin mouth. A year ago, she'd been halfway to a first class medical degree at Cambridge when somehow – a kind of mental collapse? she still didn't know - the full horror of the Syrian refugee crisis seemed to reach out and demand her on-the-spot presence *without delay*: come exactly as you are, ask no questions, don't even stop to gather your things. She dropped everything as if in response to a divine command, qualified precipitately as a nurse and joined MSF.

By contrast, Jean-Marc was the finished article: a graduate of the *Université de Montpellier* with four years' surgical experience, an established ability to subordinate moral importunity to practical possibility, and the authority of a conventional career-path behind him. Tall, with short hair, small ears and perfect teeth, he ate leisurely as if making the most of his fare.

Nine hours earlier, the Odyssey had come across a Zodiac, a rubber dinghy with sixty people aboard. Ninety minutes' later, it had been hailed by a German commercial vessel with three hundred and forty people to transfer. Since then, there had been one baby delivered, six broken limbs mended, a variety of minor surgeries, and all the routine treatment of dehydration, scabies, dysentery, fuel burns, excrement-caked flesh. The ship was an ex-merchant vessel, chartered from a firm in Bonn and with a crew of Croatians who tended to keep their distance from the refugees. Behind the mess was a small morgue and three operating rooms. The hospital was a portable cabin on deck. Right now, most of the migrants were down in the hold. The ship was on its way back to Messina.

After satisfying their initial hunger, the two medics talked about the problems and practicalities of the latest rescue for five minutes, then got up. Before they parted, Jean-Marc took Mabel's arm.

"I've been thinking about Libya again," he said brusquely. "I've changed my mind."

"About what?" Mabel said.

"You're not coming. It's too dangerous."

"Er, hang on, I think we - "

"We can't talk about this now. I just wanted to prepare you. We'll discuss it later."

They parted without further comment and went to their respective duties. Thankfully, the ops were all done. What remained was aftercare and encouragement. She felt too angry to offer much of the latter. Then, recognising this, she felt guilty. She was a nurse. Her personal issues had no place here.

But still.

What the hell did he mean, *you're not coming*? Who was *he* to decide what *she* should do? If she wanted to go to Libya … she would. Wouldn't she?

No. No, she wouldn't.

Because he was right. The time of reckoning had come. Completely out of the blue. But it had. She'd always known it might.

She could see what it entailed. Even through a film of bitter tears. He'd get back together with Rima, obviously. Rima was his wife, she'd given birth to his son; he'd believed she was dead, killed in an airstrike near Daraa on her way to the border – and now here she was again, in Libya, a full year later.

Of course he'd go back to her. It was the right thing. He had to do the right thing.

And she had to let him.

Why hadn't Rima called him before? Why wait a year?

Because she'd been injured, that's why. And she believed he was dead.

And neither of them *was* dead. They were both *alive* and now they had a whole shared *life* together in front of them! *Hooray!* It was the happiest of happy endings.

For everyone except poor, pathetic Mabel Mordred.

She was due a fortnight's holiday next week. They'd been planning to go to Libya together, fetch Rima and Hassan and … What?

Actually, what specifically *had* they been planning to do? In that war-zone? More particularly, what had *he* been planning to do? "Hi, Rima, I know you're my wife, and this is my son, and I know you thought I'd been killed and so on, but I'd like you to meet the new woman in my life. She's ten years younger than you and she's called Mabel."

"Hi, Rima. I'm Mabel. Sorry I slept with your husband, but in all fairness, you were supposed to be dead."

What then? *Rima, I want a divorce* was unthinkable. Either Jean-Marc could see that or he couldn't. If he could, he should have spoken up by now. *Mabel, it's over* would have been his best option, brutal but moral. If he couldn't, he probably wasn't worth sticking around for. Either he was a thug or an idiot.

A complete bloody mess. But at least her immediate course of action was clear. She had to cut all ties with him.

Love – what did that have to do with anything?

Thirty minutes later, she turned in for an hour's sleep. She was the only person aboard who had the luxury of a single cabin – 'luxury': big enough for a bed and a foot of floor-space - and only because she was so young and everyone here felt a little sorry for her, the once exceptionally promising doctor cut down, by her own hand, to ten-a-penny nurse-status. She climbed into her bunk and cried.

After an hour, the knock at her door she'd been half expecting. She'd exhausted her well of tears now and had her words prepared. Might as well get it over with.

"It's not what you think," Jean-Marc said when she opened the door.

She scoffed. Of all the hackneyed phrases.

"It's over," she said, returning cliché for cliché.

"Rima re-married."

"Er, what?"

"She thought I was dead. She met another man. They married. Obviously, she's got to 'divorce' me, but we were never married under French law, so that shouldn't be too problematic. The boy's almost certainly mine, of course. She wants me to help her get her new family into Europe. It's the least I can do."

"Why - why didn't you tell me any of this before?"

"We never get to talk here. Not properly, of course we don't. Can I come in?"

She stood aside. He sat on the bed, pulled her down next to him and kissed her.

"What's she doing in Libya?" Mabel asked, disengaging herself. No good allowing herself to be seduced. She had to think. It might well be bullshit.

"I don't know what you mean," he said.

"I mean, everyone knows nearly all the Syrians are going north now. Egypt's turned inhospitable and Libya's a basket-case. Everyone we've been picking up in the Med for months has been Eritrean, Libyan or sub-Saharan. Why did Rima risk bringing her son to the Maghreb?"

"You'd have to ask her husband. They're southern Syrians, from just above the Jordanian border. It was probably easier to head that way rather than Turkey. Maybe they went south and just decided to keep on walking. After all, Zaatari's full, the

Mrajeeb Al Fhood camp's got a reputation." He shrugged. "It's academic, anyway. They're here now. I've got to get them out."

"I thought we were going to do it together."

"I wasn't thinking when I said that. I don't want you getting harmed. It's dangerous enough for me. Your presence won't achieve anything."

"Why can't they get on a boat? And we'd meet them?"

He smiled. "We're not a pickup service. Even if we were: cash. They haven't any."

"What's your plan exactly?"

"I'll have to get Rima and Hassan out first on the pretext that we're married and he's my son. Her husband will have to come later. He accepts that."

She took a deep breath and exhaled slowly. "Where does this leave *us*?"

"I love you. You know that. Look, I really can't tell you how sorry I am. If I'd had the slightest suspicion that Rima might be alive, I'd never have got involved with you – or anyone. For both our sakes. As for 'us', you're entitled to have second thoughts about me, I agree. All you have to do is say the word and I'll pack my bags. After this mission, you never need see me again. It'll be horrible – for me – but I'll understand."

"I don't want that."

"I love you, Mabel. Just give me a few weeks and I'll sort everything out, I promise."

"Does Rima – know about us?"

"It was the first thing I told her. A confession. But – but she was delighted. That's the main reason I thought it'd be good for you to accompany me to Libya. She's desperate to meet you. I let her enthusiasm get the better of me, I'm afraid, but now I'm seeing things in a more sober light, I realise it's a bad idea. She says the media's exaggerating the dangers, but it isn't. She's just got used to conflict, that's all."

"I hope I *can* meet her. Not necessarily in Libya."

"We can Skype her any time you like. It's probably a bit late now, but tomorrow."

"Does she speak English?"

"A little. And you've got a little Arabic. Together, you'll bridge the language barrier."

"What part of Libya's she living in?"

"Tripoli."

Mabel nodded. Everywhere in Libya was bad, but it could be worse. Like Sirte, where ISIS was. Or Benghazi where General Haftar's LNA was having it out with the Revolutionary Shura Council.

They didn't say any more. Magically, it was beginning to feel all right again. Outside, the wind picked up. The thrum of the engine and the sound of happy voices somewhere along the corridor augmented her reassurance. There was nothing more to say, not yet. She lay on the bed, and he lay beside her. After a few minutes, they fell asleep. It had been an exhausting day.

They awoke to the blare of the klaxon that doubled as an emergency call. Outside the cabin, people were running. The door opened with a bang and Bjorn stood there, a forty-something Swede with black hair, circular-lens glasses and a goatee. His job was to round up the sleepers.

"Come on, Lovebirds!" he barked.

Difficult to tell whether there was disapproval in his voice. No reason for it. Everyone aboard knew about them. They leapt up as if they'd been doing something wrong only because they were half asleep. They put one foot robotically in front of the other and followed their colleagues to the upper deck.

"We can't take any more passengers surely," Mabel heard Jean-Marc saying. "We've got a full complement."

"Captain's scuppered his ship," Bjorn replied. He left the corollary unspoken. In that case, except in the most extreme circumstances, 'full' or not, MSF was bound to help.

It happened a lot. The captain of a particularly clapped-out migrant boat breached his hull to force a passing ship into a rescue-mission. A severely overloaded unreliable vessel could only make headway so long as its load remained evenly spread. Once people realised they were sinking, they panicked. For that reason, usually, lots of them drowned.

When Mabel and Jean-Marc emerged on deck, it was dark. They could just see the boat's outline off the starboard bow, going round in ever decreasing circles like an insect whose abdomen had been crushed. People were yelling and screaming, lots already in the sea.

The Odyssey came alongside and ropes were thrown, lifeboats lowered. The distressed vessel was a wooden fishing sloop, almost underwater now. In the deck's centre, people clambered out of an exit from the lower levels. No one was helping: the reverse: they seemed to be standing on each other, or dragging one another down or backwards in an effort to get out before the boat sank, pulling them down with it. Mostly, the little that could be seen of them through the gloom, they looked manic.

"Look after this for me," Mabel heard someone next to her say. A phone was thrust into her hand. Whoever it was grabbed a rope and jumped off the side. A second later, he was on the deck of the doomed boat, taking people's arms and wrenching them to safety from the hold. It was a lost battle for most of those down there: they'd probably already drowned.

She looked at the phone then at the person doing the heroics and suddenly she realised it was Jean-Marc. Her stomach flipped and she shouted his name at the top of her voice as if that would help.

Looking back later, she thought she must have had a premonition. At that precise moment, something unheard-of happened. The boat's deck seemed to split lengthwise. Everyone aboard lurched in every direction and mostly ended in the water. The boat sank as quickly as if someone was pulling it from beneath. Jean-Marc and everyone in his immediate surrounds simply disappeared below the surface.

Meanwhile, the Croatian crew were forcing their way between the medics and the rails. They'd seen Jean-Marc and they weren't about to allow a repeat performance. Ropes and lifejackets and rubber rings, yes, and they were happy to help. Personnel, no.

The first migrants were already coming aboard now. Bjorn grabbed Mabel by the shoulders and made her look at him.

"You've got a job to do," he told her firmly. "OR2. Go now."

She looked at him as if he was mad.

*"Now!"* he yelled.

Of course, yes. But couldn't he see she'd be no good until – that she had to - ?

But she was already moving in the required direction.

She was in shock. She recognised the symptoms. She'd be no good to anyone like this and five minutes later, Bjorn himself clearly reached the same conclusion. He found her as she was putting on a pair of surgical gloves and told her to go to the mess. One of the Croatians had been told to keep an eye on her. A tall muscular man in a blue overall, he sat her down solemnly at one of the tables, took up position opposite her and folded his arms. He didn't speak. A cup of strong tea appeared apparently from nowhere.

Thirty minutes later, Celine appeared in green surgical kit and gloves. Celine Dufour: they'd spent an hour talking back in Messina while they were waiting for the Odyssey's all-clear. She looked emotional. She sat down next to Mabel and took her hand. She wiped her eyes with her free sleeve.

"I've some terrible news," she said.

Mabel lost track of time after that. They took her up on deck to see Jean-Marc's body before its transfer to the morgue. But this was a major disaster: lots of people had died, and it would probably be on the front pages of all the newspapers tomorrow.

It wasn't until she got back to Messina and she was finally alone for the first time that she realised she had his phone. She waited till a day later, when she was on the bus to Rome, to access it. She sat next to an old man in a beret. Outside, the scenery passed in a haze of olive groves and arid hills. *5 new messages*.

None from his parents, thank God. No, they were all from Rima.

Rima. All that was left of Jean-Marc now.

Her mind went blank for a moment and then it was like a shaft of light had burst in. Suddenly, she knew exactly what she had to do. My God, it was so obvious.

And she was travelling in the wrong direction!

*Episode 3: Four weeks before the present day. St John's Gardens, London, 1pm*

A shady meeting in a park, a brief exchange of information, an abrupt departure – the stuff of espionage stories everywhere. Only this one was different. Yes, they were spies; yes, their behaviour followed the rubric, or it soon would. But they both worked for the same organisation, and in the same department, and at the same pay-scale. Two well-dressed women in their early thirties; one blonde, petite and straight-backed; the other much taller, dark-haired, with more of the *haute couture* about her, even though her clothes were understated: a beige skirt-suit and matching heels.

"I take it there's a problem between you and John," Annabel, the blonde woman said when her friend sat on the bench next to her.

"You could say that," Phyllis replied evasively. She hadn't planned on meeting a colleague here, but there was no escaping once their eyes met. And Annabel was the last person she wanted to talk to about John. Was her being here an accident? Who could tell? The one thing everyone said about her was that she was opaque. Even her husband agreed.

"What do you have in your sandwiches?" Annabel asked.

"Fish paste. You?"

"Cucumber. Always the same. Three slices per sandwich. And a tiny little film of butter."

How to keep a conversation about cucumber sandwiches going? Not possible. But they couldn't just sit here in silence. In the course of wondering how to obviate the silence, however, quite a lot of silence actually occurred, and when the time came to break it, Phyllis realised it wasn't so objectionable. She held her tongue. She could very happily spend the next ten, fifteen minutes – however long it took – like this.

"What about your drink?" Annabel asked.

"Water."

"Me too."

More silence. Annabel removed a small plastic bottle from her bag and took a sip. She put the top back and resumed her cucumber sandwich. The clouds parted. She put on a pair of sunglasses. Not at all the sort of thing Phyllis would have expected: the frames were subtly heart-shaped. Probably best to pay them a compliment.

"They look very stylish," she said.

"Miu Miu 54 RS Noir," Annabel replied. "Hand crafted in Italy."

"Wow."

"They're no reflection on me. I didn't even choose them, Tariq did. He paid two hundred pounds for them, which is a complete waste of money, but I couldn't tell him that, because they were a present."

"No, of course not."

"Don't you tell him, please. If you see him."

"I won't."

Annabel laughed. "Sorry, I don't know why I said that. What has John done?" she went on, reverting to her original subject. "You two seemed to be getting along so well together. I had really high hopes for you. I trust it was nothing to do with the villa?"

"The villa was lovely, thank you. No, it was nothing to do with that."

"You don't have to tell me. It's just, I'm probably your closest colleague, added to which I'm female, and I know John pretty well - what a complete oddball he can be - so I thought I might be able to empathise, and you might appreciate that, and it might make you happier."

"Thank you."

"Obviously, if you choose to confide in me, I won't tell anyone."

All the time she spoke, Annabel looked straight ahead – even with her sunglasses on it was possible to tell that – and so there was no eye-contact designed to facilitate a confession. It was all completely impersonal, and almost certainly genuine. Annabel was constructed in such a way that, on a deep level, she probably wasn't remotely interested in The John and Phyllis Problem. And yet she really did want to help. She considered it her duty.

"It all went very well for a while," Phyllis said, biting the bullet. "Then I went to meet his family."

"Always a testing time."

"Oh, you betcha."

"Surely, you've met them before?" Annabel said. "Hannah, the pop impresario? Charlotte the bespoke candle-maker? There's another one, as well: a prize-winning novelist. Julie, I think."

"Julia. That's right. And another. Mabel. She wasn't there."

"And his mother and father, of course. Where did you meet them? At home in Hexham? Or were his parents in London to see *Seven Brides for Seven Brothers*?"

"I didn't know that was on."

"I'm not sure it is. I simply chose it as an example. They love coming down to London to see a show and meet their son. His mother always gives him a twenty-pound note as a goodbye-present when she's on her way back up north. 'Towards the electricity bill', she says. Incredibly touching. Anyway, what did they do wrong?"

Phyllis raised her eyebrows in a 'what *didn't* they do wrong' way. "I went to his parents' house in Hexham. First mistake. I was outnumbered six-to-one on unfamiliar territory. And they're all hard-line Remainers. And mostly Labourites. I counted at least two Corbynistas."

"Whereas you're a proud Conservative and committed Brexiteer. I see the problem."

"I didn't *have* to say anything. I could have held my tongue. I suppose."

Annabel laughed. "Did alcohol play any part?"

"A small one, but none of us was drunk. They just went *on* and *on* about what a disaster it was, and how you'd have to have been *stupid* to vote Leave, and what the chances were of provoking a second referendum so *justice* could actually be done, and so on and so forth. In the end, I just snapped. It didn't start off as a blazing row, but it quickly escalated into one."

"I wish I could have been a fly on the wall. It sounds hilarious."

"Maybe one day it will be. Right now, it's too raw."

"I didn't think John was a passionate either-sider. I always imagine him more worried about pigeons and donkeys."

Phyllis shook her head. "At least he's not like bloody Hannah or self-satisfied Charlotte or stuck-up Julia."

"So you dumped him. He didn't dump you."

"Correct. We're too different. Oh, I'm sure he can *live* with the fact that I'm a Brexiteer and I'm not a vegetarian and I don't give all my money to Oxfam and Christian Aid. But for how long? There comes a point at which you've got to ask: what's the actual basis of the relationship? If your values are that different, you're probably heading for a fall."

"The sex was all right, though?"

Phyllis rolled her eyes. "People always say that as if it's a significant consideration. I'm an attractive woman, Annabel. I've been a bloody model, for God's sake. I expect good sex as standard. It's not necessarily any kind of gateway to a meaningful future."

"John's miserable, if it's any consolation."

"I know he is. I know we both are. But I'm not a teenager. I've got to consider my future with *this*." She tapped her temple.

They lapsed back into silence again. Annabel finished her sandwiches and drank more water. "Our meeting here was no accident," she said eventually.

Phyllis sighed. Of course it wasn't.

"I meant what I said about wanting to help," Annabel went on. "You *are* my friend, Phyllis. Probably the best I've ever had."

Phyllis turned to look at her. She felt both deeply moved and betrayed at the same time. She suddenly wanted to cry, which was rare for her. "Ruby Parker asked you to have a word with me for some reason," she hazarded. "Is that it?" It was all it could be. Annabel didn't run errands for anyone beneath a Head of Section. She certainly wouldn't be here on John's behalf.

"That's right," Annabel replied.

Phyllis ground her teeth, then sat back. "I'm listening."

"You noticed the younger sister, Mabel, wasn't there when you met the family. The fact is, right now, she's in Libya. 'Unknown abductors' have commandeered her phone – almost certainly militiamen of some stripe, although that doesn't say much: there are about five hundred miniature armies in Libya now - and they've been in touch with John. They don't know he's a spy, obviously, because Mabel doesn't know. But they do know he goes abroad a lot, and they're convinced they can use him. He 'sells machine parts', if you remember: that's what he tells his family. To cut a long story short, they're demanding money – lots of it - and gun-running. For starters. Anyway, Blue are sending a rescue team. Knowing Blue, it'll probably go wrong. The point is, John's been making noises to suggest he wants to go out there alone. Ruby Parker's having none of it, of course. She's fobbed him off with the Blue op for now, but I understand he's already issued her with an ultimatum. She wants us all to keep an eye on him."

Phyllis put the last of her sandwich away. She didn't feel hungry any more. "My God. Poor John."

"Poor Mabel."

"She didn't go over there – to Libya - voluntarily, then?"

"Stranger things have happened. But no. She was lured by the wife of a man she was in a relationship with. The man died unexpectedly, right in front of her eyes, shortly before she left Europe, just under a fortnight ago. The theory is, the woman presented herself as a would-be migrant, and Mabel went to help her get into Italy. We don't know how genuine the woman is. In all likelihood, she's been kidnapped too. It's a booming industry in Tripoli."

"I'm not re-starting my relationship with John, if that's what Ruby Parker thinks. That wouldn't be right. What sort of 'ultimatum' did he give her?"

"A resignation one."

"That's it then. He's leaving. She's not going to cave in to blackmail. I wouldn't."

"That's the strange thing about John Mordred and Ruby Parker. They're two of a kind. Both incredibly stubborn."

"What a tragedy," Phyllis said sadly.

"As I say, she wants us all to keep an eye on him."

"With a view to what?"

"Stopping him going, of course. Not stopping him resigning. That's a done deal."

"It's utterly bloody childish. As you rightly say, they're two of a kind."

Annabel stood up. "Well, I'm heading back to Tracy Island now. Coming?"

"I'll just sit here for a moment, if that's okay. Get my thoughts together."

"Would you like me to stay?"

"No, no: you go ahead. I won't be long." It was the last thing she wanted. And she could tell Annabel wasn't serious. She'd delivered her package; time to get back to the sorting office. No, best to be alone.

Annabel left without a backwards glance. Phyllis gave the rest of her sandwich to the pigeons. She knew she wasn't supposed to, but it was what John would do, and she didn't know quite how she felt about him now. After that meeting with his family, she'd felt sullied somehow. The things she believed in – the essential decency of Theresa May, the merciful escape Brexit had been, the sordid grubbiness of Jean-Claude Juncker – had been trampled. Well, apart from the last one. And John hadn't stood up for her. He'd been more interested in 'keeping the peace'. Which meant he was on *their* side, really. Obviously he was.

As for MI7, Ruby Parker would regret digging her heels in as soon as he was out of the door – she probably thought he was bluffing – and from then on, things would get progressively worse. And Annabel was no kind of friend. Of her other colleagues, Edna and Ian were seven years younger than her. Alec was ten years older. The work was okay, but she could do better.

The more she thought about it, the more she could see that although there were lots of courses open to her now, her best by far was to take a leaf out of John's book. Time for a fresh start. The country had got one, and fate had thrown her an identical opportunity.

The key to resigning was to make it absolutely clear that hers was an independent decision. She wasn't doing it out of sympathy for John, much less in solidarity with him. No, she'd taken a good look at herself and decided she'd be better off striking out on a fresh path. Some kind of business venture; it didn't matter what. She could plan that while she was seeing out her notice. And she could go anywhere. She'd had her fill of London. Somewhere provincial where people were a bit friendlier.

Anywhere but Hexham.

## Chapter 2: Whoops, There Goes the Ground

Mordred took the lift to the first floor and turned left along the corridor that led to the rear of the building. Not a moment to lose: Ruby Parker had just ordered his immediate detention.

Till now she'd held the fewest cards. She'd accepted he was about to resign, but didn't know the precise time or manner. Your classic phoney war. She didn't want to be the one to make the first real move – all those agents watching his flat notwithstanding - because there was always the slim possibility he might have a change of heart. Even today, going into her office, the humble climb-down was still a theoretical possibility, otherwise she'd have had a roughneck visibly on hand to escort him to the police, down in reception.

Only when the clock stopped ticking on his notice and the word 'goodbye' passed his lips – those two things together, not either singly - could she be absolutely certain. She'd be on the phone right now, mustering a posse.

Its purpose, of course, would be to convey him into the waiting arms of the counter-terrorism officers on the ground floor. Naturally, no one could prove he was on his way to Libya, even less that he was in thrall to terrorists – GCHQ had full remote access to his phone, and all his conversations were being monitored at his own request. No, he was in the clear as regards all that. What they *could* legally do was hold him for fourteen days without charge. By which time, going by last time's fiasco, Mabel would be dead.

Not that anyone in MI7 would intend that, obviously. Yet they'd all walk away when it happened.

He didn't have that luxury.

One of the first rules of effective spycraft: always do startling things in plain sight. Well, not always. Sometimes. About 30% of the time. He walked deep into the building – probably the last thing they were expecting - and took out six metres of high-tensile wire he'd stowed in his pocket earlier that week, plus a pair of heavy-duty gloves.

He carried on past colleagues' offices, desks, standalone workstations - *hello, hello again, hello* – until he reached the west wall. He threw open the window to Thorney Street. He secured the loop he'd made to the opening-restrictor-stay and climbed out. There were a few surprised calls behind him, but, hey, this was John Mordred: he did odd things.

Four metres to the ground: he probably didn't need a mooring. Still, it should reinforce their preconceived idea that he was incompetent, which would be useful later. He disengaged the wire with a deft flick of the wrist and rolled it up as he walked. He thrust it, and the gloves, into his pocket. At either end of the street, Annabel and Alec were on their way towards him with walkie-talkies, as expected. They accelerated. He broke into a run.

Page Street, directly ahead, looked clear – of course it did. They'd foreseen something like this and organised an ambush. What they didn't know was that he'd anticipated their anticipation. For now, just run as fast as you can: forget your pursuers and concentrate on what's ahead. His worst fear was that they might set Edna on him, the school panther. She could probably outrun him within a hundred yards, although if he threw obstacles in her way – well, she was relatively new to this job: that didn't seem fair.

But then he remembered: Edna had pulled a ligament. Thank you, God.

Which didn't make any difference to the possibility of an ambush. Phyllis, yes, it'd be her. She'd stick out a well-timed, shapely foot, and when he went sprawling: *Why the hurry to LEAVE, John? Much better to REMAIN*. Then she'd laugh humourlessly.

No, she wouldn't. They'd had a tiff, that's all. He loved her. They still had an understanding of sorts. One that precluded that kind of thing. He hoped.

There were men at the end of Page Street, waiting for him. So far, so good. He pretended to recalculate and leapt over a couple of bins into the side-street they were obviously shepherding him towards.

He found the expected open door to his left and slipped inside. They were probably rubbing their hands with glee now.

They obviously had no idea how thoroughly he'd studied this building. Memorising the architect's plans; locating the exits; learning the name of each worker in every office, even gauging the proximity of adjacent buildings for a viable rooftop-to-rooftop.

As soon as he entered, he saw the possibility of a bonus. The cleaners' cupboard was open. He went in. No handle on this side, but he grabbed the edge and pulled it as far shut as it would go. To his relief, it wasn't one of those doors with a life of its own.

Alec was ten years older than him, and they'd probably be evenly matched in a fight. He could outrun him, though. Annabel was another matter. He didn't know how speedy she was, but there was absolutely no possibility of besting her in combat. She'd have him for breakfast.

"Could he have gone in here?" he heard Alec call, theatrically, from outside.

"I don't know," Annabel replied, equally artificially. "Go in and have a look. I'll go to the end. If I can't see him, I may come back."

Sure, yes. She'd be waiting right outside. Alec was just the squeeze-guy. The police would blockade the front; to evade them, Mordred would have to back up and fight past Alec; Annabel would join Alec. Checkmate in three.

But with game-plans like that, you never reckoned with a cleaners' cupboard.

He waited till Alec was just outside, then he slammed the door into him. He followed up with a deft kick to the head. He leaped over the unconscious bulk and banged the exit on Annabel while she was on her way in.

She'd be bloody furious next time they met. If they ever did.

According to the script, Counter-terrorism should be coming now, or at least half of it. But that didn't matter either. All part of life's rich tapestry. He went leisurely upstairs to the first floor, walked across the landing and knocked on the door of Office 14. Credibility now was of the essence: one reason he was wearing his best suit. Without waiting for a reply, he opened the door and walked in.

A spacious office with white woodchip wallpaper, framed landscapes and an elderly man at a desk dictating to a middle-aged woman with a laptop. Fourth time he'd been in here; first time with occupants.

"Morning, Nigel," Mordred said breezily, closing the door gently behind him. "Morning, Linda. May I just ask, can either of you smell burning? How was Eastbourne, incidentally?"

Nigel and Linda looked nonplussed. Their embarrassment at not even recognising him when he obviously knew them intimately was just what the doctor ordered. He smiled while each waited for the other to provide a clue as to who he was.

He opened the window casually - crucial not to make any sudden movements here, and of course to keep as quiet as he could – and looked down into the street. Five policemen gathered directly below, next to the doorway, in a clutch. Their body-language said they thought the chase was over.

Perfect. He hadn't been ten-pin bowling for a while, but he understood the basic principle. Everyone did.

"Do we – er? ... Have we met?" the elderly man said, cautiously genial.

"Excuse me just one moment, Nigel," Mordred replied. He took the wire from his pocket, unravelled it and found the pen-mark indicating the exact distance from here to four feet above the ground. He put his gloves on, attached the loop to the window restraining-stay and jumped.

The height was great enough - and he spread himself sufficiently - to knock all five officers down under the impact.

Because the wire was adapted to stop him hitting the ground, he experienced a severe jerk, but no more than in the six practice-runs. He punched one of the men who was groggily getting up, then found his feet and ran.

He zig-zigged through the alleyways and found Regency Street, then up Fynes Street to Vincent Square. He slowed to a jog – he wasn't being followed – and climbed inside the grounds.

Vincent Square wasn't a public space; it belonged to Westminster School. And for that reason, once you knew where the CCTV cameras were and how to avoid the patrolling support staff, it was ideal for concealment. He crossed to the thicket where he'd buried his change of clothing and two hundred pounds in cash.

Disguise, disguise, oh the possibilities. The convention was to go as far the other way as possible: if you wore a suit, then a T-shirt and baseball cap, and vice-versa. To avoid that cliché, he'd brought another suit, a dark, double-breasted one. He cut his hair – one of his most recognisable features - and shaved his scalp, and put on a pair of plastic-framed glasses and a dark trilby. He crossed the field by the perimeter trees and left via the north fence.

He couldn't find a taxi, so he hopped on the first bus he saw. Ten minutes later, he was in Oxford Street. Not his first choice of destination – quite the opposite - but he could see from the route map between the wall and the ceiling overhead that, if he stayed on, he'd get ever closer to Thames House. He had to change, find a bus that went north.

MI7 would be trying to get a lock on his phone now. They couldn't succeed so long as it was switched off, so he was safe for the moment. It wouldn't hurt them to find out where he was, because he wouldn't be staying here, and he had to put one part of his plan to bed.

Four days ago, he'd arranged to meet his two older sisters in Selfridges for breakfast. MI7 knew he'd resign today; an appointment with family members an hour later was meant to put it off its guard. Since it was paranoid by nature, it would still set a trap for him in Page Street, that had been obvious. But it would be a half-hearted one, and he'd evade it.

And he had. So far.

He walked down the street towards Marble Arch with Selfridges behind him. He switched on his phone and pressed 'call'. None of his family knew about Mabel. As far as they were concerned she was still merrily hauling migrants from dinghies. So he expected Hannah to sound more cheerful than him. At least, until she found out she'd been stood up.

"John, you're *late,*" her voice came. "Charlotte's gone out onto the street to look for you. There's a limit to how long we can stay here with the queue like this. Do you want to meet in Starbucks or something, instead?"

"I can't be there at all, I'm afraid. Something's come up at work."

"Oh, fabulous," she replied sardonically. "Have the Americans and the French run out of machine parts again?"

"I'm really sorry. Look, I can't talk now. I promise I'll make it up to you."

"For God's sake, John, I've bought you your *favourite.* I'm sitting here - "

He switched the phone off and put it in a public bin. He wondered what she thought his 'favourite' was. How did she do it? Always make him feel guiltier than he'd budgeted for?

Still, this wasn't the time or place for recriminations. This was about Mabel.

"John! *John!*" A woman's voice behind him.

Charlotte. Bloody hell. Short, stout, hennaed hair, pink-framed glasses and the usual shapeless T-shirt, skirt and zip-up top combination.

"John, you dropped your phone in the bin by mistake!" she exclaimed, beaming and trotting over to hand it back to him. "I knew it was you by the way you walk!" she said before he could ask. "Oh, my God! What have you - ? Where's your *hair*, John?

Take that hat off, come on, show me! Oh, my GOD!" she went on, when he did as she asked. "What's the - ? And why are you wearing *glasses? Bald!* And *glasses!* Have you – you haven't got – the - *the big C,* have you, John? Oh, my *GOD!"*

She seemed simultaneously overwhelmed with concern and utterly traumatised, and it wasn't clear which would get the upper hand, or whether they'd collide in her brain and cause an explosion. She held his phone at arm's length as if it was infectious. A few passers-by looked at her, shocked at the brutality of her public diagnosis.

"I'm fine," he said weakly, accepting the phone. "I've got to go."

He really did. She was about to ruin everything. MI7 might well have discovered his location now. Pure instinct kicked in and he ran away, the phone feeling like a white hot bar in his palm.

After ten seconds, he looked hurriedly behind him – he'd lost her, surely – then spotted a red double-decker about to pull away. He was past caring about its destination: for all he knew, it might even be the one he'd just alighted from. He thrust his phone into another City of Westminster bin and slid through the electronic doors just as they were sealing.

The bus pulled out into a miraculously clear lane and accelerated. He paid ten pounds, didn't tell the driver where he wanted to go or whether single or return. He was focussed on just one thing. He ran up to the top deck to see if he could spy his sister.

It was worse than he could possibly imagine. A middle-aged Chinese tourist fished Mordred's phone from the rubbish, looked quizzically at it, then all around himself, solicitously, as if to locate its rightful owner. Then Charlotte appeared from nowhere and leapt on him.

Even from behind the thick glass, he heard her yelling, *"That's my brother's phone! Help! HELP, everyone! HE'S GOT MY BROTHER'S PHONE!"*

Then the bus went up a gear and gathered speed. It turned left onto Park Lane and Oxford Street and disappeared from view.

## Chapter 3: Another Gloomy Fenella Sunset

Mordred didn't expect any more trouble from MI7. They'd tried to stop him leaving Thames House; they'd experienced a humiliating failure. But that was probably the end of the matter. Everyone knew he wasn't conniving with terrorists; they knew he was no danger to the public; he was on record as saying he quite liked the Queen, but not enough to have her babies. In short, he was a harmless enthusiast. The Joint Intelligence Committee, or whatever it was Ruby Parker sat on once a fortnight in Whitehall, wasn't going to commit millions of pounds – probably what it cost nowadays – to standing in his way. If he wanted to go to Libya and get blown up, good luck to him. He might even take a few of the scumbags with him.

On the other hand, there was no room for complacency. The police would have been told to look out for him, and just because his photo hadn't 'top priority' stamped on it, it didn't mean he wasn't vulnerable.

Four weeks and two days beforehand, he'd made necessary arrangements to leave the country. Right before letting MI7 know he'd been contacted about Mabel. At that stage, he wasn't being monitored, and was free to do roughly as he pleased. He'd booked a hotel in Brixton for the afternoon and evening of his actual resignation; then he'd called a friend, a wealthy Central American heiress named Fenella Decristoforo-Salvaterra, whom he'd met on a work-related trip to the Caribbean eighteen months previously. She knew what he did for a living; they were in each other's debt in a variety of ways, and they were roughly the same age. Tomorrow, she'd welcome him aboard her yacht, the *Chalchiuhtlicue* – after the Aztec water goddess, apparently – and introduce him to the co-conspirators she'd promised to round up for his excursion to Libya. At his own recommendation, she hadn't been in contact with him for over a month, so right now anything was possible. He hoped there hadn't been a hitch.

After leaving Charlotte behind in Oxford Street, his bus had taken him all over London. He decided to cut his losses at Trafalgar Square. As he alighted, he got the odd impression Nelson's Column looked slightly awry. A kind of divine comment on something, maybe, he didn't know what. As usual, the place was packed. Easy to blend in, and easy to get elsewhere. He strode to Charing Cross and caught the Underground to Brixton via Stockwell. He checked into Rhoedam Lodge under the name Mirek Sobotka – pretending to be Czech with a poor grasp of English - and spent the afternoon sitting on his bed reading Daniel Hannan's *Why Vote Leave?* His room had all the usual fixtures and appliances. It looked like it had been furnished in the 1960s, but it was clean and it smelt nice. Of lavender.

He thought he got the Leave business now. It didn't look half as bad as he'd originally thought. Conservatism was going to be harder to swallow, but he could try. He might have to if he was going to get her back.

No, he couldn't go that far.

Could he?

Mind you, he wasn't much of a one for the socialists either, although he probably preferred them. Conservatives tended to prefer their friends and family over ideals – even, sometimes, ideals like justice. Socialists were the opposite. At their extremes, they both went badly wrong in opposite ways. We were all going to die in the end. Care for the poor, be kind to animals, cherish your friends and family, try not to let those things get in the way of each other. He was a nonentity, anyway. It probably didn't matter what he believed, providing he was nice to orphans.

Every so often he put his book down on the bed and had a prolonged chuckle. When he'd landed on those policemen this morning and they'd all gone flying, what must it have looked like? More Buster Keaton than Bond. Story of his life, really. Still, it had worked. Must try it again some day.

At five o' clock, he went down into the lounge and ordered cheese pie with potato sticks sautéed in sunflower oil, accompanied by sugared, crushed marrowfat peas. He was the hotel's only guest. The proprietor, a large man with a walrus moustache and a white apron, didn't seem inclined to speak, so Mordred enjoyed his food in silence. Afterwards, he went upstairs, watched three hours of TV – there was no mention of him on the evening news: no 'suspected terrorist magnificently deploys early 20th century silent-comedy escape technique' – then read more *Why Vote Leave?*

At half past seven, a young man in a motorbike jacket knocked on his hotel door. A sealed envelope by courier for Mr Mirek Sobotka. Nothing to pay, but Mordred handed over five pounds anyway, and said *děkuji* – thank you - three times. He showered and ordered a taxi to Victoria Coach Station. Once there, he retrieved a travelling bag from the left luggage office and went to Canary Wharf. He walked into the shopping centre, wandered around for ten minutes keeping a constant eye on the time, found the public toilets, entered a cubicle, unzipped the bag, changed into the clothes and put on the sunglasses. He waited for a minute, then heard someone come into the next compartment and knock four times on the dividing wall: two long, two short. He passed the travelling bag across – presumably the unseen occupant was dressed identically to him – and exited. He wore a straw-coloured suit, an open-necked oxford shirt and tan slip-ons.

He went straight to the marina where four middle-eastern men were waiting for him outside a coffee shop. They were all in their fifties with trimmed beards, and they wore *thobes*, long sleeved, ankle-length garments. It was beginning to get dark now. He smiled at them; they got up and sauntered in a group to a well-lit displacement motor yacht, seventy metres long and moored in between two rather smaller others, *The Mendoza* and *The Flighty Breeze*. *The Miss Watkins*, actually the *Chalchiuhtlicue* but re-named temporarily in Mordred's honour and registered to a false owner in Vancouver. They walked aboard on a gangplank. The captain and his two crewmen made ready to cast off. They gave no indication that they considered Mordred a newcomer. One of the men from the café opened a door to a cabin and he and his three companions went through. Mordred followed them.

He found himself in what looked like a five-star hotel room. There was a bed, but also a lounge suite, a dresser, fitted wardrobes and a minibar. Fenella sat on the sofa opposite an old woman. They were reading what looked like novels, but stopped and rose when the men came in. Fenella wore a plain black dress, matching heels and a diamond necklace. Her hair was dark, her face thin and her eyes were narrow, almost as if she was squinting. The old woman muttered something and left, edging discreetly round the men.

"I'm so glad there were no problems," Fenella told Mordred. "This is your cabin. The *Chalchiuhtlicue* is a bit of an improvement on my last yacht, and it enables me to play the hostess a little more effectively. It'll resume its real name when we dock in Monaco."

"I'm very glad to be here," Mordred replied. "I can't thank you enough for your hospitality."

"How is Ms Ruby Parker?"

"A little more frustrated now than the last time you met her. I'm sure she doesn't suspect your involvement."

"As far as I know, no one in London even knows I'm here. May I introduce my friends? Muammar Khalifa Al-Azzabi, senior agribusiness consultant for GNT; Mohammad Al-Taher Al-Juhaimi, CEO of LibAc oil; Nouri Said Younis, junior minister for Migrants and Displaced in the Government of National Accord; and Mustafa Kahiry, a founding member of the Free Egyptians Party. Gentlemen, this is John Mordred, former British intelligence officer and one of my dearest friends. Incidentally, we cast off in thirty minutes' time." She turned to Mordred. "We'll put you ashore in Rochefort early tomorrow morning. From there it's a light aircraft journey to somewhere in Libya. About a hundred and fifty kilometres south of Tripoli. I don't know the details. These men do. Obviously, it won't be an official flight. I take it you haven't brought your passport?"

Mordred grinned. "I barely escaped with the clothes I stood up in. However, all's well that ends well."

"Except that it is only just beginning, Mr Mordred!" Muammar Khalifa quipped, putting his hand warmly on Mordred's shoulder.

"I only hope the rest will go as well as the beginning," he replied in eastern Libyan Arabic.

The smiles dropped from the four men's faces. One by one, they turned to Fenella.

"Is this a joke?" Mohammad Al-Juhaimi asked.

She met his indignation with a smile. "I told you he was good."

"You told us he was British," Mohammad Al-Juhaimi said, still sounding a little affronted.

"I'm a languages-expert," Mordred replied in English. "I can also do the western Libyan dialect. I know a little Tamazight – enough to get by – and I can speak Italian with twenty-six regional accents. Not all at once, obviously. I only wanted to demonstrate that if your plan involves me blending in with the local population, it shouldn't present difficulties – at least, not of the linguistic variety."

"John's actually a born and bred Briton," Fenella said. "And an insufferable clever-clogs. What did you actually say?" she asked him.

"I said, 'I only hope the rest will go as well as the beginning'."

"Well, consider your point made," she replied. "We'll stick to English now, shall we?"

Maria arrived with glasses of tea and announced that dinner would be served in an hour. For the next ten minutes, everyone sat in a group making small talk about the British weather and the declining standard of London cake and coffee, then one by one the men made their excuses and left. Their wives and children were aboard elsewhere and they had to perform *Maghrib*, the penultimate prayer of the day, with them before eating. Suddenly Mordred and Fenella were alone.

"I take it you've no idea what we've come up with in terms of a plan for you," she said.

"Whatever it is, I'm very grateful."

"We're meeting again after dinner to discuss the details." She stood up. "Shall we go outside? I'd like to admire the view."

There was nothing romantic between them - there never had been - but somehow their friendship was deep enough to make that irrelevant. She was a widow; she'd lost her whole family in tragic circumstances. He spent much of his life alone, and in danger, and pondering the worth of existence generally. The meeting of those things couldn't entirely explain their connection; at bottom, it was opaque. But they could sit or stroll in silence together for hours on end and feel more fully contented than during virtually any time they were apart. The odd thing was, they didn't especially crave each other's company. They hadn't seen each other for over a year now. And yet both intuitively knew that their paths would cross and re-cross for the rest of their lives.

She led the way across the room and out of a door opposite to the one Mordred had arrived through. She brought her book with her. *We Should All Be Feminists*. They walked along a short corridor and took an elevator to their destination. When they stepped out, the boat was already moving east along the Thames. She stopped at a tall locker and removed an overcoat. The sun was setting and the sky, clear of clouds, had turned purple. They stood against the western rail and watched the London skyline slowly recede.

"This is a free country again," she said, hugging her book. "How do you feel about that, John?"

"You mean Brexit? I don't know."

She laughed. "You don't think it's a good thing?"

"It doesn't really matter what I think. It's happening. My family was against it. I thought I was."

"I think it's excellent. Now you need to control immigration. Stop the influx of foreign cultures."

It was his turn to laugh. "I didn't know you felt that way."

"I'm a woman."

Normally, they saw eye-to-eye. He wasn't familiar with this new Fenella. And here he was, unemployed and accepting her hospitality. How to react?

"What you've achieved in this country," she continued before he could reply, "is complete legal equality between the genders. You prosecute rapists and female genital mutilators and homophobes and racists. Britain just won't stand for those things, at least in public life. Lots of other cultures would like to remove that intolerance. Don't be fooled by their exotic dancing and flavoursome cuisine and electrifying music."

He breathed an inward sigh of relief. Back on the same wavelength again.

But something about her demeanour told him she thought it wouldn't stay as it was; that sooner or later, the West would succumb to the same barbarism that still infected much of the rest of the world; the savagery that, since it mainly affected women, most people – including even most women, since they were usually conditioned by men - didn't even notice. He was suddenly reminded of how Nelson's Column had looked earlier that day - subtly off the perpendicular - and something of her gloom overran him.

"What's your book like?" he asked her.

She stopped hugging it, looked at the cover and laughed. "You must think I'm pretty transparent."

"Just because you've been influenced by it, it doesn't mean it's the book talking. It happens to me a lot."

"We're living on a tiny little peninsula of gender and post-gender freedom at the end of history," she said. "And because we send probes to Mars and Jupiter, we imagine we're invulnerable. Those men you met downstairs. They don't exactly despise me, but they don't know how to take me. Their wives and daughters are women. I'm some kind of halfway creature." She turned to him. "I'm *so* glad you're here, John."

He put his arm round her waist and kissed her hair. She didn't react, except to relax a little and lean on the rail. They resumed looking at the city.

After five minutes another mammoth yacht passed them in the opposite direction, lights ablaze, hard trance music blaring. Old men danced with bikini-clad young women on the top deck while further down, couples in formal eveningwear stood holding drinks. Someone launched a firework and there was applause and laughter.

Fenella watched it go by as if she were a zoologist observing insects in a glass case.

"Russians," she said neutrally.

A few seconds later, it was as if it had disappeared into a black hole. Nothing remained to indicate it had ever been there, much less that it still existed. They stood looking at London again. In the distance, a foghorn blew.

"Don't get killed in Libya, will you?" she said.

"No."

"Not that it matters too much, I suppose. This life isn't the only one."

"No. But I'll still try not to."

The last embers of the sun died behind them. The purple went out of the sky and dark blue took its place. The grotesque neon lights of the big commercial buildings acquired an unwanted pre-eminence, but overhead, stars appeared one by one, and the earth suddenly seemed ancient and small. Nothing much mattered. They'd all die in the end.

Downstairs, Maria was calling them to dinner.

## Chapter 4: Two Sisters in Search of a Younger Brother

The Chinese tourist grappled with Charlotte for about five seconds, then decided to cut his losses. He released the phone and ran away. Passers-by – those who'd seen – shook their heads. *You're a bloody appalling advert for the UK*, they seemed to tell her. One man muttered 'bloody Chav' at her. But it didn't matter in the slightest – no, not at all! - because she'd rescued John's phone!

Then the tourist came back, but with a policewoman.

It had been quite a nice day up till then. She'd met Hannah at the hotel and they'd sauntered over to Oxford Street and sat in Selfridges with a bath bun and a cappuccino each, waiting for their little brother. Then *this* nightmare. Luckily, the tourist didn't know any English, so he couldn't get through to the policewoman or anyone else. Charlotte had stuffed the phone in her bag by now. While he tried to mime, 'I was assaulted by this woman', Charlotte tried to mime, 'I didn't mean it' to him, only with a parallel explanation in English for the benefit of the policewoman.

"I walked into him by mistake, and I dropped my phone," she said, "It went in the bin, and he probably thought it was his – I get that now - and he picked it up, and he was about to run off with it, and I thought he was a mugger, so I grabbed him. I couldn't make him understand. I didn't mean to hurt him. I'm not a chav, really, I'm an honest woman. I'm a tourist. I run a respectable candle-making business in Devon. *Charlotte's Candles*. I don't go round stealing phones."

The trouble with this explanation was, firstly, that it had to compete with Chinese protest and Chinese mime, so probably the policewoman didn't get all – or any - of it, and secondly, the tourist didn't look like mugger: he looked like a tourist. He even had an expensive camera round his neck. Realising that she was about to be asked to present the phone, Charlotte decided to pre-empt matters. She took her own phone out of her bag. "This is what he tried to run off with," she said.

"Is this what you were fighting over, sir?" the policewoman asked the tourist, ignoring the fact that he clearly couldn't speak English.

The Chinese man nodded vigorously. He followed up by producing more throttling and wrestling gestures, but less angrily. Obviously, he believed he was finally getting through.

The policewoman turned her back on him. "Is there any way you can prove it's yours?" she asked Charlotte. "Any selfies or anything?"

Charlotte was on the verge of answering that she had *literally loads*: it was all she ever took, apart from her cat, Bastet, and her husband, Marcus, and her toddler, Seth, and her candles, when two complicating events occurred simultaneously. Firstly, the tourist's family arrived. Two teenage daughters, a wife and two grandparents. They surrounded him and he began to relate his tale; more solemnly, this time, and without the aid of mime.

Secondly, Hannah arrived. "What the hell's going on here?" she asked.

The policewoman turned to her. "Do you know this - "

"I think John's got *cancer!*" Charlotte blurted out, ignoring everyone except her sister. She burst into tears and fell melodramatically to her knees. After a stunned moment, the two Chinese daughters came over and crouched next to her. One put her arm around her shoulder.

"What are you talking about?" Hannah said. She obviously had no idea which aspect of the situation to deal with first, or even what the situation was, or whether it had any aspects. She put her hands to her temples.

Charlotte raised her head to look at her. Her face was already tear-stained, and she removed her spectacles to wipe it. "He was *completely BALD!*" she yelled. "And he was really, *really thin! And he was wearing GLASSES! And he RAN OFF!* I'm telling you, *he's had CHEMO!*"

She couldn't say any more for sobbing. Meanwhile, the attitude of the passers-by hadn't substantially changed. She still wasn't a very good advert for the UK, but for slightly different reasons.

One of the teenage daughters returned to her parents and grandparents to explain what had just happened. They all looked devastated. The policewoman went through Charlotte's phone looking at her selfies and her cat and her candles. Hannah got on her haunches and rubbed Charlotte's shoulder.

The Chinese man came over, bent down and uttered what, going by his face and tone of voice, was a profuse apology. Charlotte threw both arms around him and kissed him and cried even harder.

He lost his balance, fell over and smashed his camera.

Two hours later, the two women sat on a bench in Trafalgar Square with a view down Whitehall. Hannah crossed her legs and checked the download chart on her phone. Next to her, Charlotte ate a cranberry and brie baguette and tried to ignore the pigeons and seagulls. The sun was out, but there was little warmth in the air. The forecasts all predicted rain within the hour.

Whereas Charlotte was short, stout and wore clothes primarily as a covering - and mainly allegedly-slimming black - Hannah was tall, thin, blonde and aristocratic-looking. At thirty-five, she was two years older than her sister. She liked ankle-length dresses and gold studded flat sandals, otherwise, she wore clothes to make a statement, mostly an anti-capitalist one. She managed a successful band called Fully Magic Coal Tar Lounge, and, paradoxically, given her political views, owned a substantial amount of land in the Crown Dependency of Jersey. In her defence, all her wealth had come to her either by accident or as a by-product of pursuing a vocation she'd identified as early as fourteen. This year, for the first time, she'd appeared at the tail end of *The Sunday Times Rich List*. She was married to a middle-aged paediatrician called Tim, and had a year-old daughter called Lek.

Charlotte burped quietly. "I'm sorry," she said. "I've got to have food when I'm worried. It's not a sign that I don't care. It's the opposite."

"I don't understand why he would have left it till *then* to stand us up," Hannah said, putting her phone in her bag. She put a pair of sunglasses on. "I mean, he made the arrangement ages ago. Why leave it all this time? Why wait till we're both in London? Why ring us from virtually outside the café?"

"I would have thought that was obvious. He was going to announce it to us and he got cold feet at the last minute."

"What? Just us two? At a fancy cafeteria? Over breakfast? That's not the way you reveal you've got a potentially terminal condition!"

"This is John we're talking about."

Hannah sighed. "Yes, that's true."

Silence. The words, *He's not quite right in the head* remained unspoken because they weren't an entirely accurate expression of what either woman felt. But the accompanying silence was because neither could think of a better expression.

"I was hoping this would be kiss-and-make-up time," Hannah said. "I despise his bloody cow of a girlfriend, but if she makes him happy, I'll just have to get over it."

"I didn't like her either," Charlotte said. "Too showy. I mean, how can you trust a woman that turns up in a suit and heels?"

"It wasn't a suit. It was just a jacket. She had a pretty bloody good dress underneath, even I can see that, and I'm not a dedicated follower of fashion. Understated, but glamorous. I honestly don't know what John's doing with her. It's a complete mystery."

"She was a slag."

Hannah grimaced. "I think that's a bit strong."

"Sorry. I'm worried."

"When I said I couldn't see what he was with her for," Hannah went on, "I didn't mean her political views. I meant, she seemed the sort of woman who could pick and choose her men. And given the world on a plate, she'd probably choose Tarquin De Shit of PriceWaterhouseFuckingCooper. Not John-Who-Loves-Poor-Defenceless-Woodlice Mordred."

"What do you call people who love Theresa May?" Charlotte said.

Hannah sighed irritably and ignored her. "I've been thinking about 'Phyllis' a lot actually. I'm not sure that was her real name. It doesn't sound like one. How many Phyllises do you know of our age? It's the sort of name a grandma has."

"Old English names are coming back, though. There's a Noah at baby Seth's playschool and an Enoch - "

*"Noah?"*

"It's quite popular now. Especially since the Russell Crowe film. Anyway, you were saying? About 'Phyllis'?"

"Who calls their kid *Noah?"*

"For goodness sake, stop showing your age. Anyway, your kid's called Lek!"

"Don't start. It's a Thai name."

*"So?"*

Hannah sighed and took a second to re-focus. "I think 'Phyllis' might have been a professional escort. Posh women often do that sort of thing. It looks good on a CV. They don't necessarily charge much."

Charlotte wept. "I really love John," she said, taking her spectacles off and wiping her face. "We've got to find him and tell him it's all okay."

"You've got his phone, right?"

"We can't contact him on his *own phone*. Anyway, the fact that he put it in the bin probably means the cancer's got his brain. So it's probably a tumour."

"I think we're running *way* ahead of ourselves here, dearest," Hannah said. "So he shaved his head. Lots of men do nowadays. And he's getting older. He turned thirty last year. He may be having a premature mid-life crisis."

"Why would he put his phone in the bin?"

"By the same token, why would it indicate that he had cancer? Look, think about it for a minute. If he had a brain tumour that was serious enough to affect his behaviour, and he'd had chemotherapy, he'd be in hospital right now. They wouldn't have discharged him to go and meet his sisters in Selfridges."

"So what's *your* explanation then?"

"Lots of men nowadays think being bald is stylish. I know Tim does."

"But Tim *is* bald."

"Maybe John's trying to change his image. Change of image, change of phone. And the reason he didn't want to meet us was exactly the reason he gave. He was summoned away by work."

"Call him then. If he's changed his phone, he won't necessarily have changed his sim card. He'll still have the same number."

Hannah took out her phone and pressed 'call'. "It's gone straight to voicemail," she said after a second.

Charlotte removed his phone from her bag and switched it on. "Try again."

Hannah obliged. The phone Charlotte was holding began to ring, so she hung up. "Give it to me," she said.

She went straight to Contacts while Charlotte leaned over to see what she was doing.

"There's only one number in there," Hannah said. "*Phyllis*."

"So I see," Charlotte said.

Hannah laughed. "Bloody good job. I'd have killed him if he'd thrown away a perfectly good phone with my details in. Or any of ours. Don't you see? This probably means it's all perfectly harmless. If he threw it away because he had a brain tumour, it'd have been a spur of the moment irrational act, like a spasm. The fact that he went through and deleted all his contacts means it can't have been that. It must have been premeditated. *Ergo*, he's bought a new phone."

"I'm still not convinced."

"Why not?"

Charlotte shrugged. "I'm just not. Call it a woman's intuition."

"Bullshit. Anyway, last time I looked I was a woman too."

"I didn't mean - "

"And it gets even better. The fact that he didn't bother to delete 'Phyllis' means he doesn't care whether anyone finds her number or not. Which means he must have finished with her."

"But she must be *actually called* Phyllis. Unless she lied to him. But she wouldn't lie about her name and give him her number. And she's probably not an escort. He wouldn't have 'Phyllis' on there if she was. He'd have the name of the agency."

"Maybe. Perhaps they did have a bit of a fling. Who cares? The point is, it's obviously over now."

"I'm still not convinced."

"You keep saying that."

"Maybe we should ring her. Phyllis."

Hannah hooted. "Never in a million years. No, let sleeping dogs lie, that's my philosophy. Seriously, I'm switching it off again now, in case *she* tries to ring *us*."

"Shouldn't we just throw it away, like John did?"

"No way. Next time I see him, I'm going to rub it in his face. I'm going to be like, *Don't you realise Oxfam's crying out for these?*"

"Okay, okay, so we've got a good theory. He's changed his image and he was called away by work, and it was so urgent he couldn't even pop his head in to see us, even though we were literally only one hundred yards away. And he'd spent a lot of time on his way to Oxford Street deleting all his numbers - save one - with a view to ditching his old phone, because it was too much trouble just transferring the sim card, it's much better to start again completely from scratch, and he was in such a hurry to get to work, he actually *ran away* from me, and that's all very plausible and everything, but, for some reason, I'm still not convinced."

Hannah took a deep breath and rubbed her chin. "I see where you're coming from," she said eventually. "Something's not right."

"Quite a lot of things, actually. Nothing's right." She started to weep a little again. "I know he's in trouble."

"You're freaking me out. Stop it."

Charlotte removed a large piece of quartz with two points from her bag. "Do you know what this is?"

"One of your … crystals."

"My *twin* crystal."

"Please. Let's not argue about stones again."

"That's John," Charlotte said, indicating the left-hand, smaller point.

"You and John aren't twins."

"That's not what it means. I've got one for you as well. And Seth, and Marcus, and Mum and - "

"Yeah, yeah, get the picture. And John's half's playing up, I suppose."

"Yes. Sort of. It's more complicated - "

"Spare me. Look, here's what we'll do. My guess is that John will be getting on a plane somewhere now. He'll probably ring me on his spanking new device once he's airborne, or maybe when he's landed, apologise for this morning. But I may be wrong about that. He didn't specifically say he was going abroad. Anyway, I happen to know where he lives. We can go round there this evening and knock on the door. I don't think it'll come to that, though. I think we'll hear from him well beforehand. I'll keep my phone switched on."

"Okay."

"And when we have heard from him, I think you should put that crystal in the bin. It's not good for you."

"My *John* crystal?"

"How much does your bloody bag weigh? You've got a crystal in there for every member of the family? It must be doing your back in!"

"It keeps me fit."

Hannah laughed.

They went to the Shard while it rained, then shopping at Canary Wharf. After five, they admitted to each other that they were anxious. They ate at the hotel and Hannah ordered a taxi to take them to Islington. It took her a while to find where he lived – for some reason, he hadn't given her his address, and she'd never asked for it. She'd only been round there once or twice, and even then, uninvited.

But eventually, she remembered it looked out onto a bus stop and an electricity substation. Bus stops were plentiful, but substations – locating one of them might hold the key. It was getting dark now. They needed to go quickly.

It took them thirty minutes. Nowadays, Islington had an independent existence of tree-lined side streets and all-night shops, and people spoke of its culture the same way you might talk of Sussex or Cornish culture: not signifying much, but distinctive enough for those who lived there to feel proud. It was supposed to be a different country to the capital, yet the people were no friendlier. No one seemed inclined to answer a question about a missing electricity-substation-plus-bus-stop combination.

Eventually, they asked someone who acknowledged their existence. A bald, middle-aged man in a worker's overall. For all they knew, he might be an actual electrician.

"There's one two streets away," he said. "Go down here, then turn left at Plain Close, then right, into Drivers Street. It's on your left. It's fenced off, though. You can't get to it."

"Is there a bus stop near it?" Charlotte asked.

He didn't know. There was an overriding creepiness about the whole thing now. Dusk was coming in. If John actually lived here, there was a possibility they might just see him by chance, out shopping, or walking home from work. But neither thought they would. They each sensed he was nowhere close by. Not only that, but that he wasn't quite safe.

When they got to his block, there was a removal van outside. Their hearts sank. They went over, but it was as if they already knew the answers to the questions they were going to ask.

"Let's just go in," Hannah said. "The gate's open. Pretend like we live there."

Charlotte nodded. They put their heads down and crossed the block threshold without being challenged. They went up to the first floor.

Hannah turned to her sister and swallowed. "This is John's," she said.

It was the flat that was being cleared. It had been furnished when he took it. He'd never added much in the way of personal possessions. The two removal men looked as if they were about to finish up.

"Excuse me," Hannah said, addressing the older of the two men. He was on his way out and didn't break stride to indulge her. "My brother lives here."

"Not any more," the man said.

"Do you know where he's moving to?"

"Sorry, not allowed to say. Data protection. You'll have to ask him."

He locked the front door and went downstairs and left the building. Not only did he not seem to want to answer Hannah's questions, he seemed actively averse to it. She followed him as far as the road, hoping at least to see the name of the removal firm written on the side of the van. She might discover John's whereabouts that way, somehow.

But the van didn't have any signage at all. The two men got into the front cabin, started the engine and drove off at speed, as if frightened the sisters might actually sprint after them, shouting obscenities. Charlotte did the complete opposite: she clutched her twin-headed crystal and whimpered slightly.

"Something's very wrong," Hannah told her. "I think it's time to go to the police."

## Chapter 5: A Plan For All Seasons

After dinner, Fenella sat talking to the wives of her guests about cars and holidays. If Mordred was honest, he couldn't imagine two subjects less congenial to her, yet she gave nothing away. The men separated slightly from the women to talk middle-eastern politics. Mordred had participated in similar discussions before and, at an early stage, the focus usually turned on Israel. What then followed was a series of denunciations of Knesset foreign and domestic policy, more or less passionate, combined with a vigorous denunciation of America's complicity, and sometimes Britain's too – although Britain was usually considered too puny to be a significant player.

This discussion was different. The initial focus was on the tension between Saudi Arabia and Iran. It was agreed that the former couldn't make an internal transition to anything much: thanks to decades of over-reliance on oil, it had evolved a completely artificial social structure with no serious opposition other than from lethargy and disillusion. The recent government reshuffle would change nothing. Iran, on the other hand, was much more dynamic. Even after the mullahs went, its foreign policy objectives would remain the same. Turkey was the new variable. The liberal preacher, Fethullah Gulen, blamed by President Erdogan for the failed coup, was merely a conduit: Erdogan's real target was Kemal Ataturk, and he wasn't above initiating a Cultural Revolution to expunge all traces of him. Turkey and Iran were the future of the bipolar Sunni-Shi'a middle-east. Israel, meanwhile, was merely a distraction. In an ideal world, it ought to be possible to accommodate it, providing the Ultras didn't get the upper hand. The problem was, hatred of it had become a kind of half-phoney higher ground that neither side dared relinquish.

Mordred got the impression this wasn't a new discussion, and none of the four participants was saying anything the others hadn't already heard from the same lips many times before. And yet neither was it solely for his benefit. He'd often heard it said that women liked talking for its own sake; men talked to exchange information. He'd never found any evidence to support that. As far as he could tell, both sexes talked because they were social animals, and talk was a means of bonding.

At a certain point in the discussion, the four Arab men exchanged meaningful glances. Al-Juhaimi stood up, and the others followed suit. The women seemed more or less oblivious.

"Come with us, John," Al-Azzabi said.

They left the dining room by a door that led to the corridor running the length of the middle of the ship. A few seconds later, they were in one of the men's cabins. Very similar to Mordred's but with a strong smell of sandalwood. Glasses of tea awaited them on a coffee table, around which the seats had been arranged. Mordred found himself subtly guided to an armchair. The others sat facing him. For a moment, no one said anything. The way three of the men looked at Al-Azzabi, though, it looked like he'd been selected as spokesman.

He tossed a large envelope on to the table and looked at Mordred. "Papers. And my family connections. Learn them. One thing you'll soon discover about Libya. You're more of a person if you have more of a background. In there, you'll find a complete list. Parents, grandparents, uncles, brothers, cousins, nephews, along with their marital status, numbers of offspring, occupations. Of course, in addition to that, there's the usual documentation. Passport, driving licence, that sort of thing. Not that too much of it is relevant in my country any more. Still, you'll probably be stopped at some stage. Bits of paper with the relevant stamps never did anyone any harm."

Mordred looked through it all as they spoke. He wanted to ask why they were helping him. In an ideal world, it would be because of their attachment to Fenella, but he didn't think that was it. *Those men you met downstairs. They don't exactly despise me, but they don't know how to take me*. Even factoring in her pessimism, there had to be more to it than that.

"Tell us about yourself, Mr Mordred," Mustafa Kahiry said. "We've all heard something about you from Miss Salvaterra, but we've yet to hear your own version of events. What takes you to Libya? Just your sister? Or do you have a wider remit?"

"I'm no longer working for British intelligence," Mordred replied as sweetly as he could. He didn't want to offend them, but it was crucial to get off on the right foot. "If that's what you're implying."

The four men looked at each other. They didn't actually chuckle, but clearly only politeness prevented them.

"Please don't take this the wrong way," Mustafa Kahiry said, "but we've learned to be sceptical of the assurances of the British. Both in history, and more recently."

Mordred smiled. Try again. "My sister's an aid worker. She went to Libya about a month ago on the understanding that she'd be picking up a migrant woman who was supposed to be the wife of a colleague of hers. Perhaps predictably, she was kidnapped."

"And we understand you're going to rescue her, yes?"

"Correct."

"You do realise Libya's a big country? Even taking into account the fact that most of it is desert."

"I have ideas as to where she might be."

"Go on."

"I've spoken to some of her colleagues at MSF. I've found out a lot about her over the last few weeks, and more about the man she was supposedly in love with – a certain 'Jean Marc Bouchet' - than she probably knows herself. He was married to a Syrian woman called Rima, whom he met in Daraa. After a barrel bomb fell nearby a year ago, he thought she was dead, but, of course, she wasn't. At least, that's the accepted version. She turned up in Tripoli just before Jean-Marc's death. Then she lured Mabel over there. Following intelligence from migrants in Sicily, a group of British secret servicemen and special forces identified a *mazraa* – a warehouse for kidnapped refugees, mostly from sub-Saharan Africa – in Tripoli's Gorje district, about a week ago. We mounted a disastrous rescue-attempt and we were forced to pull back and abort. I say 'we': I wasn't involved. In any case, 'we' still don't know whether she was in there or not. It's irrelevant. If she was, they'll have moved her. If she wasn't, well, you can't get any further back than square one."

"And?"

"And what?"

Nouri Said Younis laughed. "Excuse me, John, but I thought you said you had ideas about where she might be."

"In Tripoli," he said.

The men looked portentously at each other. "And what makes you so sure?" Al-Azzabi asked.

"Her captors want guns," Mordred said, "so presumably it's a militia of some sort. It can't be ISIS, because they'd have secured her in their stronghold in Sirte before making demands. But they wouldn't make demands: it's not their style. Beheading people on Youtube: that's their style."

"So it's not them," Mustafa Kahiry said.

"There are supposedly few national groups left in Libya," Mordred went on, "so whoever has my sister probably doesn't have the connections – possibly even the capacity - to transport her across the country. All of which indicates that she's likely still in the capital. And of course, that would make perfect sense. Most Westerners don't appreciate the situation on the ground there. Anywhere else, once you'd foiled a rescue-attempt, you *would* relocate a few hundred miles away. But in Tripoli, there are always lots of alternative no-go areas. You might even move just down the road. And Western intelligence will be looking anywhere except there."

"It's a good argument," Mustafa Kahiry said.

"Extremely sound," Nouri Said Younis agreed. Their words were at odds with their tone. They sounded sceptical.

"And yet?" Mordred said.

Al-Juhaimi took a deep breath as if preparing to perform an unhappy duty. "Miss Salvaterra told us about your predicament nearly three weeks ago. We set to work interviewing rescued migrants at the southern tip of Italy to find out if anyone had information about your sister. Or rather we farmed out that task. Within a week, we knew your sister was in Tripoli. We thought we had enough information to give you a reliable lead, but, at that point, the failed rescue-attempt changed the situation irreparably. Since then, we've been working overtime to establish her new whereabouts."

"In a word, we believe she's six hundred miles away in Benghazi," Nouri Said Younis said.

Mordred felt his eyebrows involuntarily bounce. "How - certain are you?"

"You were right to infer she's not being held by ISIS," Al-Juhaimi said, ignoring the question. "However, she is in the hands of Islamists of another persuasion. We believe that the militants who originally kidnapped her exchanged her for weapons and an alliance. The group who inherited her then shipped her east."

"Any guess as to its immediate intentions?" Mordred asked.

"None whatsoever," Al-Azzabi replied. "Presumably, her phone was part of the deal, so you'll probably hear from them presently."

"Where did you get your information? I mean, whoever told you this must be pretty well informed."

"Your sister's move from A to B," Mustafa Kahiry began, "involved people-smugglers, men who knew how to traverse the checkpoints and negotiate the tribal jealousies involved in a six-hundred-mile land journey from west to east. Occasionally, such people – well, their boats fail at sea, and they end up very reluctantly on the shores of Italy. Then they're looking at prison sentences. They'll talk, given the right inducements."

"In order to operate successfully," Al-Juhaimi said, "the people-smugglers have to form networks. In practice, that means they get to find out something of what the others are up to. If they're sharp, they'll usually be able to deduce a lot from a few whispered sentences. We spoke to a man of this calibre. He described rumours of a contract to drive an Englishwoman from Tripoli to Benghazi. Two hundred thousand dinar."

"And you spoke to this man when?" Mordred asked.

"Yesterday," Mustafa Kahiry replied.

"Of course, if she can be moved once," Al-Azzahi said lugubriously, "she can be moved again. It's not inconceivable that ISIS will eventually come into possession of her. Then, much as it pains me to admit it, they'll probably do what you say: execute her on webcam. They tend to see that sort of thing as propaganda gold, easily worth more than the half million or so dinar whoever now 'owns' her has invested. Her present holders could stand to make a handsome profit."

"Do we know whether she actually reached Benghazi?" Mordred asked.

"That's your job," Nouri Said Younis said drily. "When you get there."

It was Mordred's turn to look sceptical. The others apparently detected it.

"Is there a problem?" Mustafa Kahiry said.

Mordred smiled. "No, not at all."

"We can make preparations for you," Al-Azzazi said, a little too eager to change the subject, "but you probably need a plan. I assume you have one."

"Plans never work unless they take into account conditions on the ground," Mordred said. "That means advance reconnaissance, and till now I didn't even know I was going to Benghazi. The difference in this case is that I'm the one surveying the territory, and formulating the plan and carrying it out. Normally, that would involve at least three different departments. Hopefully, I'll make a few friends along the way, but I'm not counting on it. This is my sister. I wouldn't be doing it unless I was desperate."

"You're saying it's a matter of honour," Mustafa Kahiry suggested.

Mordred swayed his head for a moment to give the impression he was weighing his words. "I wouldn't put it like that. It's nothing to do with anyone's reputation. I see what you mean, though. It's not necessarily an emotional thing. More a matter of family duty."

The four men looked at each other. It seemed to be an answer they liked. Something hard and objective, not shot through with sentimentalism.

"You're probably wondering why we're going to all this trouble for you," Mustafa Kahiry said. "You seem an intelligent man. I'm pretty sure you've worked out it's not because we've been seduced by the undoubted charms of our hostess."

"If you're after British state secrets, I don't have access to them," Mordred returned, trying to create the impression of a light-hearted quip, yet uncomfortably aware he may have identified the heart of the matter. "And now I've resigned, that's highly unlikely to change."

"Your name is Omar Zeidan," Al-Azzabi said, apparently without rising to his challenge. "You're the youngest son of Ali and Fatima Zeidan of the Magarha tribe from Fezzan. If you don't know anything about the Magarha or Fezzan, it's all in the documentation. The real Omar Zeidan was killed by ISIS four weeks ago in Sirte, probably at roughly the same time your sister was abducted. We have permission to act on behalf of the family. If questioned, they will vouch for you. They'll swear to the world that you're their son. And their other sons will do likewise."

"In return," Mustafa Kahiry said, "they don't want British state secrets. They want revenge. I'll tell you the truth: they are gambling that you will not be able to complete your mission without spilling the blood of militants. And they've been given to understand that you're good."

Mordred took a breath. "I'll be perfectly honest with you. I'm not into killing for its own sake. If I can get my sister out without killing anyone – ISIS or not – I will."

The four men beamed.

"We very much hoped you would say something of the sort," Mustafa Kahiry said. "The parents of the man whose identity you are assuming would not – what is the American phrase? – *have it any other way*. The prophet Muhammad himself, peace and blessings be upon him, said: 'The major sins are: to ascribe partners to Allah, murder someone, disobey one's parents, and take a false oath'."

"On the other hand, if I do have to kill them, I will," Mordred said. "I just won't enjoy it, that's all."

"That, too, is acceptable," Al-Azzabi said.

"I take it I'll be under the command of General Khalifa Haftar," Mordred said. "And I'll busy myself gaining intelligence on Islamists, which he'll then follow up by destroying their positions with his 'Libyan National Army'?"

"That's precisely right," Nouri Said Younis said. "Although it's not 'his' Libyan National Army," he added, hurriedly. "It's *the* Libyan National Army."

"My apologies," Mordred said. "That's of course what I meant."

Something felt wrong about nearly all of this. However, he'd already let his guard slip once. He couldn't allow them to discover he was suspicious now. Maybe he wasn't. Perhaps he was being paranoid. But then, paranoia had always been kind to him in the past. The guardian angel of all spies everywhere. Or perhaps their worst enemy, one of the two.

"The General's chief of staff will brief you in more detail when you arrive," Mustafa Kahiry said. They were suddenly eager to get rid of him. They didn't say anything, but it was written in all their faces.

He was happy to oblige. "Not long now till we reach Rochefort," he said, standing up and suppressing a yawn. "I hope you won't mind if I turn in. It's been a long day, and I need my beauty sleep."

They looked delighted, though they made a play of wanting to detain him. Three minutes later, he was in his own room.

And he knew exactly what was going on.

To be absolutely fair to her, Ruby Parker had warned him weeks ago that something like this might happen. *It would be different if you'd passed your sell-by date, John, but you haven't. Once you step over the threshold of this building for the last time, you won't necessarily be safe. Technically, you'll be 'available for hire', and some people have effective ways of taking advantage of that.* To which he had the perfect reply. Why should anyone find out he'd resigned?

At that point, it was a reasonable question. In an ideal world, even now, there'd only be a handful of people in Thames House who knew he'd gone, each one perfectly capable of keeping his or her mouth shut. All Ruby Parker had to do was play it discreetly.

But no, she hadn't gone down the subtle road. Her preferred highway involved an entire unit of anti-terrorist police officers, a forced escape through a first-floor window and a frantic sprint against Annabel and Alec. He might as well have arrived at work trailing silver balloons and wearing a pink top-hat with 'Bye!' written on the front. Probably everyone in London knew he'd resigned now. It'd be in *Metro* and *The Evening Standard*.

His room contained an alarm clock – the very thing he most needed. He set it for three o'clock, two hours hence, then undressed, turned off the lights and got in bed. He thought he might be too annoyed to sleep, but he wasn't. When the alarm went off, he knew instantly where he was, but he also wondered where the time had gone. And then an internal bell ding-ed: he remembered where he'd last seen Al-Azzabi. Yep, made sense.

Just about everyone should be asleep by now. He needed to find Fenella, which was a problem since he didn't even know where her room was. There was a phone on his bedside –

presumably an internal line – but obviously, it might be bugged. As might his room. And hers. He had to think.

First of all, where would her cabin be? The mark of a good host was to keep yourself apart from your guests a little, forestall the impression you're keeping a beady eye on them. He knew where at least one of her guests' rooms was; and it was likely the four men and their wives were accommodated in neighbouring cabins for company. Going by what he'd seen at dinner, the wives, in particular, seemed to get along well together.

His room was a little way apart from theirs. Given that she'd said she was so glad he was here, it seemed probable she'd want to be closer to him than to them; or rather that she'd use him as a kind of barrier to keep them at a distance. If he turned left outside instead of turning right to where the four men were, he should find her. If the worst came to the worst, someone had to be piloting the vessel. There had to be staff. He could just ascend to the bridge ask the captain. Or the chef: he or she would probably know. Mordred was a guest. He'd hardly be denied that sort of information.

He dressed and slipped outside into the corridor. Weird how you could feel the ship's movement, yet it was like being in a hotel. No sign of sea or sky or even anything nautical. He walked ten paces to what looked like the only cabin in this direction and knocked on the door.

Fenella answered. He expected to find her bleary-eyed and encased in some sort of *robe de chambre,* but she was dressed as if for company, although she'd changed since earlier in the evening. A beige frock and pearls. She even wore shoes.

"John," she said, as if his being there was the most natural thing in the world.

"Er, hi," he replied.

"Would you like to come in? Maria and I are playing Chinese Ten. The card game." She held the door open wider. "Neither of us has slept for years, and it helps pass the time. It's easily modified for three players."

"Could I have a word with you on the top deck?" he asked.

"I don't see why not." Again, uttered as if it was a perfectly reasonable request. Most people would have said, *what the hell about, at this time at night?*

She stepped outside without getting an overcoat, then he remembered: she kept one permanently up there. Nor did she say goodbye to Maria; instead, she kissed her fingertips and extended them slightly into the cabin.

"This way," she said, walking away from his cabin and the lift.

They mounted six sets of metal steps, each steeper than the last. At the end of the second, they passed through double doors to the outside. A full moon hung high to their right and a gentle breeze blew. The boat seemed much livelier now, more really at sea. The ocean was black and invisible except where the moonlight caught the tips of the nearest swells. There was no sign of land.

When they reached the top deck she removed her overcoat from the locker and put it on. She turned her back to the rail and faced him. "What's this about? Although I think I can guess."

"Where did you meet those men?"

"They're friends of friends. They were recommended to me by people I like and trust, and who would have no reason to deceive me. What's the matter with them?"

"They're Egyptian secret servicemen. General Intelligence Directorate, to give it its full name."

She laughed. "Dear God. What makes you so sure?"

"I've actually seen a picture of Mr Al-Azzabi. And the others were lying to me when they said Mabel is in Benghazi."

"Lying? How do you know that?"

"I'm trained to recognise deliberate falsehoods in people's faces. I say 'trained'. It's not entirely something you can learn."

She smiled and said nothing for a moment. "I know that when Maria was young, her mother kept a stray monkey called Juno. Truth or lie?"

"Lie."

"Very good. One of the last things I did before I set off on this voyage was to order a new skirt. True or false?"

"True."

"Because I'd seen something very similar on Channel Six."

"False."

"Maria won our last game of Chinese Ten."

"False. You've got to take into account that I'm doing this in conditions of reduced light. And that we're probably wasting time."

"What do you want me to do, John? Throw them off at the next port?" She laughed again, as if nothing could be funnier than that she'd been duped by Egyptian intelligence officers. "That's a serious question, by the way. And while we're on the topic, what's their motivation, or don't you know?"

"You've got to remember that I've done one or two things in my life that were quite dangerous and come out alive. I've crossed swords with a few villains and won. Intelligence services around the world aren't very generous in giving out information; mostly the people that run them aren't very bright and they prefer to play safe, so when they hear someone on another side's been exceptionally lucky – as I have – they habitually ascribe all sorts of martial virtues to him. It's always complete bullshit. Right now, what they want is to insert me into General Khalifa Haftar's army in the hope that I'll win the second Libyan civil war for them, thus clearing Egypt's westernmost border of Muslim Brotherhood clones."

She was still delighted, by the look of her. "And you'll win this war single-handedly, will you?"

"Supposedly. I can't think of any other motivation they might have. Put it like this. If, after all, I am a complete dud, they haven't lost anything because I'm completely expendable."

"And they've had a nice luxury cruise with the perfect little Mexican hostess." Her mood had changed. She looked angry now. "As if Donald Trump wasn't enough. What do you want me to do? Obviously, you have to get away from them."

"You said there was a plane at Rochefort waiting to take me to Libya. I assume it's theirs rather than yours."

She sighed. "They offered. It would have been difficult, although probably not impossible, for me to procure such a thing. But as long as they think you're their dupe, you can avoid them. At least, with my help. Do you still have your passport?"

"I've a very good forgery in the name of Mr Mirek Sobotka."

"If it helps, I can give you money and hire a car to take you to the nearest airport. Alternatively, I can arrange for someone to drive you to any point on Europe's southern coast. Or a train. Anything."

"Money would be good, for a start. And a car to the airport. I'll catch a plane to Algeria."

"Algeria?"

"I'll have to make careful preparations. Once these four men realise I've gone, they'll know I'm on to them. Egyptian intelligence attempting to suborn an MI7 officer when the ink's not even dry on his resignation probably won't go down well in London. Not when Egypt and Britain are supposed to be friends."

"And the best way of keeping that quiet would presumably be to kill you."

"Correct." He didn't voice his next conclusion: given that he'd spoken before thinking earlier, they'd know he was in Tripoli.

"It'll keep me on my toes," he said. "I'm walking into minefield as it is. Besides, let's not rush to pessimism. Their second best way of keeping me quiet would be to rescue Mabel. For what it's worth, I don't think they're murderers. They might well find me and try to make amends. We might end up working together, after all. Just not on their terms for their purposes."

"I'll talk to them after you've gone. Right now, I need to speak to my captain. Ask him to change course, discuss the best way of getting you ashore."

"Be careful. There may be bugs - even on the bridge."

"Pack what you need for a getaway and come and knock on my door again in an hour. After you've gone, I'll speak to all four men. If they become unpleasant, I can tell them you held me at gunpoint."

Ninety minutes later, as she watched him depart for the French shore in a motor-launch, she steeled herself to speak to her remaining guests, the Egyptians. It could wait till morning. They wouldn't believe she'd been coerced; they knew enough about her and Mordred to realise force would have been unnecessary. But she'd tell them that anyway. They couldn't argue, not as her guests.

But they wouldn't be pleased. The most pessimistic prognosis was likely the most accurate. Eventually, somewhere else, they'd try to kill him.

Which left her no alternative. She'd have to call Ruby Parker.

## Chapter 6: The No. 2 Ladies Detective Agency

"What's the point of reporting him missing?" Charlotte said. "The police won't care."

She and Hannah stood outside John's flat. Darkness had almost fallen now, but this was an outskirt of the capital so it hadn't entirely closed down. While it was ten times brighter than any provincial suburb, it felt gloomy thanks to the inescapable – but probably deceptive - sense of brilliance and perpetual motion only a few miles away.

"I don't think we should tell mum or dad," Hannah said. "Ring for a taxi," she commanded Charlotte. "No, I'll do it," she went on, changing her mind. "I don't want us to end up getting mugged as well. That would be the icing on the cake." She took her phone out.

"We can't tell Julia or Mabel about John. They can't be trusted not to blurt it out."

"Julia won't care. Or she will, a bit: in a rarefied literary novelist kind of way. In any case, she's not going to come back from Norway, and even if she did, what can she do? And Mabel's doing important things, besides which, she's just a kid. No, we're going to have to get to the bottom of this one alone. Are you up for a few more days in the capital? On me, obviously."

"I'll have to ring Marcus and ask him."

"Do it. - Oh, yes, hello," she said, her voice changing. "Is this Robson's taxis? Yes, I wonder if you could send a car to pick us up and take us into the City? We're in Islington, at the junction of ... Yes, easily. We'll walk down there now." She put her phone down. "We'll talk about it at the hotel, then - "

"Hi, Marcus," Charlotte interrupted, "this is your wife. Yeah, I know, I love you too. Yeah, I *am* missing you. I can't wait to come home. It's been terrible here without you, I'm counting the hours. Listen, do you mind if I stay in the capital for a few more days with Hannah? Something's come up ... Oh, nothing, really.

How's Seth? Great, that's really great. Well, I'll get off then. I'll ask my angel to look after you both."

She put the phone back in her bag and started to cry.

Hannah rolled her eyes. "Follow me," she barked. "We've got to get to the taxi." She took her own phone out, tapped the screen and put it to her ear. "Hi, this is Hannah," she said. "Lexingwood, that's right. *Sister-in-law Hannah,* that one. The point is, John's disappeared. We weren't going to tell anyone, but Charlotte made such an *arse* of admitting that she missed you a second ago, that I felt I'd better put it in a bit of context. That's right, Marcus: just so you don't go looking for another woman on the grounds that your wife's gone right off you. Exactly, it wasn't just 'nothing', like she said, and she should probably have started off by asking about Seth, but you know what a complete arse - "

It took Charlotte a moment to realise what was going on. First, she wiped her eyes and stopped weeping sufficiently to aid comprehension, then she had an attack of mortification and had to stop walking to put her hands on her head, then she ran to catch up and made a lunge for the phone.

"I was *joking!*" Hannah said, showing her the screen to prove it. "But it would have bloody well served you right." She laughed. "*I'm missing you every second, Marcus, I can't wait to get home, but PRECISELY NOTHING'S come up, so I've decided to stay here a little longer*. Bloody hell: imagine if *he* did that to *you*? Phone him back!"

They were both laughing now. They sat down on a bench to recover, then Hannah remembered about the taxi so they set off again at a half-jog. Charlotte rang her husband.

"Tell him he's welcome to come to London with Seth if he wants!" Hannah called back. "Tell him I'll pay! And I'll ring Tim when we get in the car!"

When they arrived back at the hotel, they shared a bottle of wine and retired to bed for a 'think'. Charlotte's angel spoke to her through dreams so, all being well, in the morning they'd have at least a plan, and possibly a solution. They were staying at The

Beau Brummel in Mayfair, a converted eighteenth century townhouse with three floors, long ago extended at the rear, and whose rooms were just like home: the ceilings were exactly the right height and every hint of a fire precaution had been discreetly merged into the fixtures and furnishings. Marcus and Tim had decided not to join them.

At breakfast the next morning, the two women ate muesli and drank Earl Grey tea. The hotel dining room continued the homely theme: small round tables with plain white covers, wooden chairs, old-fashioned lampshades and a slightly cramped feel. There were three other sets of guests, two American and a German.

"I still think we should go to the police," Hannah said. She poured herself another cup of tea. "I know what you're saying. They'll just be, like, *He's an adult, he's allowed to move house, and we're not convinced there's any reason for anxiety,* in the oh-so-soothing voice of the rookie Community Relations Officer. *Let us know if there are any developments* and so on and so forth. My point being, if we've been to them, and they *do* give us all that - "

"Which they *will.*"

"At least we can say we've been. Otherwise, let's say something happens and we *haven't* been… "

Charlotte pulled a sour face. "Then they'll be all, like, *Why the hell didn't you come to us, we'd have cleared it up yonks ago, you stupid pair of useless cows*. Yeah, I know what you mean. *Now it's all your fault.*"

"I don't suppose you got any clues in your dream last night?" Hannah asked and was instantly transported back to a time years ago, when she and Tim used to ask Charlotte what the angels or the crystals or the stars or the runes or the I Ching or the tealeaves said. The highlight of their day. Things weren't quite so good without him here.

"Well, I did actually have quite an intense dream, actually," Charlotte replied.

"I assume it needs interpreting."

"I was walking through this cornfield, and there were loads of bulls in there – about fifteen - and they were all eating this little gooseberry bush. I kept thinking, 'I've got to find the farmer and tell him what's happening', but I didn't know how to. There was an abbey in the distance, and it was probably Whitby abbey because I could smell the sea air. Anyway, all the bulls suddenly stopped eating the bush and started coming towards me, but I had a wand made out of one of those giant thistles you often see in ornamental gardens, and I was pointing it at them, and every time I did, they turned into different animals: a snake, I remember; a beaver, a rabbit, two spiders. All the time this was happening, I was completely naked. At the end, it started to rain."

"Hmm… interesting," Hannah said, even though she'd stopped listening after 'there was an abbey in the distance'. She never knew what anything in Charlotte's dreams meant, only that if Freud was alive he'd have a field-day.

"The meaning'll come eventually," Charlotte said. "We've just got to keep thinking about it."

"Hopefully, you'll have another tonight."

"God, yes. I won't be able to stop having them."

"Maybe we're being completely stupid. If John has moved – which obviously he has – he wouldn't necessarily tell us. But he would tell Mum and Dad."

Charlotte's eyes nearly popped onto the table. "Who wouldn't necessarily tell us either! Yes! Of course!"

"So all we've got to do is ring Mum and ask her, ever so casually, in passing, whether she's heard from John recently."

"Genius. Why the hell didn't we think of that earlier?"

"It's probably natural to over-complicate when you're worried."

Charlotte opened the teapot lid and poured the reserve boiling water in. "Maybe."

"There's no point doing it yet. Thursday's her Hospice Shop day. And Dad's no use, he won't know anything."

"Besides, if we ring her during the day, she'll think it's odd. She'll suspect something's up."

"Tonight, about eight?"

"Perfect."

"Perfect is right. Our booking runs out today, and we can't extend our stay. The Beau Brummel's highly sought-after. A waiting list of four weeks, and that's low season. No, if we're going to stay on, it'll have to be somewhere else."

"What if everywhere's booked?"

"There's always somewhere. The great thing about the internet is you don't have to tramp the streets asking if there's room at the inn. But if the worst comes to the worst, I'll get the manageress to recommend us a place." She took a sip of tea. "And if even that fails, I've friends who live here: I can call in a few favours. We'll be fine." Her expression darkened. "Having said that, us having to stay on after tonight would mean it's bad news. It would mean Mum doesn't have any answers."

"But she probably will have. He's bound to have said something to *Mum*, surely?"

"There's something decidedly uncanny about this whole affair, Charlotte. I'm not optimistic."

"What shall we do today? I don't suppose either of us feels much like holiday-type things."

"Practicalities first. Let's find another place to stay, then we'll chill. Have a facial or something. Watch a bit of TV. Just to pass the time."

"Meditate. Ponder my dream."

Hannah reached across the table and put an affectionate hand on her sister's. "Yep."

They waited till twenty-past to phone, mainly because eight o'clock might look too on-the-dot. They were paranoid about looking suspicious now, and although they'd never intended to, they spent dinner planning their campaign. Charlotte would phone. Pretext: Hannah's got two tickets to *Mandela* in the West

End, but there's a catch: it's tomorrow night. Of course, there was no chance the two senior Mordreds would be able to make it in twenty-four hours. A London show took months of careful planning, even after the tickets had been procured. A polite rejection would open the field to general chit-chat and a put-Hannah-on, probably lasting around an hour. If they hadn't taken the old lady for every last cent of relevant information at the end of that time, their names weren't *Les Sœurs Terrible*.

They'd found a new hotel in Russell Street, The Edward VII Metropole. Not quite as grand as the place in Mayfair, but comfortable, though everything about it was bulky or creaky. Big skirting boards, heavy doors, garish wallpaper, thick pile carpets a little upturned at the edges, ostentatious landscapes in gilt frames, large brass light fixtures. It didn't look as if it had been decorated since the 1950s; or rather it did – nothing looked overly aged – but only by someone whose taste rejected every succeeding decade. They had adjoining rooms.

At eight-twenty they sat together on the sofa in Hannah's room, put the phone on speakerphone and rang. Their mum picked up, good start. Then a setback. She couldn't talk too long, she was going out to a Church meeting. Luckily, things came to a head much faster than either daughter had anticipated. Of course it was impossible for Mum and Dad to make London for tomorrow night, but that needn't be the end of the matter.

"Why don't you give them to John?" Mum said. "He lives in London. Or are you still not speaking to each other?"

"You mean, to take his girlfriend?" Charlotte said, suddenly departing from the script.

"Look, I know you don't like her much. But that's only because she's got different views. It always amazes me, left-wingers - "

"I'm not a left-winger. Well, I am. But - "

"They – *we* - want 'everyone to come together and forget their differences', but as soon as we come across a Tory, we can't possibly have anything to do with him or her. It should have occurred to you that this Phyllis and you might have far more in common than you imagine. Did you ask her if she believes in angels, for example?"

"Come on, Mum, you could tell by her *outfit* that she didn't believe in angels!"

*"What?"* Mum laughed. "She didn't have her *angel-believing outfit* on? Is that what *you* wear then? An angel-believing outfit? Here, I'm putting your dad on. Say hello."

Putting Dad on was what happened when Mum began to despair. She usually had to go and sit down for a minute. Hannah mouthed 'give it to me' and snatched the phone.

"Mum!" she said. "It's me. Hannah. I just wanted to say hello."

"I was just about to put Dad on."

"Well, don't. I actually think it's a very good idea to give John these tickets."

Mum laughed again. "Have you been listening all the time? How are you, love?"

Charlotte stood up petulantly, and went to sulk on the hard wooden chair in the corner.

"The trouble is," Hannah went on, "it works both ways. I don't believe there'll be that many die-hard Tories queueing up to see a musical about a left-wing hero."

"Rubbish. Mandela's world-historical. You see, here we go again, stereotyping. I know lots of Tories who'd love to see Mandela. Anyway, if she doesn't want to go because she's some sort of closet racist, I can't think of a better way to put John off her, can you? If that's what you want."

"It isn't. Not necessarily. Not unless it's for his own good."

Mum sighed. "Look, love, John isn't like you girls. You're a billionaire, Charlotte's doing amazing things with that candle-making business of hers, and she's an excellent mum into the bargain – *did you hear that, Lottie?* – Julia's won literary prizes, Mabel's a medical genius and a saint and it's only a matter of time before she returns to Cambridge. John's not like that. He's just an ordinary man, and not doing particularly well for himself. And now his boss has taken a shine to him, and he's going out with her - "

"Er, what?"

"Oh, come on, Hannah. Put two and two together. One: where might John go to meet someone sophisticated like that? He's hardly the world's greatest socialite. So work, probably. A chance meeting. Two: remember her jewellery and her designer labels? She's got to be in a better position than him, at the very least his 'line manager', as the term is nowadays. Three: she's a Tory, so it might even be that she's connected to the ownership of the business: the boss, or the boss's daughter. She seemed to know a hell of a lot about the export-import balance and so on. It all adds up."

"I hadn't thought about it like that."

"Look, I'm going to be blunt because I'm going out in a minute. I need you to get in touch with him and make amends. And before you ask 'why me?', because it was your fault. I don't care how you do it and how many concessions you have to make. Just swallow your pride."

"Have you heard from him recently?"

"Not at all since the almighty bust-up. Obviously, I've tried ringing him but his phone's always switched off." She sighed. "Which isn't his style at all, but love does strange things to people… Anyway, I'm worried. And the longer it goes on, the worse it's going to get. Please, just bury the hatchet. It'd be a much better present than a night watching *Mandela,* lovely though that would have been, really."

"You're right, of course. I'll ring him tonight."

"If he's serious about this woman, we may have to make a few adjustments at get-togethers. Other families do it. It's called tolerance."

"Toleration."

"I'm not getting at you, Hannah. You mean the world to me, you all do, you know that."

They reassured each other about kindly intentions, expressed mutual love, promised eternal loyalty, and hung up.

"Well, that was a bummer," Charlotte said, from the corner.

"It was shit," Hannah agreed. "Not only did she put her finger on the probable truth, but now we're going to have to ring 'Phyllis' and eat humble pie."

"What are you talking about?"

"Mum's right. Far from persuading him to dump this woman, our actions probably drove him deeper into her clutches. Some people are like that. I'm guessing 'Phyllis' is."

"Like what?"

"Possessive. Someone – let's call him 'John' - falls in love with them. They're not content to enjoy John in the normal way. No, they can only get pleasure from him insofar as he's exclusive to them. So they make him cut all ties to friends and family, then wrap him in in a cocoon of emotional manipulation and suck all the life out of him. Like one of those ghouls in Edvard Munch. Don't you see? That's where he's moved to. In with her."

Enlightenment filled Charlotte's face like a blush. "Of course. And when he decided not to meet us in Selfridges, it was probably – something had probably gone wrong with the house-move. A hitch, meaning he had to be there."

"And he actually wants to be friends with us again. He threw his phone in the bin knowing it only had her number on and that you'd almost certainly fish it out. It was a cry for help. He wants us to contact her."

"And he arranged to meet us first, then cried off at the last minute. He's experiencing an internal battle. Us versus her."

Hannah nodded. "Obviously, he's hoping not to have to choose. If we contact her, using his phone, we might be able to effect a Sisters-Phyllis ceasefire, that's his hope. Mollify her, thereby resolving his tortuous dilemma."

"Oh, my God. You don't think she's some sort of crazy woman, do you?"

"Yes. Yes, I do. But I also think we'll have to ring her."

*"Why?"*

"Because I promised Mum I'd talk to him! Weren't you listening?"

Charlotte grimaced. "Shit. I get it."

"I can only talk to him through her. That's what the discarded phone's saying. 'You either talk to me through my demonic girlfriend or not at all'."

"'But please talk to me. I love you.'"

"Don't make excuses for him," Hannah said. "He's a feckless jerk."

"Look on the bright side. When we've saved him, he'll owe us."

"Great. Maybe we'll get a twenty per cent discount on machine parts instead of just ten."

"Ten? You get *ten?* He only offered me *five!*"

They laughed then discussed the calling-Phyllis campaign for a few minutes. Who'd say the first words, how to introduce themselves, when to pop in the apology, how profuse to make it, how to explain their having her phone number at all, possible topics for further conversation in the event of an apology-acceptance, what to do if Conservatism was extolled or Socialism was slated, options in the event of an apology-rejection. Suddenly Hannah clicked her tongue and stood up.

"What's up?" Charlotte asked her.

"We took the exact same approach to Mum's phone call, remember? We planned it meticulously, then it went wrong from the outset. Maybe we should play this one by ear."

"I'm too nervous."

"Me too. Let's get a few shots of tequila, then call. That ought to do it."

"Here? In the hotel room?" Charlotte asked.

"No, that would be sordid. A bespoke shots bar. I'll order us a taxi. Leave the wretched phone at reception. We'll call when we get back."

Half an hour later, their cab pulled up. It took them three minutes across London to the heart of the financial district and a twenty-five storey building with a cocktail bar called Sammi's at the top.

Most of the building was closed down. Reception, the bar and one or two late-night eateries were its only remaining centres of life. The entrance was down a wide side-street with a spotlight.

Suddenly two men appeared menacingly from nowhere. One from in front, one behind, both male and well-built, and both wielding knives. They looked the same age – early thirties – one was black, the other white, they were clean-shaven and spoke without accents; their faces were mostly hidden by hoods and bandanas – only their eyes were visible – and they were well-built. They looked like they could run, punch, kick and make effective stabs to the heart or slashes to the throat without much effort. Somehow, no one else was around. The women instinctively froze.

"I want your phones," the foremost man said. "And your cash. Put your bags on the floor and step away. Neither of you need get hurt. Don't try anything stupid and don't tell the police. We know who you are and where you've come from."

"Do as they say," Hannah told Charlotte.

Charlotte didn't look as if she'd argue in any event. Both women put their bags on the floor. The men grabbed them and ran off.

"Bloody shit," Hannah said. "End of a perfect evening."

"At least we're still alive," Charlotte said.

They looked at each other and seemed to realise what had just happened. Suddenly, the temperature seemed to drop through the floor; their teeth chattered and they were swept by violent emotions they couldn't remember experiencing before. They hugged each other without even knowing what they were doing, trying to merge into each other's warmth. "My God, my God," Hannah repeated over and over, while Charlotte gasped uncontrollably.

They had to get back into the stream of humanity again. Hannah took hold of herself and led Charlotte back to the main pavement. This was the City of London. Creepy at the best of times, and never as populous as it should be. Right now, there were only a few people around, all on their way somewhere, heads down.

"We've got to get back to the hotel," Hannah said. "Don't worry, it's only a few minutes' walk. We're all right. It's over. We're all right."

Charlotte knelt and vomited in the gutter.

Ten minutes later, they were back at the hotel. They'd forgotten all about Phyllis and John now. All they knew was they needed the safety of a door to shut on the world, and a phone to call the police. They took receipt of the keys at reception and held hands in the lift. They'd sleep in the same bed tonight, probably ask to be transferred to a single room. Until the police had been called and that was sorted, they'd repair to Hannah's.

When they opened the door to what they anticipated would be sanctuary, there were clothes strewn across the floor. The wardrobes had been emptied and every drawer was gaping.

"Oh, my God," Charlotte said, half-hysterically. "Muggers then burglars. What are the chances?"

As an attempt to lighten the mood, it failed.

## Chapter 7: In To Africa

After reaching a sandy beach somewhere on the west coast of France, Mordred transferred to a black BMW driven by a young man wearing a hoodie and wire-framed spectacles. In the course of sixty-five minutes at a fairly constant 120km/h, they passed through a succession of tiny villages interspersed by cornfields and columnar trees. They stopped at a single light aircraft beside a gloomy hangar on an airfield seemingly in the middle of nowhere.

The driver transformed into a pilot without missing a beat. He started the plane, waited for Mordred to climb aboard and issued a pre-flight instruction to retrieve a briefcase behind the seat. Inside were two thousand French euros, a thousand US dollars, an American Express card 'for emergencies', and a pocket booklet with Fenella's number disguised amongst a set of other figures. Outside, it was a clear breezeless morning. Perfect flying weather. They took off as the sun rose and lapsed into silence as the French landscape gradually lit up ten thousand feet below. One by one, the stars disappeared. Soon, they were over the Mediterranean.

She'd taken excessive precautions. He wasn't sure he'd be able to use the credit card – surely there hadn't been time to index it to his Czech alias – but it was a nice thought, and full marks for trying.

Which was the wrong way of looking at it. She'd had no formal training in intelligence. At that point in his development, four or five years ago, he'd been an imbecile. Her provisions for him spoke convincingly of her acumen and even suggested an intellectual gulf where he occupied the lower end. If she'd been the falling in love kind, he'd have been her slave by now. Only the certainty that she wasn't – not any more - stopped him drawing up the customary ledger of optimistic versus unthinkable outcomes and committing to achieve at least one of the former.

They landed in Algeria at 07.15 on a desert runway with literally nothing around except another hangar, a few sandy tracks and four cars, none of which looked up to the work involved in leaving the vicinity. He transferred from the plane to a Jeep and a different chauffeur. Within an hour, he was in a second-floor hotel room in the centre of Algiers. As was his custom, he swept for listening devices – between the bed, a free-standing wardrobe and a bare table and chairs, it wasn't too difficult - then locked the door, closed the curtains, laid down and slept. The city was already awake.

Five hours later, he awoke, washed in the communal bathroom at the far end of the corridor, and walked into the city. His first concern was to find out if he was being watched or followed, although he quickly came to the conclusion he wasn't. The heat was stifling. He needed a change of clothing to enable him to pass as a local, and a ride to the border. Normally, he'd swap a prearranged hotel first thing, wherever he arrived. On this occasion, Fenella had arranged his lodgings, and it wasn't impossible that she'd have given away something to her 'guests'. He didn't think she herself was in any danger: a boat like the *Chalchiuhtlicue* needed a lot of staff, and they were unlikely to stand by while their owner was threatened. Besides, the Egyptians hadn't seemed the extorting kind. No, if she'd let details slip, it'd have been inadvertently. In any case, this time it didn't matter. He wasn't going to be around long enough to make a target. Not in Algiers, anyway.

The hardness of shadow in the streets made the buildings look misleadingly tall and distorted, and the space in between them deceptively narrow. In the fluctuating sun and shade, pedestrians seemed to bounce or they walked with intensity. Mostly, they seemed to be shopping, or selling, or guiding clients, or solemnly discussing, or looking for something just out of view. Buses roared. Turks, Berbers, Arabs, Sub-Saharans sat motionlessly, eyes alert, apparently expecting something obscure. In the administrative district, office workers mingled with shepherds. Men in ties and sunglasses sat in pairs on walls or benches eating *tunisiennes*. Horns peeped continuously and innocuously. Insects chirruped in place of birds. A fragrance of oregano and diesel filled the air. Dogs roamed.

And of course, he was seeing all this through the eyes of a foreigner. Unaccustomed eyes, pathologically attuned – at least for the moment - to the exotic. For someone newly arrived from Britain, it was impossible to get past the palm trees, the tribal headdresses, the occasional dromedary, things most locals almost certainly never saw, not because they never entered their field of vision, but because they never made it as far as their consciousness. As so often abroad on some kind of intelligence mission, the feeling of menace and the sense of being on holiday merged. And then the loneliness. An odd kind of exhilaration, mostly unpleasant.

He bought a change of clothing in one of the markets and hired a taxi to take him to the Libyan border. The problem now lay in obtaining Libyan or Algerian papers. There were undoubtedly men here who specialised in forging identities: from what he'd heard, too many Sawahari Arabs wanted a passage to Europe for there not be a market. For the time being, he had to discard his old clothes and don his new ones: a white woollen cloak or *gandoura* over a cotton shirt. Since he wasn't being followed – yet – and since his initial inspection, that morning, had turned up nothing suspicious in terms of bugs, it was probably safe to change in his hotel room. A last visit.

When he checked in at reception, there was a package awaiting him. A small flat envelope, with what felt like a passport inside. Fenella's work? He tore it open. It was what it appeared to be. An Algerian passport - in the name of Omar Ouyahia Abu Farafisa, with his photo.

This wasn't Fenella's doing. It was too perfect and too swift for that. And she didn't have any sort of photo of him, much less one that could serve for a passport. No, there was only one person this could be. Ruby Parker.

The implications sank in drop by drop, and for a few seconds, he felt almost giddy. Good or bad? Something prodded him hard in the lower back and a voice whispered, in English, directly into his ear. "This is a gun, Mr Mordred, and I'm not remotely afraid to use it. We'll begin by going to your room. Try not to make any sudden movements."

Nouri Said Younis, one of the men from Fenella's boat. As if by magic, Mustafa Kahiry appeared at his other side.

Pure melodrama. In these sorts of scenarios, it was never a good idea to act your part. It gave them confidence, making them more likely to act theirs – in this case, shoot.

After drawing the implications of the passport, he already felt giddy, but this drove his sense of unreality to a new level. He suddenly found himself acting out the advice of *The Manual of Effective Spycraft,* a book that existed solely in his imagination and which he'd invented last year to tease his former MI7 colleagues with. Quoting it in the canteen was supposed to expose their ignorance.

According to the *Manual,* the thing about a corny line like, 'I've a gun and I'm not afraid etc.' was it came from a script. It meant your adversary was convinced he had a good screenplay and that other members of the cast will do their artistic duty. It meant the last thing he expected was to be smacked in the face with an open fist. In an especially propitious situation, the *refusnik* might even be able to seize the weapon while his adversary is on his way to the skirting boards.

Or not.

*Situations in which he might not # 1.* Supposed adversary never actually had a gun. He recited a corny line because he's a fan of black and white American movies, and he knows you have a sense of humour.

And now, you've broken his jaw.

*

Half an hour later, Nouri Said Younis lay on the bed in Mordred's room with his head in a bandage, courtesy of a medic from the Egyptian consulate. Mustafa Kahiry took charge of Public Relations and, after a minute, Mohammad Al-Taher Al-Juhaimi arrived from the street to assist. There was never any question of calling the police: 'Abu Farafisa' – significantly, they were already using Mordred's alias – was a friend, and the whole thing had been a tragic misunderstanding. Since Younis could no longer talk, there seemed little point in his remaining at the hotel – better to get him home - but he seemed to believe the whole thing was his fault, and his being *in situ* would serve as an act of contrition. Once Mordred realised the true state of affairs, he was equally mortified, but without the inconvenience of being unable to talk. He kept his apologies to Arabic with a local inflection.

It took a full hour for the situation to settle. Tea was brought. At last, Mustafa Kahiry thanked the innkeeper for his help, then politely requested that he and his staff leave. He closed the door when he heard them descend the stairs at the end of the corridor. Extra seats had been brought in for the show. Mordred sat on a chair in the corner by the window; Nouri Said Younis lay on the bed trying to look chipper, but obviously in great pain – his eyes still watered; Mustafa Kahiry sat in an armchair in front of the wardrobe, and a sofa had been laid on for Al-Juhaimi, parallel to the bed. For a few moments, silence carried the day, broken only by the din of the street.

"So *Abu Farafisa,*" Mustafa Kahiry said eventually, in Arabic, "how are you finding Algiers?"

Cue for a Bond-type witticism, but he couldn't think of one. "Very nice," he said.

"You're probably wondering what we're doing here," Al-Juhaimi said.

A second cue for ditto. Still couldn't think of one.

"Not really," he said.

Was this the suave prelude to some sort of interrogation? It couldn't be. He realised he was being monosyllabic, and probably sounded a bit like a petulant child. Which didn't reflect his feelings at all. If anything, he felt slightly stupid and guilty, more so when he looked at Younis.

"After you left the *Chalchiuhtlicue,*" Mustafa Kahiry said, "our hostess came to see us. She didn't mince words, but neither did she seem particularly angry, although I admit she was entitled to be. She told us what you told her, I suppose: that we're high-ranking officers from the General Intelligence Directorate in Cairo, and that we'd planned to use you in our campaign against Islamism in eastern Libya under the command of General Haftar. She was frightened we might attempt to expunge all traces of our duplicity by attempting to kill you – I assure you, such a possibility never entered our heads, though, from her point of view, and yours, it could have – and to forestall that, she'd been in touch with the head of British intelligence Red section in London, a certain 'Ruby Parker'."

Al-Juhaimi smiled. "Don't look so shocked that Ms Salvaterra mentioned her by name. We have a dossier on Ruby Parker in headquarters as thick as a man's torso. Although surprisingly little hard information. I imagine a similar dossier exists in every capital of every major country in the world, more or less extensive, depending on the efficacy of their sources."

"Of course, Egypt and Britain are friends," Mustafa Kahiry continued. "And we'd like it to stay that way. A few high-level phone calls between your Foreign and Commonwealth Office and its equivalent in Cairo soon resolved the apparent disjunct. In a word, thanks partly to us – although we're not so conceited as to attempt to take credit for it – you now enjoy the full confidence of your government, *and* we've been ordered to assist you in every way possible."

"The perfect combination," Al-Juhaimi said neutrally.

"What did Ruby Parker say?" Mordred asked.

"Too junior to be part of the conversation," Mustafa Kahiry replied airily.

She was probably fuming. Although to be fair, she was a bit like Mr Spock on *Star Trek*. Emotions didn't usually figure. She'd looked angry at him leaving, but that was probably affected: a stratagem to bend him to the logical course. But the bottom line was, he was almost certainly still fired.

"What were you planning to do in Algiers?" Al-Juhaimi asked. "Just out of interest?"

A third opportunity for a Bond-type quip. Bloody zilch *again*. There'd never be a film about him.

Although perhaps when he dictated his memoirs, sitting in a wheelchair in a retirement home in Riga, he'd have come up with something. He could re-write history.

A sin, usually. But if it meant a film …

"I didn't have a full-fledged plan. In these sorts of situations, plans aren't drawn up in some sort of mental boardroom with a map spread out on a table. You start off with the germ of an idea and you grow a plan organically."

"And what was your 'germ of an idea'?" Mustafa Kahiry asked.

Al-Juhaimi turned to his colleague and spread his palms. "Does it matter? This isn't an interrogation. I would imagine it's the same one you or I would have. Get into the conflict-zone, assess the conditions, follow up the leads, make projections. One day at a time."

Mordred nodded. "I was going to enter Tripoli dressed as a middle-class Algerian or Libyan, depending which passport I could obtain at short notice. Then ingratiate myself with as many influential locals as possible. Travel about from one compass point to another. You're right: the same 'plan' anyone in this room would come up with. Hardly worthy of the name, really."

"Trial and error," Al-Juhaimi said. "Likely to prove expensive when there's a time-factor built in. I understand her captors have been in contact with you."

"They made one phone call. Now I've got a list of times and dates when I'm required to contact my sister with a disposable phone. When I do, I'll be given another phone number to ring. Providing I've transferred money, I get to speak to her for ten seconds. Obviously, they know my money will soon run out. Then I pay in guns."

The men looked at each other. "That doesn't sound like ISIS *at all*," Mustafa Kahiry said. "Daesh is the richest terrorist organisation on the planet. It doesn't need anyone's pocket-money. It certainly wouldn't take the risk of running an errand boy. No, these are simple peasant boys by the sound of it. Amateurs."

"That was MI7's conclusion," Mordred said. "The problem is, firearms help level the playing field. If you're up against ten gunmen, you've always got problems, however wet behind the ears they may be in other ways. Perhaps why we botched it."

"When is the last date on which you've been told to contact them?" Mustafa Kahiry asked.

"A week from today," Mordred replied. "By that time, I'm to have a consignment of rifles in Nice."

The men chuckled.

"Amateurs! *Amateurs!*" Al-Juhaimi exclaimed.

"Of course, they *could* be ISIS," Mordred said. "I'm not ruling that out."

Mustafa Kahiry shook his head dismissively. "I can't see how."

"I believe John's right," Al-Juhaimi said. "ISIS isn't like McDonalds. A person is ISIS if he says he is. He may not have established formal links with the mother-ship yet, but providing he's declared allegiance, that's enough. And the way things work in Libya right now, he might change his mind tomorrow. Or he might not. Or he might actually establish those links and the fate of John's sister gets upgraded to immediate execution. Everything's in flux."

Mustafa Kahiry shrugged. "When do you next have to call these guys?"

"Two days' time," Mordred said. "Noon GMT. Look, I'm pleased our respective governments have reached an agreement, but I'm rather anxious to get on for obvious reasons. I apologise again for breaking Nouri Said's jaw - "

"An occupational hazard," Mustafa Kahiry said.

"But I need to know if and how you can help me. I've a taxi booked to take me to the border soon, and I don't want to be late."

"We've cancelled it," Al-Juhaimi told him. "Because what we've got for you is so much better," he added hastily. "Your sister isn't in Tripoli, by the way. She's in Tanarej, a fishing town forty miles east of the capital. We don't know exactly where, but our intelligence is reliable. With your help, we'll find out, obviously."

"What makes you so sure?" Mordred asked.

"Your rescue-attempt wasn't entirely unsuccessful," Al-Juhaimi said. "As always, a few militants were injured. Of course, the British stood no chance of picking them up. Yours was a straight-in, straight-out operation. Luckily, we don't have that handicap."

"We removed them to Tobruk for interrogation," Mustafa Kahiry said. "General Haftar was only too happy to help, of course, as he always is. Anyway, the prisoners all independently said the same thing. Tanarej."

Mustafa Kahiry leaned back like he was about to begin telling a story. "We've worked together with British intelligence to produce your new passport. Omar Ouyahia Abu Farafisa works for Sonatrach, the state-owned Algerian oil company. He's looking to expand the firm's interest in Libya by smoothing the way for partnerships and - "

"I don't mean to sound ungrateful," Mordred interrupted, "But I don't actually know anything about oil. I'm not sure I could pull that off."

"Don't worry," Al-Juhaimi said. "You're just there as a PR man. You meet the relevant people, shake their hands, drink pomegranate juice, smile a lot. You don't need to know the technical details."

"The sad truth is, you're a little *corrupt,*" Mustafa Kahiry said.

## Chapter 8: Après La Double Whammy

Hannah and Charlotte abandoned their plan to call the police. They tidied away the clothes that littered the floor, and sat side by side on the bed looking silently at the carpet. They both remembered *Don't tell the police, we know who you are and where you've come from.* Of course, bag-snatchers always said that, it didn't necessarily mean anything. But the burglary coming right on top of the robbery added a new dimension of menace, and raised the claim's credibility.

Somehow, it made it doubly ominous that the burglars had taken nothing valuable. Like they'd been looking for something specific.

And they'd obviously got past the hotel reception desk. In and out, and no one had noticed. Even now, as far as the two women knew, they were the only people in the entire building who knew a burglary had even occurred. Hannah's words at breakfast that morning - *There's something decidedly uncanny about this whole affair* – returned with renewed force.

They pondered whether to ring their husbands, but decided against it. Tim and Marcus wouldn't understand. They'd just be like, *Ring the bloody police, you've GOT to*. It'd end in a row and make matters ten times worse. Instead, they both rang their phone and credit card companies, cancelled their cards, then sat in silence again.

"Do you remember what the muggers said?" Charlotte asked eventually, in a hoarse voice.

"I know," Hannah replied.

"No, I mean the *first* thing. They said, 'I want your phones'."

Silence, as the unspoken insinuation filtered through.

"No, that's not possible," Hannah said eventually.

"As if they asked for our cash and our bags as an *afterthought*."

"You mean, you think…? No," she repeated. "That wouldn't make sense. Sorry, Charlotte, can I just check we're on the same wavelength? You're actually suggesting they were after *John's phone?"*

"You wouldn't go, 'Give me your phones' then, 'Oh, and by the way, I'll take your cash too while I'm at it. No, I'll tell you what: why don't we just go the whole hog? Go on, give me your entire bags. Save you the trouble of getting everything out.'"

"You'd probably be edgy if you were robbing someone. You might not come across as articulate. Burglars get nervous. That's why they defecate on the carpet."

"I can't see any faeces in here."

Hannah sighed. "No."

"If you were a bit panicky, you'd have learned your lines. It would be, 'Get down on the floor and gimme your bags!' It wouldn't be… well, how they said it."

"What the hell could they want John's phone for?" She suddenly had an epiphany – a bad one – and leaned forward and let breath out as if she'd been winded. *"Because there used to be something on there*. Something bad. And he wiped it. And they're after him, and they think it's still there."

"And that's why he moved out of his flat. He's running away."

Hannah laughed without humour. "No, no. This can't be right. We keep inventing stories. We can't just keep on like this. A few hours ago he'd moved in with 'Phyllis' and she was manipulating him. Now he's on the run from we don't know who." She laughed in the same way and stood up. "The *CIA?* We can't keep doing this!"

"A few hours ago, we hadn't been mugged and burgled. And remember what you said this morning: 'There's something utterly uncanny about this whole thing'. Your exact words. And that was then. *Then,* before we'd been through the - the *terror mill."*

"This ends now, Charlotte. We're going down to reception – together – and we're going to get that phone and we're going to bring it back up here, and we're going to ring 'Phyllis'. And then, depending on how unhappy we are afterwards – but I'm not optimistic - we're going to the police."

"Do you think that's wise?"

"These people always go, 'Don't tell the police'. It's bullshit. Remember *Happy Valley*? Remember the kidnappers? As soon as the police got involved, good things started to happen. Not before. I'm only not ringing the police *right now* because I'm curious about 'Phyllis'. I only didn't ring them earlier because I was in shock. But I'm getting over it now. I can see things more clearly. We've got to. It's a no-brainer."

"What worries me is if someone *is* after John's phone."

Hannah groaned. "More complications. What now?"

"They must know *we've* got it. Otherwise, none of tonight is explicable. By now, they'll know *they* haven't got it, which must mean *we still have*. They're probably watching us. Next time, they'll be angrier. They might even be standing outside the door right now, waiting for us."

"That… That is a very good point. We need reinforcements. Not the police, not yet. I've got friends in London. I can hire protection at the drop of a hat. I'll ring Tim, too. Might as well now."

Charlotte picked up the bedside phone and put it to her ear. "Just checking the line's not dead," she explained.

"And is it?"

"No. Not yet."

They rang Tim; Charlotte called Marcus; Hannah called her PA, Ruth. She asked her to access their shared contacts, ring ten friends and instruct them to drop everything and get to the hotel for a party. And order some food in too, please. And come yourself, and bring Alan. No expense spared, no. Go as wild as you like.

Within forty-five minutes, the room was full of men and women who probably had better things to do, but couldn't risk ignoring a summons from Number 12 on Hammill's 100 Most Influential Women in the UK list. Four young men accompanied her to reception, where she claimed the phone she'd left earlier.

"Did you ask for it to be given to a young man in his early thirties?" the receptionist asked. "Only, we had a caller earlier, while you were out, asking for 'the package you'd left at reception'. He claimed you'd instructed him to pick it up. I said we'd have to verify that, and when I wouldn't hand it over, he became quite unpleasant. Rightly or wrongly, I didn't give it to him. I couldn't. Company policy. And occasionally, the management likes to stage tests to see if its employees comply. I'm sorry if that caused any inconvenience. As I say, it's policy, and standard practice in London hotels nowadays."

"I didn't ask anyone to collect anything on my behalf," Hannah said. She was on the point of asking the receptionist to keep hold of the CCTV, she was about to ring the police. When it occurred to her she couldn't ring the police. The time for that was over.

She and Charlotte had just been mugged and then burgled. How to explain that they'd tidied the room, waited an hour, and now they were having what, to all appearances, was a get-together with a few friends *right on top of the evidence*? If it had only been one of them, that might just have been explicable. It's difficult to put things in context if you're alone. But two of them? At best, they'd look like idiots; at worst, liars. And for what? So everyone on Facebook could go, *Hannah Lexingwood's desperate for publicity!* So she could be struck dead by a Force 12 Twitter storm?

There was only one thing for it. She had to go back upstairs, get Charlotte alone somewhere, ring 'Phyllis', then take the phone back to reception and hand it in again with the words, 'Probably someone will come and ask for this. Please give it to whoever'. Plus, perhaps, that instruction in writing. Then posted on all social media. *I've just handed a lost phone in at The Edward VII Metropole.*

Then run.

Ten minutes later, they stood together in the locked bathroom of their adjoining rooms. Hannah held her brother's phone plugged into her charger; Charlotte held his twin crystal. They felt as frightened now as at any point in the evening. Being mugged hadn't been scary – not the actual process, because it hadn't sunk in until afterwards. Even then, there had been too many other emotions: revulsion, mainly, then horror, self-pity, indignation, self-loathing, fury, a bunch of other feelings - none pleasant - that didn't even have names. Right now, their knees were almost knocking.

They'd decided that Hannah would be the first to speak since, looking back, although The Family Dinner From Hell had begun as a slightly strained discussion between the three sisters and their brother's girlfriend, it had quickly *descended* – that being the only appropriate word, in retrospect – into a bitter argument between Hannah and Phyllis. Hannah therefore had to do the making-up. Besides which, she'd promised her mum.

"Countdown," Charlotte said breathlessly. "Three, two - "

"From ten."

"Ten, nine, eight - You know those bulls in my dream? They were the muggers."

"This is nerve wracking enough," Hannah replied. "Please."

"I'm just saying. Only because we might be able to use my dream to find out what's going to happen."

"How?"

They looked at each other.

"You're right," Charlotte said. "Seven, six - "

"Stop."

"What now?"

Hannah unlocked the door and peered into her hotel room. She'd ordered six pizzas, three plates of canapes and enough wine, beer and orange juice to keep thirty guests entertained for about three hours. Casually-dressed young men and women sat or stood about in groups as if they were at an insurance company reception do. In the background, low-volume music by Madonna. Oh, how Rock and Roll had progressed since the days of Keith Moon. She clapped her hands to get everyone's attention.

"Excuse me," she said, "but did anyone here vote for Brexit?"

Silence. In the centre of the room, two men and a woman turned to look sheepishly at a third man with a beard. He wore an open-necked white shirt and pink trousers and looked as if he hoped a hole would open in the floor so he could be swallowed up.

"Efan did," the woman said, pointing.

"Would you mind coming with me a moment, Efan?" Hannah asked.

Suddenly, his evening had imploded. As he crossed the room, blushing and trying to avoid eye-contact, the others hissed slightly. When he was in the bathroom, Hannah closed the door behind him. He looked like he was about to be executed.

"I'm really sorry to do that to you, Efan," she said. "I'll make it up to you, I promise. What do you do for a living?"

He said something, but it was asphyxiated by hoarseness and possible nervous constriction of the larynx. He cleared his throat and tried again. "Sound engineer."

"I need you to give me your best argument for Brexit."

"Oh," he said. "Erm… Sorry, my mind's gone blank. Erm…"

"If you do it I'll give you five pounds," Charlotte said, obviously mistaking his incapacity for reluctance.

"It's okay," he said. "I've got five pounds."

"He doesn't need five bloody pounds!" Hannah told her sister, raising her voice.

Enlightenment seemed to dawn on Efan's face. Of course! They'd been taking drugs. He'd forgotten that Hannah Lexingwood was Old School.

"Right," he said. "Let's see. Britain's trade with Europe is declining; its trade with the rest of the world is increasing. For the sake of our future prosperity, we need to make our own trade deals, but we can't while we're part of the EU. We're being forced into a political union that isn't democratic and isn't in our interests, and we're paying through the nose for it. We're the world's fifth biggest economy - "

"That's great, Efan, thank you," Hannah said. "Really appreciate it. I'll catch up with you later. Contrary to what you might think, we're not high on illegal substances, and I never forget a favour. What's your surname, by the way?"

"Featherstonehaugh."

"Okay, I probably will forget that. Let's swap numbers instead."

They did so. She opened the door to release him back into the room. Everyone regarded him with distaste. She saw him pick up his coat and leave.

*"Ring bloody Phyllis,"* Charlotte said when they were alone again.

Hannah hesitated a moment then pressed 'call'. She took a sharp breath, as if her dialling finger had ambushed her. They had it on speakerphone, so they both heard it begin to ring immediately. Charlotte held up a pair of crossed fingers. It wasn't clear whether she was signifying, *Good luck,* or *Hopefully, she won't be there.*

"John?" came a plummy voice at the other end. Phyllis. She sounded baffled.

"This isn't John. It's his sister, Hannah. I'm ringing to apologise for my behaviour at dinner that day we met. I know it was a while ago now, but I've thought a lot about it since. I had no right to talk to you the way I did. You were a guest in my parents' house and I behaved abominably."

"John's *sister*? Hannah Lexingwood?"

"That's me, and I really am sorry. This isn't a wind-up."

Silence. "Well, thank you." Said in a tone that suggested astonishment rather than the digging in of expensive heels plus the possibility of an upcoming gloat. "That's, er, very kind of you."

More silence.

"Thank you, er, Hannah," Phyllis said at last, in the same tone. "Can I ask why it is you're, er, ringing me on John's phone? Not that it matters, only I thought it was him. You don't have to tell me, of course. I won't keep you, by the way. Thank you again for the apology."

"He, er, gave it to me. Upgraded his. And it still had your number on." She was aware that there was an unacceptably high proportion of 'er's in their conversation, and moved to adjust. "I wonder if we could go out for a drink sometime? Maybe?"

"That would be lovely. Well, Ciao."

Charlotte grabbed the phone. "Don't hang up! This is his other sister, Charlotte. I wanted to apologise too. I was no better than Hannah."

"Er, sorry, I may have got the wrong end of the stick," Phyllis said in a noticeably colder tone. "Is this your idea of a joke? Have you been drinking, by any chance?"

"No!" the sisters exclaimed together.

Hannah grabbed the phone again. "Look, I swear it's not a piss-take. And I honestly meant everything I said about apologising. I can even see where you were coming from, and how you might be right. After all, Britain's trade with Europe is declining; its trade with the rest of the world is increasing. For the sake of our future prosperity, we need to make our own trade deals, but we can't while we're part of the EU. And yet" – she'd uttered two long sentences without taking a breath, but couldn't keep it up – "even if that weren't the case… Look, I'll come to the point. Do you know where John is? We're frantic."

"John? No. Why would he be with me?"

"Because you're his girlfriend, aren't you?"

Phyllis chuckled. "We split up, shortly after that dinner. I've no idea where he is now. You must have some way of contacting him, surely?"

"Shit, no. Sorry to keep swearing. He's disappeared. Normally, I'd phone him, but, well, he hasn't got his phone. I have. And I …"

"Don't take this the wrong way, but I'm not sure how you get from that to his supposed disappearance."

"We were meant to meet for breakfast yesterday morning, only he didn't show up. Then Charlotte bumped into him in Oxford Street and he was trying to throw this phone away. This one: the one I'm holding in my hand right now. Luckily, Charlotte retrieved it, and he actually *ran away* from her. We haven't seen or heard from him since. And the phone's been wiped of *virtually everything* except your number. Which is why we thought you and he might still be together. Anyway, then we went round to his flat in Islington, but it was being cleared by removal men. And Mum hasn't heard from him since that dinner. But the worst of it was, Charlotte and I were out tonight and we were mugged. The muggers asked for our phones before our bags. And when we got back to the hotel, we'd been burgled. Burgled on top of being mugged! We're pretty scared right now. We're actually ringing from the bathroom and I've invited twenty or so friends round, not because I actually want to see them, but because I'm shit-scared of sitting alone with just Charlotte and – hang on, I've forgotten where I - "

"How we'd taken the phone to reception," Charlotte whispered.

"That's right: fortunately, we'd handed John's phone - this one: the one I'm holding now - in to reception before we went out. But when I went to claim it, the receptionist said someone had been in and asked for it. Whoever it was said I'd given him permission. But of course I hadn't."

"So someone's after John's phone," Charlotte whispered.

"So someone's after John," Hannah said. "That's all it can be. He's obviously in some sort of big, big trouble. We just wondered if you had *any* idea – any *at all* – what it might be. Or how we could help him."

"It sounds awful," Phyllis said. "But I'm afraid I've no idea how to proceed. Have you been to the police?"

"We daren't," Hannah said. "We were dazed when we got back from being mugged. We actually tidied the burglars' mess. Then we invited people round. The police will never believe us.

Apart from anything else, I manage a number of successful bands. I'm always making things up. It comes with the territory."

"I'd advise you to go to them anyway," Phyllis said. "At the very least hand the phone in, tell them it's lost and you'd like to be kept informed of a claim. If you're really worried, I'd hire a private detective. It's not for me to advise you about ways forward, of course, but believe me, there are men and women out there who know how to get to the bottom of a situation like this."

Hannah stopped biting her lip and nodded vigorously. "That's a really good idea. Before I go, could I just ask, do you know where John actually works?"

"He always played his cards a little close to his chest in that respect. I didn't want to come across as prying. Sometimes, for silly reasons, people can be a little bit embarrassed about the jobs they do. I judge people by their characters, not their careers. From the little I managed discover, I gather he was a company rep of some kind. And as you may already know, we met on Match.com. We hadn't yet reached the point of meeting each other's friends. In fact, I was surprised when he asked me to meet his family. Part of me thought things might be moving a little too quickly. I'm sorry I can't be more helpful."

"You have been helpful. And I meant everything I said earlier. I'm really sorry for all I said that night, and I know I speak not just for myself and Charlotte, but for the entire family."

"It takes two to tango. I was unreasonable as well. Would it be too much to ask you to keep me updated? I liked John a lot, and I'd hate to think something had happened to him. Add my number to your own phone before you hand it in to the police. Please."

"Definitely."

She hung up and turned to Charlotte. "Sound advice," she said. "And a really nice woman. Bloody bloody EU *bloody* referendum! For about a month, it turned us all into flesh-eating zombies." She sighed. "I don't feel so powerless any more. Private detective it is. The best money can buy. I'll ring one now, then we'll take the phone to the police!"

*"Now?"* Charlotte said. "But it's late! They'll all have gone home."

"Not for me, they won't. I've got contacts who'll get me any home number I ask for *and* smooth the ground in advance for a courteous reception, and I can well afford to pay time-and-a-half, or triple- or quadruple-time, if need be. I'm not prepared to wait till tomorrow morning. I want to get to the bottom of this right now, and I don't care if I have to tip the whole of London out of bed."

## Chapter 9: The Petroleum Facilities Guards

Mordred arrived at Mitiga International Airport, five miles east of Tripoli city centre, at three in the afternoon. During the flight, he read the Sonatrach briefing papers – the Algerian government had apparently agreed to corroborate his cover – and drank lemonade. On his arrival in Libya, five bodyguards in pale suits transferred him to a waiting Mercedes where he sat beside a small elderly man in a *checheya* hat and a blazer. "Mohammad Reza," the man said, introducing himself with a smile and a handshake. "Your guide."

"Pleased to meet you," Mordred replied.

They set off at high speed for the city centre. Skyscrapers, long curving highways, whitewashed buildings, fountains, a turquoise sea, it looked like any prosperous Mediterranean city, apart from the fact that mingled with the Roman ruins, more recent ones kept appearing. The sun shone, the Unity government was in place, for now a semblance of peace held sway. Mordred recognised the five That El Emad Towers and Martyrs Square from a backpacking visit, years ago, in a previous life. People went about their business apparently heedless of the recent chaos.

He disembarked at his hotel, the Auroria, just around the corner from the old town. The old man told him to be downstairs in the lounge in twenty minutes, he was meeting four minor government officials about The Treaty of Oujda.

"Don't worry," the man added. "I'll do the talking."

In his room, Mordred shaved, including his scalp, and changed into the new suit that had been provided for him. Fifteen minutes later, one of the bodyguards was at the door. He escorted Mordred downstairs to the lounge, where he was introduced to the four officials, all academic-looking middle-aged men in brown suits. Small talk was the order of the day. Mordred had no idea what the Treaty of Oujda was, and he hadn't been told to find out. He left the talking to his guide, as instructed, and made complimentary comments about Libyan hospitality.

He had no idea who his guide was, but the deference the others treated him with strongly suggested he was anything but a conventional tour conductor. Likely, he was connected to the oil company, Sonatrach, and a 'guide' only in the literal sense of making sure Mordred didn't put a foot wrong.

After an hour, the reception was over. Mohammad Reza re-approached him. "Thank you for your help, Abu Farafisa," he said, apparently without irony. "Please join me in my room in ten minutes."

The purpose of the ten minutes grace period was unclear, but according to the plan he'd reviewed in Algiers, pretty soon he'd be moving on to Tanarej. Then he'd be more or less on his own. Just him, a huge pile of money and a gun.

Fifteen minutes later, Mohammad Reza sat on a stool in his own room. The bodyguards were elsewhere, with at least two of them posted directly outside in the hotel corridor. Mordred sat opposite his host, in an armchair, with a revolver and the obligatory glass of tea on a low table beside him. He wore a shoulder holster, which he'd been given three minutes ago. The old man had explained the gun's details: how to use it, how much penetrative power it had, even a little about its manufacture and the complex history of its kind. Mordred had listened without taking much in. He wasn't much of a fan of firearms. Nevertheless, he accepted they were necessary from time to time.

"That is you and me done," Mohammad Reza said finally. "The important thing is, you now have contacts in the Tripoli government; men who have seen you in the flesh, and think they know who you are. Personal introduction counts for a lot in this part of the world. Your having been seen in my company will serve as a kind of security, should things go less well than intended. Your car is waiting outside. When you reach your place of residence you will find instructions for your meeting with the

PFG. Tell them whatever you like, but don't be too specific. As things stand, the Algerian government has no intention of cutting it a deal. Of course, things may change. Ibrahim Jathran may turn out to be a key player. Stranger things have happened in Libya. So while you're not to make him any promises, don't categorically deny him anything either. It's unlikely you'll actually meet with him in person in the first instance. Perhaps not at all, if you're lucky."

Mordred finished his tea, put the gun in his shoulder holster, then stood up and offered a handshake, which Mohammad Reza accepted warmly.

"Thank you again," Mordred said.

"Best of British," the old man replied drily.

The 'Petroleum Facilities Guards' had been a real organisation pre-2011 under Colonel Gaddafi. Since the beginning of the second civil war, it had morphed into a spectrum of rebels led by a Commander Ibrahim Jathran, himself a former revolutionary. It still controlled most of the oil export terminals in the country's east. Such was the state of Libya that no one seemed to know how closely allied Jathran was to the Unity government, whether he was for or against General Haftar in the west, or even the extent of his personal control of the PFG. It was rumoured that some elements of the movement wanted to distance themselves from him. The Americans and the British were neutral about him because, although he was a potentially complicating factor in any long-term peace settlement, he had scored several successes against ISIS. Mordred was scheduled to meet his representatives tomorrow morning for an hour's prevarication in the guise of a strictly off-the-record exploration of ways in which Algiers and the PFG could cooperate to their mutual advantage. After that, he was free to go his own way.

The car journey to Tanarej was better than he'd expected – a smooth highway from which the ocean was visible for most of the way. His driver was one of the bodyguards from Tripoli, and two cars, front and behind, formed armed guards. As before, they drove fast. They reached their destination in just under twenty minutes.

Tanarej was big enough for someone not local to blend in without exciting comment. Its official population was twenty-one thousand, two hundred and sixty, but it was a long time since a census had been taken. It had a large harbour, partly man-made, partly natural, with a functioning coastguard, and it was a hub for migrants with their sights set on a future in Europe. Fishing boats were not always what they seemed – or rather they were: they were fishing boats some days, migrant-carriers another, then fishing boats again. Or maybe migrant-carriers again. A few men had made fortunes exploiting this opacity. Brown rocks, crystal clear water with fish visible in abundance, a vibrant waterfront and a picturesque array of bleached white, low buildings meant this used to be a prime tourist destination, and all being well, that it probably would be again one day. As it was, behind the picture postcard scenery, militias operated, and kidnappings and shootings were far commoner than any rational travel agency could countenance.

Mordred hadn't booked into a hotel here, partly because that trade had all but upped sticks and made for the hills, but also because he wanted to give the impression of someone prepared to settle in to the community, such as it was. In any case, there was only one fully-functioning hotel left in town, a relative high-rise called the Hotel Mediterranean. Financially, given the situation in Libya, it was probably hanging by a thread. His home was a villa on a hill overlooking the town. It stood in its own high-fenced grounds. It was owned, via a variety of judicious intermediaries, by the Egyptian government, and it had come into its possession yesterday. It was fully furnished.

As soon as he arrived, he introduced himself to the dogs – four Bull Mastiffs – using the techniques he'd been shown by experts. He fed them, spent time with them, called them by name, played with them, gave them treats in exchange for obedience, took them for several walks round the grounds, singly then in pairs, on leashes. Two hours later, he released them to patrol. In the morning, he'd have to go through the whole routine again – and again until he was certain of their loyalty – so he needed to begin from a position of caution.

Once inside the house, he closed all the shutters. At great expense, the windows had been replaced with bullet-proof glass long before Cairo took possession of the property. Still, no harm in playing safe. He performed only the most cursory of sweeps for surveillance devices. The place was inevitably going to be full of them, but since he intended to be alone here, there wasn't likely to be much worth listening to.

In the kitchen, he found what he assumed were the instructions for his meeting with the PFG. A single sheet of paper, which didn't mention the organisation by name, and whose wording required a significant amount of reading between the lines. All apart from the location: a café called *La Fiodora* in the town centre.

He had no doubt he was working for the Egyptian government now. They'd even left him a phone on which he could contact them. Meanwhile, all that spiel about phone calls to and from London was almost certainly fabricated.

On the other hand, he didn't think they'd try to dupe him twice; not now Fenella knew. What they had in mind was something different, something better suited to his temperament and less likely to raise hackles. They were going to help him find his sister and earn his boundless gratitude. Then present him with an *And now there's something you can do for us, John, if you feel so inclined…* plea.

It might even work. He'd always been a sucker for all-out niceness; do anything to return a really big favour.

In any event, it meant Mabel really was here. Somewhere in this town.

And to make matters even better, he could already feel it.

The next morning at nine-thirty, he took a taxi to the town centre, a small square surrounded by cafés and brasseries and a few boarded-up premises in front of which opportunists had erected stalls. It was busier than Mordred expected, but no one appeared particularly happy. It looked more like a transit-point from one part of the town to another than a location significant in its own right. At the far end, a goat stood looking nonchalant.

The rear section of *La Fiodora* had been set aside for the meeting. Mordred entered through a serving area with a counter at one side and tables and chairs across the other. There were no customers. The proprietor, a large man with a round head framed at the bottom by a double chin, seemed to recognise him and gestured for him to come this way. Mordred followed him along a dark corridor and up a flight of stairs. They emerged into a dusky room – all rooms in this part of the world were dusky – with three men sitting at a table, smoking cigarettes. They all looked to be about ten years younger than him: that is, in their earlier twenties, or possibly even their late teens. They wore western casual gear: zip-up hoodies, sweat pants, T-shirts, trainers, and sported downy beards. They were a strong indication that the Petroleum Facilities Guards expected no more of this meeting than the Algerian government did. When Mordred entered they stood up slowly, like teenagers acting a part, and offered churlish handshakes and *salaam*s, as if they'd just emerged from a sulk about not asking to be born. Mordred removed his *checheya* but stopped short of sitting down. He noticed three rifles propped against the wall.

"How's it going, Abu Farafisa?" the first man said. Something in the way he framed the question – American-informal, slightly insolent - indicated he was testing the waters, seeing what, and how much, he could get away with. And little though the men knew it, the PFG stood happily behind them: it had calculatedly deployed three boys as a means of carrying out the same test.

Which cliché to respond with? (1) *I don't make deals with boys; let me know when you've found someone I can do business with?* or (2)

*Is this some kind of joke? I'm not here to play games, gentlemen. Good day*? Difficult to know. Maybe a combination of the two.

"Who the hell *are* you three?" he said eventually.

The boy-men exchanged looks. Not what they'd budgeted for. It took them a second to adjust.

"Who do you think - " one of them began.

"I was told to expect the PFG for a meaningful discussion," Mordred continued.

"We *are!*" the man who'd asked him how it was going exclaimed, standing up. "The PFG," he added by way of clarification.

"Prove it then," Mordred said. "Which of you can explain thermally enhanced oil recovery methods?"

"Er – what?"

"Let's try another then. What are surfactants?"

At this point, a less patient militia would have shot him dead, but these boys had obviously been to school. They looked at each other like they were collaborating in a quiz and might still stumble on the right answer and win a car. In reality, 'We just guard the oil, we don't produce it' would have put the ball firmly back in Mordred's court, but luckily, it didn't occur to them.

"Look," Mordred said gently, trying to lower the temperature – he was outnumbered three to one, four counting the proprietor – "I don't mean any disrespect, but if the PFG doesn't want a discussion, that's fine by me. I'll be on my way. Don't even think of using those guns, by the way. The Algerian *Département du Renseignement et de la Sécurité* has been active in this town for years, and I'm not a person of no consequence. It has the building surrounded."

The boys looked like the buzzer had gone and they were going home with nothing.

The proprietor chuckled and gestured for them to leave the room. They picked up their rifles and slouched out.

Mordred hadn't anticipated this. *He* was supposed to be leaving, not them. They could hardly exit together, that would be undignified.

"Please sit down, Omar Ouyahia," the proprietor said. "*Abrar, TEA!*" he yelled downstairs. "I'm Nasser Ragai of the PFG," he carried on, as Mordred tentatively took a seat. "I'm a lieutenant; not that ranks have the precise signification they used to, not anywhere in this country. I apologise for the prank. It backfired. The thing is, we have nothing to offer you, but we – I – didn't realise you'd take offence so quickly. Or even that it would end up offending you. I thought it would be an effective way of demonstrating that we're not interested in your offer. Not yet, anyway. The PFG can't afford to look less than one hundred per cent patriotic right now. A deal with the Algerians – *any* deal – might be used by our enemies to discredit us."

A middle-aged woman in a long-sleeved T-shirt and jeans and no hijab appeared. She set a tray on the table with two glasses of tea, spoons and a bowl of sugar.

"*Enjoy,*" she said using the English word, and left as unobtrusively as she'd arrived.

"That's fine," Mordred said. "And I understand."

"If there is anything else we can do to make your stay in Tanarej more comfortable, just say. Or are you leaving?"

Mordred dissolved a teaspoon of sugar in his tea and took a sip. "I'll be staying here for a while."

"The one thing I could have offered you was a bodyguard. But unless you were bluffing when you said the Algerian secret service was looking after you …?"

Nasser Ragai's questions were none-too-subtly designed to pump him for information. Presumably he'd be passing whatever he discovered on to whatever rank trumped a lieutenant, and hopefully, it would be common knowledge in Tanarej before the end of the day. Things were looking up.

"I was bluffing about the details," Mordred admitted. "Yet I do have bodyguards. They've been told to keep a discreet distance.

They are very much hired hands, nothing to do with my government."

"That's interesting. You should be safe here, anyway."

"I live in the house on the hill. I have the appearance of a wealthy man. I'd have to be mad to go round without bodyguards."

"Indeed. So you actually planned for your stay here to be an extended one?"

"I did."

"May I ask why? I mean, there are far safer places for a holiday than Tanarej. A wealthy man might have his pick. Anywhere in Europe, for example."

"May I speak in confidence?"

Nasser Ragai got up and closed the door. "Of course."

"I represent a consortium of expatriate Libyans in Algiers. We're looking to get into the people smuggling business."

Nasser Ragai looked as if he couldn't believe his ears. He quickly hid his discomfiture behind a sip of tea and a nod. However, the two gestures occurred so close on each other that he actually dripped a little down his front. "You mean, taking Eritreans and Malians and Syrians and Nigeriens to Italy or Greece in boats?"

"Anyone who wants to go, yes."

"I see."

Mordred smiled. "Don't look so disapproving. We're doing it to make a profit, yes, but not an exorbitant one. Our primary aim is to make the whole process more benevolent."

"I'm not sure I understand."

"There's nothing intrinsically inhumane about taking a group of people from one shore to another. Quite the reverse, if that's what they want. And of course, they do want it. No one boards those boats unwillingly. But keeping migrants in stinking warehouses for weeks on end; casually taking advantage of your power to rape the women; holding men and women for ransom; sending unseaworthy boats out, overloaded boats - all those things are wrong. What we're aiming to do is bring Islam into the equation. As the Prophet, peace and blessings be upon him, said, 'Beware of the supplication of the oppressed, for there is no barrier between it and Allah.'"

Nasser Ragai nodded. His attitude had softened. "Everything you say is true. There are lots of bad men."

"The Libyans with whom I'm associated in Algiers, by the grace of God they escaped the revolution with their lives. They therefore know what it is like to have to flee. Some of them did bad things in their past lives. Some of them even supported Gaddafi. But as the Prophet said, 'No forgiveness will be shown to those who cannot forgive'. I don't judge them and nor should anyone else."

Nasser Ragai seemed to emerge from a trance. "Well, Omar Ouyahia, I hope your bodyguards are as effective as your speech. As you rightly say, there are lots of men in this town and farther afield, who earn a lot of money from the migrant trade, and who won't take kindly to a newcomer on their patch. Much as I admire your motives – and I mean that: for a moment, at the beginning of our conversation, I thought you were the worst kind of rogue – I know there are men who'll stop at nothing to discourage you."

Mordred smiled and stood up. "'No calamity occurs on Earth but is inscribed in the Book of Decrees'."

"Be careful."

"Thank you for the tea. And thank your wife too." He bowed just slightly from the neck and went down the stairs.

A moment later he was out in the sunshine again. Clouds were building up on the horizon, but they'd probably clear before they reached here. Nothing could survive the full force of this heat for long.

Next stop, the harbour.

"In confidence, I've already contracted to lease my boat out," a fisherman told Mordred, an hour later. "I can't break my word."

They sat in the cabin with the door closed so no one around could overhear their discussion. The fisherman was thin, old and weather-lined. He wore a long-sleeved white button-down shirt, a loose-fitting grey waistcoat and a black beanie. Outside, the ordinary business of the harbour continued: fishing-boats small and large came and went, men checked moorings, crossed gangplanks between boats, mended nets or sat and smoked on the waterside. On shore, behind the hundred-odd vessels rocking gently, men and women marched to and fro as if going somewhere crucial. A ship's hooter sounded somewhere in the distance.

"Who have you leased it to?" Mordred asked.

"I can't say. It's for another fishing-trip, you understand. Nothing else."

"Of course, and I fully appreciate that once you've agreed a deal, it would be dishonest to go back on it. However, next time you're offered eighty thousand dinar, I want you to remember me. *Omar Ouyahia Abu Farafisa*. I'll give you double whatever you're offered. I live in the house on the hill."

"The big house? With the dogs?"

"That's right."

"What did you say your name was again?"

"*Omar Ouyahia Abu Farafisa*. Write it down."

"I can't read or write. But now I know where you live - "

"I'll come and see you again in three weeks' time. Don't lease out your boat again until you've spoken to me. I'm confident I can offer you the best deal in town."

"I hear you've already spoken to Khamis Hirazi," the fisherman said suspiciously.

"Who is Khamis Hirazi?"

"He owns that boat over there. The blue one. *Heap of shit,* as the Americans say. Which means it's not very good," he added translating helpfully into Arabic.

"It's not a competition," Mordred said. "I'm not looking to hire your boat *or* Khamis Hirazi's *or* those of any of the other five fishermen I've been to see this afternoon. My plan is to hire them all together. Simultaneously."

The fisherman cackled. "You must have a lot of migrants lined up!"

"Africa's a big continent."

"And you must be very rich!"

"I'm not doing it for the money. It's a form of *jihad*. A striving for spiritual betterment. Would you do me a favour, Samir Al-Bousseffi?"

"Of course. If I can… "

"Next time you see the men who've hired your boat for eighty thousand dinar, would you tell them I'd like to meet them? I'm fairly sure we can do a deal."

"Buy them off, you mean?"

Mordred smiled and stood up. "Thank you for your time."

As he walked home at eight o'clock that night, deliberately making a target of himself, he didn't think he was in too much danger. It'd be different if he was a lone wolf. Then it would simply be a matter of eliminating him, problem solved. But being part of a pious consortium with apparently limitless wealth made him someone to be reckoned with. The herald of a possible new order, even. Killing him might provoke his backers to war, and the way Libya was right now, you could hire guns to snuff out people smugglers as easily as you could say *As Salaam Alaikum*. No, they'd want to sound him out first, at least find out what they were up against before they triggered a conflict they might bitterly regret. The great thing was, he'd indicated a willingness to talk.

As he got close to his house, he heard the dogs barking. They must have scented his return, and they were probably hungry. He picked up his pace.

A car pulled up alongside him and ground to a halt. Its back door flew open and Mordred turned to see a middle-aged man in a suit jacket man pointing a pistol at him.

"Get in, Abu Farafisa," the man said.

## Chapter 10: A Hard Night's Night

Sometimes, an apparently insignificant detail about how you think of, or recall, something can open a world of insight to your least known feelings about it. As Phyllis put the phone down she told herself it was the worst time to hear something like that from *John's sister*. Then it struck her as odd not to think of the caller as *Hannah Lexingwood* even though Hannah Lexingwood was famous and something of a minor fixture in the national psyche. Somehow, even after their break-up, John meant far more than the celebrity-in-her-own-right or even the apology.

And the news that he'd only kept one number on his phone hadn't helped. What did that mean? That he'd had every intention of contacting her? It didn't sound like an oversight. But contacting her to say what?

When the call came through, Phyllis was at home in Camden. She'd just showered after coming in from a farewell drink with former workmates. She wore her plain blue pyjamas. After hanging up, she sat alone in an armchair with a glass of milk to one side and her phone held limply in her right hand.

Her flat, like John's three miles away, consisted of a bedroom, living room and kitchen. The difference was that whereas his was owned by the government, she'd bought the lease to hers with money she'd earned modelling before her life in MI7. And unlike his, which was bare, functional and typically male, hers was expensively furnished exactly to her tastes. For a while, when things between them had been going well, she'd fantasised about him moving in with her. Had it not been for June 23, several bottles of Sauvignon Blanc, a national vindictiveness over Brexit exacerbated by quasi-religious zealots on both sides, and of course, three of his four sisters - one in particular - they might still have been together. They could have tackled the problem of Mabel as a couple.

She drank her milk and put the empty glass in the kitchen. Hell and damnation. It was the worst time for such a call in so many ways. Most trivially because she was about to turn in to bed. It meant she'd lie awake. Secondly, she was alone. It meant she'd brood. Thirdly, it was night-time. It meant being unable to go out for a walk to slough it off – she was effectively trapped here. She probably couldn't even phone or text anyone. They'd all be asleep. Finally, she'd left Thames House for the last time today. She was theoretically free. She should be happy. But the phone call made her feel like she'd walked off a cliff.

It had to be admitted: from the sisters' point of view, John's behaviour must look disturbing. And the events surrounding it wouldn't help: the mugging and then the amateurish burglary. You weren't supposed to disturb things during a burglary. Oh, it'd be MI7 all right, but almost certainly not Red department. Annabel was in charge of that sort of thing in Red. She was anything but a bungler. No, it was probably Blue or Grey.

She sighed. Even during her conversation with John's sister thirty minutes' ago, she'd considered saying, 'Hold on, I'll come and meet you', but she'd stopped herself just in time. Given what had happened to them, they were probably brimful of conspiracy theories. At some point in the day, they'd probably figured her for a villain. How would it look: *you haven't called the police yet, Hannah? That's great. Just sit still and don't do anything. I'll come and meet you*? She might as well have added, *and by the way, don't tell anyone about this phone call*. She and Charlotte would have thought about it for precisely ten seconds then panicked about her turning up with a screech of tyres and a single-action revolver. No, she'd done exactly the right thing, all she *could* have done without arousing their suspicion: tell them to go straight to the police, hire a PD and good bye and best of luck.

She brushed her teeth, got into bed and switched out the light. Down in the street behind the block, she could hear a man shouting, then an emergency services siren somewhere in the distance, and a faint parping she couldn't identify.

No, she wouldn't sleep at all tonight. She got up and went to the window. A view onto the communal gardens enclosed by the flats. In the daytime it looked well-tended and tranquil. At night, it was invisible except for a little sodium light at the courtyard's edge whose purpose she had never been able to determine. Keep cats away, maybe.

She didn't even know what had happened to John. Last she heard was from Annabel, that lunchtime in St John's Gardens. He'd handed in his notice, but Ruby Parker was determined to block it. A battle of wills; irresistible force versus immovable object.

It must have come to a head. One way or the other. The sisters' experiences weren't explicable on any other hypothesis. And of course, he'd handed in his notice before her.

She suddenly felt giddy, like looking down into the illuminated garden was giving her vertigo.

He'd gone. He'd left MI7 and set out for Libya. Or Ruby Parker had stopped him. Either one was a catastrophe.

For who?

She put her hands on her head and paced the length of the room twice. She wouldn't be having these thoughts if it wasn't night.

Catastrophe … For *her?*

Annabel's words came back. *So you dumped him. He didn't dump you.*

Just when he needed her most. Or needed someone – anyone. She'd dumped him. *He hadn't dumped her. She'd dumped him.* She went through a kind of psychological empathy exercise. Imagine you've been given terrible news about a family member; you feel compelled to risk your life to help; your partner, whom you love, dumps you…

Of course you wouldn't try to get your partner back! You're already at risk of losing *one* person you love. You're not going to sacrifice another. You've already decided to sacrifice yourself.

*John's miserable, if it's any consolation.*

*I know he is. I know we both are. But I'm not a teenager.*

Oh, shit, shit, shit! What the hell had she been thinking?

If only she'd been as bloody introspective as him. Instead, she'd decided to put him out of her mind – the conventional strategy for getting over someone – and she'd messed up big time. For all she knew, he might be dead now. All her fault.

No, no, not all her fault, but she could have prevented it.

She was getting things out of perspective. It was night time and she was alone – and tired! She was *tired!* Tired of living! *Thirty years old and tired of living!*

No, she wasn't. Obviously she wasn't. That was stupid.

Normally, in this kind of frame of mind, she'd ring her mum. She'd tell her as much as was necessary, maybe have a quiet weep over a cocoa and go to bed. 'This frame of mind' was mercifully rare.

But no, it wasn't possible to ring home, not at midnight. Bloody night time again. A big wall of darkness, screwing everything up, even in the twenty-first century.

Stop. Think. There were two possibilities: (1) He'd managed to get away; he was on his way to Libya, or (2) He'd been prevented from leaving the country; he was in detention somewhere. House arrest didn't seem likely. His sisters had been round there, and they'd drawn a big fat blank.

Which of the alternatives was it? Where was he? Schrödinger's Cat, slap bang in front of her. For a moment, she thought she was having a panic attack, like she'd walked into some kind of science fiction world, only real. She switched the lights on. She went through into the living room and switched the TV on. She went into the kitchen and switched the kettle on. She toasted a slice of bread and ate it. She had to conjure normality.

He still loved her, and she loved him if she was honest. No one better was going to come along, not on match.com or eharmony.co.uk or elitesingles, or at a dinner party or a bar or a business function, or anywhere. All the other men were duds. *All* of them, and she hadn't even met 99.99% of the world's males. *All!*

Night hysteria.

One thing was certain. If she was going to get through tonight with her sanity intact, she had to find out – at least roughly – what had happened to him.

She still had Annabel's number. Now she'd left MI7, she was supposed to have deleted it. Sod that. She pressed 'call'.

"Phyllis?" came the expected voice at the other end. "It's the middle of the night! Are you okay?"

No point in mincing words. "What happened with John?"

"Has he tried to contact you?"

"I asked first. And I'd like the truth."

"You sound a little emotional. No one's there with you, I assume?"

She laughed bitterly. "I'm utterly alone, sad to say."

"'What happened with John' is that Ruby Parker tried to stop him leaving the country by deploying counter-terrorism police officers at reception in Thames House. And he seems to have anticipated just about everything we put in place to impede him. He used a length of wire to escape from the first floor at the rear of the building, but we'd expected something like that. Alec and I chased him down Page Street and shepherded him – or thought we did – into a building where we assumed he'd be cornered. He knocked Alec over and broke my nose by slamming a door into me – I'm sure it was nothing personal; it'll mend – and escaped by dropping from the building's front window onto seven or eight policemen, one of whom now has a broken collar bone, another a cracked rib, and a third concussion. The others were too taken aback to mount an effective pursuit. I'm glad you called because I was going to ring you. We think he may try to contact you, so your phone's been tapped. Well done for telling the sisters to hand his mobile in, by the way. We've got it now. Remember, Phyllis, I didn't have to tell you any of this, but I really do see you as a friend, and I don't like deception unless it helps defeat an enemy. You're not an enemy. You're certainly not mine and I can't foresee any circumstances in which that will change."

"If my phone's tapped, surely everyone at Thames House will know you've just forewarned me. Won't you get into trouble?"

"No."

Silence. Typical Annabel. The truth, so just a monosyllable.

"Okay," Phyllis went on, trying to keep the conversation going. "Is my flat being watched?"

"No. But then I would say that."

"Not if you're my friend."

"I'm just trying to think myself into your shoes. You probably don't like me very much right now, and you'll imagine it's reciprocal, especially since John broke my nose. It isn't. The fact is, Phyllis, I know you're still in love with John, and I know you think we're persecuting him, but we're not. We're trying to stop him committing suicide essentially, because that's what this is. He's blinded by familial love and he's not thinking straight. We all get into that sort of position sooner or later, and when we do, our true friends are often the only thing that stands between us and the pit. We may not thank them for it at the time, or even ever, but that's irrelevant. My conscience is absolutely clear."

"Will I be followed tomorrow?"

"Honestly?"

*"Of course honestly!* Why would I want you to *lie?"*

"No. You won't be followed tomorrow. And if you think about that, plus the other things I've said, you may be able to deduce something."

She hung up.

Phyllis looked at her phone screen as if it might still hold something, then ran her hands through her hair. Odd, given how brief and vaguely patronising Annabel had been, but she felt slightly better now. She'd opened the box on the stupid thought-experiment cat and at least he'd got out of Thames House. That had to count for something.

What had she meant, 'You may be able to deduce something'?

Of course, Phyllis's flat wasn't being watched and she wasn't being followed, but her phone was being tapped. That meant they'd discounted the possibility of John making contact with her in person. If he tried to reach her at all, it could only be by phone.

So John had gone to Libya. At the very least, he'd left the country, but given that he'd evaded the entire British secret service, he was probably resourceful enough to make it as far as his destination. Whether he'd get any further was a moot question. Everyone's luck runs out sooner or later, and by the sound of things, his reserve of good fortune had to be running low. Something like rescuing a hostage in a war-torn foreign county wasn't a one-man mission. Annabel was right: you'd only attempt it if you were blinded by emotion. You wouldn't see it as suicide. If you thought about it at all, you'd imagine you were set to buck the trend, come out unscathed and triumphant.

Bottom line, she had to get over there and help him. Two professionals might just pull off what one almost certainly couldn't, and she'd never forgive herself if he got killed and she hadn't done everything in her power to prevent it.

She should really have been having thoughts like this three weeks ago. It felt like she'd awoken from sleepwalking and only now realised where she was. And that it wasn't anywhere like where she'd thought she was.

So: she'd already made a decision. God willing, she was going after him.

But what about putting it into effect? Another matter completely.

Re-joining MI7 wasn't an option. Although she'd left in good favour and no doubt she'd be a welcome revenant, it wouldn't give her access to John or anything within a million miles of him. Ruby Parker's thinking – probably sound – was invariably to prevent agents dealing in matters in which they had the merest whiff of a personal stake. Which is why she'd been so furious with him. Not only had he disobeyed her, he'd also humiliated her by escaping from under her nose. His name was probably mud in Thames House right now.

On the other hand, Ruby Parker had never been one for personal vendettas. The very principle of fencing off espionage projects from private concerns meant that, in consistency, however angry and frustrated she felt right now, it couldn't affect her judgement about how to proceed. More: his failure to heed instructions was compounded by her failure to make him.

She would know that. In forgiving herself, she'd likely be forced to forgive him. Whether he survived or not.

The important point was, they were probably trying to rescue him.

But they didn't know him like she did.

The horrible feeling of going round in circles. Or not even that: pulling up hard in darkened *cul de sacs,* reversing, trying again, failing again, over and over the same stupid, *boring, useless* thing with no apparent end in sight. God, if only she could look out of the window and see sunrise. She checked her phone. 12.30.

She laughed. *Twelve bloody thirty!* Time was a joke!

How else could you get into Libya? Where there's a will… Obviously no travel agent. Probably not even a private booking, not without FCO approval. She switched her phone back on. She was about to Google 'Flights to Libya' when she remembered.

It was tapped. She switched it off.

In any case, even if – let's say, in an ideal world - she didn't need the approval of the Foreign Office, she'd still need a visa. Thames House would find out and it'd be onto her like a flash.

Set off for Italy, maybe? Somehow make her own way across the Med?

Not likely. Who in their right mind would take her south now? All the traffic was one way.

If she was going to get into Libya, it would have to be via an intelligence agency of some stripe. They were the only ones going into places like Tripoli now.

Which meant it was out of the question. Russia or even America… She didn't want to work for them!

But it wasn't an option. They wouldn't have her.

But then – why had it even occurred to her?

Then she knew. Because consideration of them provoked consideration of a kind of in between possibility. Horvath, the private intelligence agency. MI7's supposed 'rival', but far too small-scale and parochial to be anything like a competitive threat, owned by retired army officers and backed by the usual slightly nefarious types in the City. A joke. Usually.

But British. They could get a person into Libya. And they'd probably jump at the possibility of hiring Phyllis Robinson.

Could she? Her heart thumped.

A deal with the devil, no other way of describing it. But sometimes, that's what you had to do.

Sometimes, it was your only option.

... But no. She couldn't do that. Really, she couldn't. There were limits, even in a situation like this.

Besides, *Horvath and John?* They'd crossed swords so many times in the past that it would want revenge. Of course it would. It would see his detachment from MI7 as a perfect opportunity to liquidate him.

Good God, that should have been her first consideration.

Still, better to realise something crucial late than never. No, Horvath needed to be kept in the dark for as long as possible. For ever, ideally.

Which meant she'd exhausted all the possibilities. *Finito.*

Suddenly, she was very tired. Like her body had required confirmation that every feasible avenue was closed before consenting to shut itself down. She switched the light off and climbed into bed. Within a minute, she could feel herself dropping off. Sometimes sleep allowed your mind to work unhindered on a problem, and you'd wake up next morning with a miraculous solution, but she didn't think that would happen this time: she'd already examined the problem meticulously from all angles.

She dreamed she was back in Annabel's villa in Capri with John. It was a nice dream, but it was interrupted by a loud beep.

Her phone. She didn't have to struggle awake: she'd been in the forces: she could go from deep sleep to fully alert at the drop of a hat. She sat up and looked at the screen.

*Message from last caller. 0770 656 7888.*

Bloody hell, that would be Hannah Lexingwood.

*Call me when you get this. I've got news! :)*

She looked at the time. 3.15. It had only just been sent. She couldn't wait till morning; it would look like she didn't care. Anyway, she didn't *want* to wait till morning.

She was bloody tired, though. All that thinking and worrying had taken it out of her. She swung her legs over the side of the bed and pressed 'call'.

"Phyllis?" Hannah's voice came, after a few seconds. She sounded pleased.

"Speaking, and thank you for texting me. Is it good news?"

"It's a development, that's all. You didn't have to ring now. I didn't expect you to get the message till morning, but I'm unbelievably tired, so I'm probably not thinking straight. Apologies if I got you out of bed."

"I don't care about that. Like I say, I'm gratified you did. Go on."

"Well, we found a private detective, a really good one, and I persuaded him to meet us. A Sir William Duggan-Strike, who's so prestigious he has a roomy office on Baker Street. His website shows his picture, lists his services and discreetly boasts of his successes. And he's reassuringly expensive. Sorry if that sounds snobby, but I'm not going to cut corners where my brother's concerned. Anyway, we met him face-to-face a few hours ago. We told him exactly what we told you. He rang around a bit and got back to us at around three. He can't find out anything about John at all. And the phone's gone from the police station: someone collected it literally *five minutes* after we dropped it off. To cut a long story short, Sir William thinks the whole thing has all the hallmarks of the British security services. Somehow, for some reason, John's got mixed up with MI5."

*"MI5?"*

"I know! My God, it's like *The Man Who Knew Too Much* or one of those old films where some perfectly innocent guy finds himself trapped in a humongous international intrigue. I don't like to make this all about me, Phyllis, but I'm pretty sure it is. I launched a big campaign against tax-avoiders a year ago, and ever since then I've been plagued by government and media infiltrators and company-bankrolled frauds, all trying to find out my next move. It's unbelievable some days."

"It sounds horrendous."

"That argument you and I had. It was a blessing in disguise, really. I'm so paranoid at this point, I'd probably suspect you of being a spy were it not for that. The good thing is, when spies are trying to get close to someone, they just nod and say yes. They don't do what you did. That's how I know you're genuine. Turns out God really does work in mysterious ways."

"So what now?"

"Sir William's 'out of his depth'. His words, not mine. He was very helpful, though. He knows a firm that specialises in John's sort of case. He's arranged for Charlotte and me to meet its directors first thing tomorrow morning, but we've already had a preliminary conversation. Horvath, it's called. It's incredibly good, apparently."

Phyllis felt her world sink about ten centimetres. "Horvath. And you told them …?"

"Everything. Just as we told it to you. They sounded raring to go."

"That's… good. Thank you for letting me know."

"We really must meet up. I'm not just saying that. We may have got off to a bad start, but I honestly feel we can be friends. Good friends."

As Phyllis hung up and climbed back into bed, she knew she wouldn't be sleeping again tonight. *God really does work in mysterious ways*. She'd just been cornered into a deal with his exact opposite.

## Chapter 11: Encounter with Bollywood

Mordred found himself facing two men, one behind the other. The foremost had a gun. The other stood six feet to his rear and looked like he was waiting to see how things turned out. A good start. If they'd meant to kill him, it'd be over by now. No, they were obviously here to take him to their Command Central, where they hung out with their friends and discussed how to expand their empire, whatever it involved.

The gunman looked about fifty, thin with a square face and a moustache. He wore a suit jacket over an Arsenal shirt, and pale trousers with black trainers. His partner was six inches shorter, dressed in the same casual style, but with long greasy hair, a trilby and his fingers covered in gold rings. Mordred couldn't tell whether this meant he was the more powerful of the two, but in his experience, the more important the man, the more he put others in the front line. So probably, yes.

The car's driver got out; the gunman handed him the firearm, then frisked Mordred, confiscated his revolver and gestured for him to get onto the back seat. The short and the tall man got in either side of him, the driver resumed position, and they pulled away. Breakneck speed but without anxiety, suggesting they were locals. But then, everyone in Libya was local nowadays. They'd stopped doing inter-city in 2011.

Since Mordred was positioned in the middle, he had a good view through the windscreen. The small patch illumined by the headlights showed they were going first down into the town, then out beyond the less densely inhabited areas, and finally up through trees along a wide dirt track. Not much to go on for future reference, and since they hadn't bothered to blindfold him, they probably knew it.

No one spoke, as was probably conventional in these sorts of scenarios. Eventually, they arrived at a white floodlit bungalow amongst what looked like eucalyptus trees. No one was waiting to meet them. When the car ground to a halt, Mordred's flankmen got out and gestured for him to follow suit. They walked him at gunpoint into the house. Still no sign of habitation. Possibly whoever lived here intended to torture him, and in classic style they were stringing out the anticipation, but it seemed unlikely. They wouldn't think he had the sort of information that needed forcibly extracting.

They emerged into a living room where twelve men sat in armchairs watching a TV. Oddly, none of them looked up when he entered. The gunman gestured for Mordred to sit down on one of three empty armchairs. He and the ring-fingered man took the other two.

For the next hour, they all watched a Bollywood film dubbed into Arabic. No one spoke. Although Mordred once caught three men side-glancing in his direction, none looked directly at him, even when the songs appeared and there was no story to concentrate on. Two men ate nuts from brown paper bags; another sipped on a straw at what looked like a giant strawberry milkshake in a transparent cup. Those established in armchairs were dressed more traditionally than those who'd picked him up: mostly in long white shirts and trousers. Most had bare feet but three wore grey ankle-length socks. There was nothing tense about their body-language, nothing to suggest they'd just been infiltrated by an outsider. On the TV, the heroine sang, to a sports arena full of old women, about her crazy love of the city in the monsoon season. The two men closest to the TV sang along quietly, although they got all the words wrong. When the closing credits finished, the man with the milkshake emitted a high-pitched fart that went on for nearly ten seconds. No one laughed or even gave any indication of noticing.

"Well, that was lovely," Mordred said, mainly because it had become obvious he was going to have to speak first.

It was as if he'd uttered an incantation to bring a roomful of statues to life. Everyone turned to look solemnly at him. He smiled at each man in turn. No point trying to be a smart-arse.

Apart from the gun and the absence of food or drink offers, he was a guest. They hadn't treated him badly. Or at least, things could have been a lot worse. *The Manual of Effective Spycraft* said to always behave nicely until someone gave a good enough reason to throw a punch, pull a trigger, release a trapdoor or detonate a bomb.

The man nearest the TV reached over to the DVD player, pressed 'eject' and took out the disk, which he put carefully back in its box. Someone handed him another. He took it out and inserted it into the machine. The menu came up below the title, *Amar Prem Aur Doddaaballaapura Mein Jangalee Phoolon*. It began to play.

Ten minutes later, a thirtysomething man in a white tunic came in with a tray and began distributing glasses of orange juice. Mordred was offered and took one. A little later, the same, but a plateful of dates. They might be trying to drug him, it wasn't impossible. But there were enough of them to compel him if that was their intention.

It had all begun conventionally enough with the gunman and the speeding car to the white bungalow, but this was surreal to say the least. How many Bollywood films were they going to watch? What was he actually here for? He could feel himself going to sleep, but it was only normal, late-night weariness. Nothing narcotic.

He'd have to say something after the credits. He couldn't take any more. Right now, the heroine was dancing on a line of waterlilies, singing about how love resembled magic. When the hero tried to copy her, he fell into the lake. Yet he never seemed to get wet - apart from his hair.

Mordred was ready to sign any confession they liked now. The two men nearest the TV were singing along ineptly and almost inaudibly again.

The film lasted just over an hour and a half. The screen returned to the start menu and the men sat in silence just looking at it.

"Great," Mordred said. "Could anyone point me in the direction of the toilet?"

The man with the milkshake rose to his feet, which seemed to be the signal for the others to do likewise. The gunman from earlier in the evening came over to Mordred with his pistol drawn and gestured for him to get up. They all filed out into the hallway. At the front door, ten of them peeled off, apparently for good. The milkshake man, the ring man, the gunman, the driver, and two others – a fifty-ish refined-looking man and an obese man in a Fully Magic Coal Tar Lounge T-shirt that left six inches of flesh above his trousers – carried on along a corridor and down a flight of steps. They went through a door into darkness. Milkshake man switched the lights on to reveal a large basement with a framed picture of a horse on the wall, a pool table in the far corner, and two sofas and a video camera facing an armchair.

The gunman told Mordred to sit in the chair. He and the other men filled up the two sofas. They didn't look happy, but so far everything had been pretty civilised. Even now, no one was positioned to start hitting him if he gave a wrong answer. He wondered what time it was. Four in the morning at a rough estimate.

"What do you actually *want*?" Milkshake said. He was in his early thirties, a little older than Mordred perhaps, with a close-trimmed beard and a double chin. "I mean, out of Tanarej?"

"To help," Mordred replied. "To begin with, we simply want to see that people are treated properly."

"What makes you think they're not already?" the gunman asked.

"We've heard stories," Mordred replied.

"About *Tanarej?"* Milkshake said, as if he couldn't believe it. "Because there are lots of other places along the coast that do migrant boats. Just about everywhere between here and Alexandria. The other way, probably, too: Tunisia. Even Algeria, I don't know. Why us?"

"It's the perfect spot," Mordred said, "that's why."

"What do you mean?" the driver asked irately.

The gunman signalled for his compatriot to calm down and take a back seat: he hadn't finished. "Ignore my friend," he said. "At least until you've answered the question I asked earlier. What makes you think we're not *already* treating our migrants well? You come in here, start trying to hire boats over our heads, and all on this assumption - "

"'Assumption' is correct," Mordred interrupted. "But it's a reasonable one. From what we know, everyone's exploiting the migrants. Why would we think you were any exception?"

"Let's cut the bullshit," Milkshake said. "What exactly are you proposing? You say you want to ensure our customers are treated well. How? By taking our business away?"

The driver grinned self-approvingly. "By taking away the business of *all* the people-smugglers between here and Alexandria?"

"On the contrary," Mordred said. "We'd rather work with you. And make you a hundred times wealthier."

"I'm a practical man," Milkshake told him. "And I can already see you're not. I'll ask you again: what are you proposing?"

"To turn Tanarej into the number one people-smuggling terminal in North Africa," Mordred said. "With you as our partners. You stand to make a fortune."

The men laughed as if he'd just delivered the punchline of the best joke that year and this was the first time they'd heard it.

"Brilliant," the gunman said. The smile dropped from his face. "Except that it's not. It'll be sunrise soon. I've wasted a long time sitting with you."

"I didn't ask to come here," Mordred said.

"Yes, you did," Milkshake replied. "You told Samir Al-Bousseffi you wanted a meeting."

"Not in the middle of the night at gunpoint."

"We gave you orange juice and dates!" T-shirt man exclaimed in a falsetto.

"You knew that killing me wouldn't be to your advantage," Mordred said, his tone changing from conciliation to annoyance. "Otherwise, let's not pretend: I'd be dead by now. Now I'm here, I expect you to listen to my offer in detail. You can let me go if you don't like it. That's your only alternative, because if you kill me you'll open the gates of hell. Not one of you will be left alive in six weeks' time. On the other hand, rejecting it will merely leave you penniless."

Milkshake sighed theatrically as if he heard something like this a thousand times every day. "Go on, then. Entertain us."

"In fact, my sponsors aren't entirely Algerian and Libyan. Ten of my wealthier backers are European. There's a school of thought in the developed world that says migrant workers are necessary for industry and a healthy economy. Only, they don't make very good headlines. Keep them *out* of the headlines by managing the routes discreetly enough, and you've a winner. The migrants pay once to board the ships; European employers pay again for what our backers envisage as a kind of short-term bonded labour, resuscitating rural areas in some of the European Union's less developed countries."

"Migrants for export?" Milkshake said.

"In the very earliest phase," Mordred went on, "my backers need to keep the scheme a secret, but they also require insurance against the possibility of it becoming public. Which it certainly will in the end, an operation on the scale they're anticipating. It needs to be done with all the outward trappings of moral goodness. Mitigate any potentially negative PR. We attract the migrants to Tanarej by offering the cheapest, most reliable and fairest service. I meant what you've probably heard me saying around town, my friends: this is compatible with Islam. We're taking people who want to get into Europe, and we're giving them a means to realise their dreams in a way that doesn't cheat or exploit them. And we're helping Europe too. Once it gets around in Eritrea and Mali, northern Nigeria and even Syria that we're offering a genuine, professional expatriation service, we'll be inundated. We'll have to expand, but our backers have the money for that. They'll do all the investing."

"Bonded labour doesn't sound very 'fair' to me," the driver said.

"Short-term," Mordred said. "The employer pays for the migrant to work a plot of land, say; the migrant agrees to subsistence-only remuneration for a limited period of, I don't know: four years? In that time, the employer recoups his investment plus a bit more. Manumission's built in. As I say, our backers don't want anything that'll cause a permanent scandal. Over time, they expect to put sympathisers in the media, using them to drip-feed information to the public, and make it part of the accepted state of things."

"So where do *we* come in?" Milkshake asked.

"In the first instance, my consortium needs local people with extensive knowledge of local conditions," Mordred said. "And we'll pay handsomely for that. By the time we get to the second instance, you'll be rich beyond your wildest dreams."

The men looked like they were becoming interested. The driver drew a deep breath and gently stroked the space just above his upper lip.

"You probably heard that I offered to outbid you on a number of boats in the harbour earlier today," Mordred said. "I wasn't entirely serious. I simply wanted to gain your attention. The point is, I can put all that money together and give you half now and half on the completion of a task I'd like you to fulfil to demonstrate your willingness to engage with us. And that, merely as a foretaste of what's to come."

"What task?" Milkshake said.

The driver grimaced. "I knew there'd be a catch."

"I'm not here to give away free money," Mordred replied.

"He said *half up front!*" Milkshake told the driver, spreading his palms. "That's not a *catch!* Let him *speak!*"

They all adjusted their bottoms on the sofa and leaned forward, as if afraid the details of the task might not reach them.

"We need the realistic semblance of law and order in Tanarej," Mordred said.

They looked at each other.

"I maybe get what you're saying," Milkshake mused eventually. "You mean these 'backers' of yours don't want to deal with robbers and cutthroats and fraudsters. No one you've seen here tonight belongs in that category. I'm not sure we can help reform those Tanarejians who do. It's a job for the police, such as it is."

The driver guffawed. "Or isn't."

"It's not that my backers don't want to be *dealing* with them," Mordred said. "It's that they don't want them to *exist*. They want to come here occasionally without any fear of being kidnapped. More importantly, if this whole scheme's going to work, Tararej is going to have to work as a safe haven for refugees. Once they get here, they've got to know that, in a sense, they've *already* made it. In that case, some of them will stay. What I'm trying to say is that ultimately, this whole project can work as a means of regenerating Libya itself. We create safety, the rule of law, fairness, equality of opportunity here; people stay and work, and the economy booms, and it all spreads outwards. We might all end up not only rich, but national heroes. It's the greatest scheme that's ever been devised: a way to get rich and make Libya an immeasurably better place."

"You haven't answered my question," Milkshake said indifferently.

"Those men we met in the other room," Mordred went on. "I say 'met'," he corrected himself, "I mean, 'watched a movie with'. They - "

"Don't forget we had orange juice and dates," the T-shirt man interjected. "That was *my* idea. I wanted to make you feel welcome."

"It was *all* your idea, as I recall," the driver sneered. "Two of the *worst* films I've ever seen!"

"The *best* films," T-shirt countered.

"The *worst,*" the driver said.

"The *b* - "

*"SHUT UP!"* Milkshake yelled. He took a few breaths. "No one else say anything. When Omar Ouyahia Abu Farafisa's finished speaking, the next and *only* voice I want to hear is mine. Then his. Then mine. *Him, me, him, me*. Does everyone *get* that?"

Everyone nodded except for T-shirt, who shrugged. "Best," he whispered, so fast that it came out as a single consonant. He raised his feet and looked at his socks.

"Omar Ouyahia," Milkshake said, "how do you propose that we deal with our local criminals, renegades and militiamen? Without getting shot in the head for our troubles?"

"A few moments ago you told me to cut the bullshit," Mordred said. "You're in charge of a very lucrative trade, and it doesn't entirely operate within the law, to put it mildly. It would be strange if none of the local gangs had tried to muscle in on your monopoly at some point. You must give some of them – the dominant ones - a cut, if only as protection money. Therefore you have a basis for dealing with them. At the very least, you're in a position to talk to them."

The men looked at each other.

"If this is going to work," Mordred went on, "we have to trust each other. You trying to milk me for every last dinar while playing your own cards as close to your chest as you can is only going to end in tears. If the deal I proposed sounds satisfactory, say so. Or reject it. But whatever you do, do it honestly."

"We can probably get them to 'talk' to you," Milkshake said. "But you'll have to offer them money, and they'll fleece you. Worse, you'll look like a fool."

"I don't plan to talk to them," Mordred said. "Not yet; it's too early. And I'm certainly not asking you to present yourselves as supporters of some kind of foreign-backed project. That would be too dangerous. All I need to begin with is a *map* of Tanarej with details of militias marked on it: numbers, weaponry, type of activity, affiliation if any, precise location. I simply want you to ask around as cautiously as you can, co-opt a few people if necessary, bribe one or two, pool your findings and report back to me. You're quite right, none of these little armies will relinquish power willingly, and talking to them without superior firepower in the room isn't going to get anyone anywhere. That's for the future, but we need to start planning for it today."

"Money," Milkshake said. "You promised half today and half on completion of the task. How much in total are we talking about, and how long to deliver the goods?"

"A million dinar," Mordred said. "And one week, but with daily updates."

"Just as well, because I don't know anything about maps," Milkshake said.

"Leave that to me," Mordred replied. "There is one other matter, but it may be best for me to discuss it with you in private."

"Now?"

"Might as well. But before everyone goes, I'd like to know your names, if I may?"

"I'm Walid al-Iddrissy," Milkshake said. "Fatty here's Hussein al Dirsi, your driver tonight was Rabea Abushnaf, this is Salem bin Hamed, Younes Omar with the rings, and finally, Hamdo Ejlal with the gun. Everyone out. Hussein, get the car ready."

Mordred waited till everyone except Walid al-Iddrissy, the former Milkshake man, was outside, and leaned forward conspiratorially. His companion mirrored him.

"I happened to be in a café this morning," Mordred said, "and I overheard a conversation about a group of militiamen who arrived here from Tripoli a short while ago, bringing with them *a European hostage*. My backers know nothing about this, and I'd like to keep it that way. Tanarej has real potential and we've already put a lot of work into preparing the ground. If these kidnappers start making a stink about holding a European at gunpoint, it could be the end. Before it's even begun. Tanarej will become a byword for terror."

"Shit," al-Iddrissy said.

"I need you to make it a priority to find out who and where these guys are so I can have them despatched without delay. Otherwise, they're going to screw it up for everyone."

"And they're not even locals?"

"They're just using Tanarej to lie low. From what I heard."

"Bastards. Okay, don't worry, I'll make it my personal responsibility to find them."

Mordred stood up. They shook hands gently and for longer than would have been customary in the west, then al-Iddrissy took Mordred's arm.

"Come for a drive with me," he said. "Before you arrived this evening, my friends and I debated how we could show you our treatment of the migrants is just. We've got a warehouse we keep them in till a boat becomes available. I said, 'Why don't we just take him over there?' Well, that's where we're going now. Then I'll come to your house and collect the first half of the money. Younes Omar and Hamdo Ejlal will accompany us. Rabea will drive, of course. If we get in a tight spot, he can reverse at top speed, spin the car, take a wild corner, all that."

"Tomorrow evening you can give me an update. Let me know how far you've got."

They went out, got in the car and set off. The sun was just beginning to come up, so Mordred was able to see more than during the incoming journey, however he was too tired to take much in. Scenery flew by in a grey whirl of trees, low-lying houses, narrow streets, dilapidated administrative buildings some bearing the imprint of gun battles, views of the ocean. After five minutes, he asked Rabea Abushnaf, the driver, to pull in so they could pray. They all got out in a pine grove and Mordred asked al-Iddrissy which way Mecca was. They performed three *rakahs* together then resumed their journey.

The warehouse was a cinder block building on the outskirts of town. They went in. Most of the migrants were already awake. They sat or slept on mattresses laid out in a line against a wall. It felt like a car park but without vehicles. Most of the migrants looked sub-Saharan, and had Mordred been asked to guess, he'd have put them down as Eritreans. Halfway along the line he came across a tall black woman and a dishevelled-looking Arab man, lying asleep on his bed. She wore the traditional black chador, but her face was uncovered. Her husband slept in his clothes: white shirt, pale trousers and brogues without socks. She sat protectively by him as if on guard. She looked at Mordred with fierce intensity.

Mordred didn't quite know whether to meet her gaze or not, how she'd interpret it. When he finally decided it wouldn't hurt to throw her a faint smile, he nearly coughed with astonishment.

Edna. Edna Watson.

And that man on the mattress was - Alec Cunningham.

His MI7 colleagues.

## Chapter 12: Horvath's Golden Hello

11am. On the first floor of Horvath headquarters - a former Victorian mansion house on London's Great Eastern Street - two men in their late sixties half-faced each other across a rectangular table. The older, Sir Malcolm Rhys-Dwyer, wore a pinstripe suit with a red carnation in the lapel. His pallid skin and unnaturally black hair – which had mostly retreated to his ears – combined to give him an unhealthy look. Although his eyes and nose were large, his mouth was small; he had thin, bloodless lips, and the beginnings of a goitre. He looked anxious.

By contrast, Sir Paul Ayton, a former Conservative party treasurer, had a shelf of hair as white, neat and apparently solid as a slab of marble. His flesh was mottled with pink and brown spots, and he wore a smug expression. He sat with one hand holding the other. When he spoke, his tone of voice suggested a complete indifference to every opposing mode of thought and life. Outside, the late morning traffic faintly honked and growled.

"So John Mordred's gone missing in a more general sense?" he said.

Rhys-Dwyer sighed. "According to William Duggan-Strike's little police contact, MI7 are as baffled as his sisters."

Ayton frowned. "This 'police contact' actually *said* that? How would *he* – or she – have access to information on that sort of level?"

"But it's the only interpretation of MI7's behaviour consistent with the facts: they lose his phone, then his sisters get it, then someone comes to collect it from the police station – someone not fitting his description. He's disappeared and they don't know where he is."

"And his sisters are actually offering us a blank chequebook to find him?"

Rhys-Dwyer smiled. "They don't know he's our arch-enemy, obviously. No, we stand to make an awful lot of money out of them, but not half as much as elsewhere."

"Yes, you said. Any takers yet?"

"Signed and sealed."

Ayton laughed. "*Never!* Who?" He held up his right palm. "Before you answer that, Malcolm, you don't look as happy about it as you should. I take it you did offer his scalp to the highest bidder?"

"We've already made a phenomenal sum out of… a government – with respect, Paul, you don't need to know exactly which – in Africa. Banked."

"So what's the catch? Your expression tells me there is one, and it's quite big."

"A long story. We found out from *Médecins Sans Frontières* that his sister went to Libya on some wild goose chase about two months ago. Where of course, she was abducted."

"Idiotic but tragic," Ayton said. "Why hasn't it been on the news?"

"Media blackout, apparently. Presumably, her connection to him. In any case, that and his going off-piste is too much of a coincidence. It's a better than reasonable conclusion that he's gone out there to rescue her."

"Alone?"

Rhys-Dwyer nodded sagaciously. "If MI7 can't even get hold of his *phone* without a hoo-ha, that's also likely, yes. Completely on his tod in a war zone, poor chap."

"What better opportunity will we get to despatch him? And you say you've already sold the rights? My dear fellow, you should be celebrating!"

"The reason Mabel Mordred isn't dead is only because she's become… useful to her abductors. Euphemistically, you'd probably say she's being kept as a 'wife'. In more literal terms, she's been repeat-raped and forced into domestic servitude. I've no doubt she's playing along and that's what's saved her life.

Unfortunately, John Mordred probably lives in a kind of 1970s-detective-programme-world where kidnappers are only interested in extorting money or guns or possibly a flight to a sympathetic country."

"He probably hasn't allowed himself to stop and think about it, poor chap. I know I wouldn't." He sighed. "I feel almost sorry for him now. I don't suppose there's anything you can do to put his assassination on ice?"

"An awful lot of money's come our way. If I'd found out beforehand…"

Ayton clicked his tongue regretfully. "Of course. It's a done deal. We're an espionage firm. We expect to get our hands dirty. Who are her kidnappers? ISIS?"

"I doubt it. No government, even the most Islamist, makes a deal with ISIS. Mind you, the way these brigades work, they're one thing one minute, another the next. Let's just say they're potential ISIS, potential al-Qaeda, potential neither – just bog-standard Islamist - potential all three, at different times as the mood takes them and the opportunities present."

"Complex."

"Apparently, the kidnappers have been in contact with John Mordred, demanding money they don't need, guns they can easily acquire in lorry-loads elsewhere."

Ayton frowned. "I don't understand. Why would they do that?"

"They want to lure him, of course. They know who he is. The government I told you about enlightened them after they took his sister's phone apart."

"I see."

"Her kidnappers had no idea they'd succeeded in drawing him. Now, they're rather jumpy. And that's where Johannes comes in."

Ayton laughed. "'Johannes'? The plot thickens!"

"Mladenov. Not his real name, obviously. The professional assassin our client government's sending to Libya to despatch

John Mordred. We go to Mordred, rather than waiting for him to come to us. Or rather, *they* go to him; we just pick up the money."

"I'm still rather nonplussed, Malcolm: waiting to discover the catch."

"It turns out Phyllis Robinson's also on his tail. She's left MI7 and she wants to come and work with us as a means of finding him. She's been in contact with the sisters. She probably knows he's in Libya."

"Phyllis *Robinson? The* Phyllis Robinson?"

"The same."

"Good God! I feel like I'm inhabiting some sort of parallel reality."

"Quite."

"I see your problem, though," Ayton said musingly. "Whether Mordred ends up dead or alive, she could be the fly in the ointment."

"She knows of our involvement, because the sisters told her. So put it this way: we can either hire her, in which case she'll expect us to get her into Libya; or we can decline to hire her, in which case, she'll probably set out for Libya alone. Either way, she's going to Libya. Once there, who knows what stones she'll turn over? His death won't necessarily stop her. We stand to lose everything."

"Hmm."

"'Hmm' is right, Paul. Any ideas?"

Ayton thought for a few seconds. "Why not partner her with your 'Johannes'? I'm sure your friendly government would be only too happy to help out. We needn't even solicit another fee. Give them her as a goodwill offering, two for the price of one."

Sir Malcolm took a deep breath and nodded. "Of course. Yes, of course. That would solve everything." He laughed. "'Two for the price of one': I like that, yes!"

"You'd have to make sure there was no double-dealing. Someone over there deciding she's too good to shoot, say, that he'd prefer her for his wife. That option would need firmly foreclosing. And secondly, you'd need to give her an appropriately rigorous interview. Feign the deepest reluctance to take her on, otherwise, she might suspect something. I think you and I should both be present in the room? When's she due over here?"

"Two hours' time."

"And there's no chance of her bumping into the two ugly sisters?"

"She's adamant she doesn't want them to know, which of course suits all parties. I told them we'd call them. I think their minds are sufficiently at rest now to prevent us having to contact them for at least a week."

"Two hours. Get on to your government, Malcolm, make the necessary arrangements. We need to get her out there as soon as we can."

Phyllis arrived for her interview in her best suit and shoes. Horvath looked nice enough on the outside – red brick, large lattice-light windows in plain white frames, a mansard roof – but she just couldn't envisage working there for the foreseeable future. Or rather, she didn't want to. She hopped off the bus ten minutes before the interview and walked the five hundred yards to the entrance. A man in a grey suit answered the doorbell. He looked to be about five years younger than her with a fashionable beard and his hair gelled into a quiff. He took her to the reception desk, took her name and asked her politely to sit, then went back to working on his PC.

Thirty seconds later, a young smart-casual woman arrived with a clipboard. She confirmed Phyllis's name, ticked something and led the way upstairs. She opened the door to an office. Sir Malcolm Rhys-Dwyer sat behind an antique desk with an Art Deco table lamp. Before him were two low chairs, on one of which sat Sir Paul Ayton. Both men were stood up in polite acknowledgement. She recognised them from past encounters, none pleasant, and wondered if there would be any residue of acrimony directed her way.

All the way here, she'd fought a paralysing misery. She didn't want this job. Or to be anywhere near it. But she wanted to help John. At least, that's what she told herself; she wasn't really sure. She lacked the determination and energy to discern her own true feelings. Maybe she expected John to die and just wanted to say she'd done everything in her power. *I've nothing to reproach myself for: look at the lengths I went to*. Maybe she was a complete cow. Or the opposite. What did it matter? Nothing mattered.

Handshakes and names were exchanged – warmth? she couldn't tell – and they all sat down.

"I trust you had a pleasant journey over here?" Sir Malcolm said.

"Yes," she said. "Thank you." She didn't like people who began questions with 'I trust': too affected. And what could you really say about a bus journey?

"I understand you've already talked to Mr Mordred's two sisters," Sir Malcolm went on. "From what they've given me to understand, he's disappeared. Now before we get down to discussing your suitability for the job, or otherwise, I think we should lay our cards on the table. That is your prime motive for wishing to join us, is it not: finding John Mordred?"

"That's correct," she said.

"You do realise," he went on, "that if we do find him, that couldn't be the end of your association with us? We'd expect something more. To be clear, if we do agree to hire you – and that's not a foregone conclusion at this point, although obviously, if it wasn't a serious possibility, you'd hardly be here at such short notice – we'd probably expect you to sign something like a four-year contract."

"Legally, it'd be difficult for us to enforce," Sir Paul interjected. "But morally, we've reason to believe you're a woman of your word. You wouldn't... 'double cross' us."

"I'll sign such a contract if it helps me find Joh – Mr Mordred," she replied.

"Good," Sir Malcolm said, as if that was the first hurdle cleared. He wrote something down and raised his head to speak to her again. "Tell me what you know about his disappearance."

"I can really only tell you what his sisters told you. He was meant to meet them in London, he cried off at the last minute, he dumped his phone - "

"You mean, *you've no idea where he might be,*" Sir Paul interrupted coldly. It emerged as a statement, not a question: one of disappointment that she'd chosen to let them down at the first opportunity.

"In Libya," she said, realising that somehow, they already knew.

"What makes you say that?" Sir Paul asked. His tone had changed. He was playing with her, but at least he was amenable again to the possibility of employing her.

"Because his sister was abducted there," she said. "I think he's gone to find her."

"Until recently," Sir Malcolm said, "you worked for MI7. We'll come to the interesting question of why you left later - "

"I can tell you that now," she said. "I was in love with John. He and I had an argument. He decided to leave because of his sister, and the fact that MI7 refused to sanction his involvement in any rescue. Since he was on his way out, I decided I might as well follow suit."

"Your interruption has led us into a diversion, but what makes you think you'll fare any better here? We're also an intelligence organisation."

"A smaller one, therefore with better chances of promotion."

Sir Malcolm looked unconvinced. "Let's get back to the topic I was asking about."

"Yes, apologies."

"Did you ever have a conversation at Thames House that actually confirmed his presence in Libya?"

"No."

"To your knowledge, was MI7 aware that he might try to *get* to Libya?"

"Yes. It attempted to stop him, I believe, but it failed."

"And how do you know that?" Sir Malcolm asked.

"The circumstantial evidence. His disappearance, his singular behaviour towards his sisters, the strenuous efforts to obtain custody of his phone."

"What do you want from us, Ms Robinson?" Ayton asked.

"I'm a fully trained intelligence officer," Phyllis replied. "I can speak six languages, I possess military capability, a medal for valour, and several years' espionage experience in a variety of different countries. I'm exceptionally good at my job, and you'd be foolish to pass me over on the grounds of a long-standing rivalry between your organisation and my former one. The loss would be entirely yours. Right now, you're my best chance of getting into Libya, and I've no doubt you have contacts that would prove useful to me. Which is why I'm applying. But I'll get into Libya anyway. If I'm killed doing so, by the way, you still lose."

The two men exchanged approving looks.

"I think we both appreciate your honesty, Ms Robinson," Sir Malcolm said. A second of silence as the men nodded to each other. "Pending the necessary paperwork, I'm pleased to let you know you're hired."

"Thank you," Phyllis said. She didn't feel remotely pleased, but at least it was over.

"A few words about Horvath before I proceed to more practical matters," Sir Malcolm said. "You may have heard some bad things about us while you were working at MI7. The fact is, most of the work you do while you're here won't be anything like what you've been used to. In tomorrow's world, multinationals will own all the power. They possess most of it now. Like all global players they need intelligence, the sort that our organisation's tailor-made to provide. As we wax, old-fashioned entities like MI7 and the CIA will wane. Eventually, governments will come to realise that. Then even they'll come to us. In twenty years' time, we'll be the overwhelmingly dominant force in the market."

"What Sir Malcom's trying to say," Ayton put in, "is that you've made the right choice. You won't regret it."

"To practicalities then," Sir Malcolm said. "Janice downstairs will talk you through the bumph. Take as long as you like to read it. She'll answer any queries, but the last analysis, I'm here all day, and I'm happy to clarify, even to modify, within reason. I know it's a fast turnaround, but you're flying out to Libya tomorrow, undercover as a journalist. Of course, we knew that's where Mr Mordred was. As part of our inquiry into the Mordred sisters' case, we spoke to MSF in Italy. We suspected it might be something like that, you see. Anyway, you'll meet your partner in Libya."

She did a double-take. *"Partner?"*

"Of course. You're new, and you're a woman. Lone women tend not to fare very well in conflict-zones. You'll be in charge. I'll make that very clear to Johannes."

No one said anything. The cue for the ending of the meeting. Smiles all round.

"If you've no further questions, Ms Robinson," Sir Malcolm went on, "allow me to say, Welcome to the firm. I hope you'll be very happy here. Again, Janice will brief you regarding travel arrangements. Otherwise, thank you for your time."

She stood up. They did likewise. They exchanged handshakes and Ayton opened the door for her.

As she went downstairs to meet Janice, she found herself shaking her head. Not enough for anyone to notice; quite involuntary, but still significant.

Something was wrong. It had all been too easy.

## Chapter 13: Day Tripper

After the *Oliver*-style visit to see how humanely the migrants were treated, Mordred went home in company with his new acquaintances. He fed his dogs then handed 500,000 dinar to al-Iddrissy with a recap of the instructions for mapping militias in and around the town. Afterwards, when he was alone, he sat thinking about Alec and Edna, specifically why they were here.

He should devise some pretext to go back and speak to them. But what? Without al-Iddrissy and his companions, it'd look like he was doing some kind of spot-check on the people-smugglers, like he hadn't believed the evidence of his eyes first time round. Guaranteed to raise hackles. No, if he returned there at all, it would have to be in the Libyans' company.

But that was also a non-starter. Obviously. What kind of conversation could he have with Alec and Edna under those circumstances? About the same as the one he'd already had: a silent one. Which probably didn't qualify as a conversation.

He wasn't thinking, though. Whatever those two were doing here, they wouldn't stay put in the warehouse all day long. The way it worked, you paid your money, you got accommodation in a supposedly safe place. A lot of the time, the advertised 'safety' didn't exist: you might be raped, beaten, robbed, or all three. But there was a sense, encouraged by the smugglers, that, however hazardous your confinement, it was at least preferable to the world outside.

If you *chose* to leave, however, they probably wouldn't try to stop you. Doing so would undermine the fiction that they were supplying a service. True, you'd have to be pretty tough: enough to know you could come back several hours later and still have your cot vacant; enough to brave it outside; enough to hold the smugglers to their promises even after they discovered you'd been awol. But that wouldn't be a problem for Edna or Alec. There were undoubtedly a lot of hard nuts in the human trafficking fraternity, but none trained like them.

Which begged the question, what were they doing with their days? At first sight, there were two alternatives: they were either looking for Mabel, or for him. But then other possibilities appeared: they'd found Mabel and they were preparing to rescue her; they were here to stop terrorists boarding boats for Europe, or perhaps *a* specific terrorist.

He got the vague impression he was missing something crucial, but tiredness was keeping it just out of view, like one of those stars you can only see through the corner of your eye. The more he dwelt on their presence in Tanarej, the more depressed he became. Presumably, the Egyptians had let slip that he was here, deliberately or otherwise. What else had they divulged? And now they knew his location for certain, what next? He looked outside into the grounds. No sign of the dogs, but that didn't mean they weren't on guard. A pair of citrus trees, three olive bushes and a bougainvillea; in the distance, dense pines and junipers. It was fully light. Right now, he was no good for anything. He needed to recuperate. He set the alarm on his new phone for noon, went upstairs, removed his clothes, lay on his bed and fell into a deep sleep.

He awoke to the sound of a gently repeating ding and hauled himself up so his back was against the wall. His heart banged hard, in a way it probably wouldn't have done had this been a mission without personal ramifications. He picked up his phone, and dialled the number he knew by heart. The same man as usual answered. Someone with an excellent command of English, yet almost certainly Libyan rather than British. Another reason to think this wasn't ISIS.

"Hello?" the voice came. "John Mordred? Is this you?"

"Speaking, yes. Nice to speak to you again. Is Mabel - "

"We got your money. We also killed your rescue team."

He'd been expecting this. He had to sound shocked. *"What?* What rescue team? I didn't send any rescue team!"

"Approximately - "

"Bu – But - There's been nothing on the news about it! What do you mean, 'rescue team'? I don't - "

"I mean, *just that,* John Mordred. You're lucky – incredibly lucky – we didn't kill your sister in retaliation, but the truth is, even without you, she's worth a hell of a lot to us. There are a large number of things for which we could barter her. Luckily, such was the ineptitude of your brigade that not one of our fighters died or was even harmed. But if it happens again, we *will* hand her over to Daesh, and they'll put her head on a spike and set fire to what remains of her body."

"I'm – I'm very sorry. I didn't know - "

"The money. Have you gathered it?"

"Er, I thought you just said you'd got it. Sorry, I didn't mean that to sound confrontational. It's just - "

The man on the other end of the phone scoffed. "You paid some of it in *early?"*

"Yes, I - "

"I don't believe you, Mr Mordred. I think the paltry amount of money we received came from your foreign army friends. They handed it over to lull us into a false sense of security."

"I – I - "

"Don't even think about lying to us, Mr Mordred. You told us at the outset you'd have extreme difficulty raising that amount of cash. We agreed to give you time. The deadline is not for another few days yet. You see, we're kind. We want to treat you and your sister with mercy. But raids on our headquarters by gangs of armed thugs make it difficult for us."

"I know, and I'm very sorry. But you've got to believe me when I say I knew nothing about it. That's not a lie, it's - "

"This phone call has already lasted too long for my liking, Mr Mordred. Can we expect the cash at the stipulated date and time?"

"Yes, yes, yes, of course. It's been difficult, but I'm fully on track."

"Afterwards, we will have another task for you."

*"What?"*

"That is the price you pay for sending in a rescue team."

*"But I won't have any money left!* You'll have completely cleaned me out!"

"This one isn't to do with cash. Just be ready. This second task, if you do well, we will release your sister."

"Could I speak to her? Please?"

The line went dead.

Mordred looked at his phone for a moment. God, that hadn't been easy. Odd, because it merely required a series of pre-determined moves as crusty as the world's stalest cliché. Question, response, question, response, rigorous as a liturgy. All that had been missing was *In unmarked bills in a trash can, corner of 66th street. And don't tell the cops or the kid gets it*. He knew the script in advance, everyone did. But your own sister, you couldn't afford to deviate one jot. Looking back, he'd given a good performance. They'd been reassured. And they could have no idea how close to actually rescuing her he was. And possibly killing them, if that's what it took. There would be no mistakes this time round.

And they'd already received money! News to him. MI7 hadn't exactly got bang for their bucks, but they'd tried, and personnel had ended up dying. On both sides. He knew that for a fact, whatever the man on the phone said. He probably shouldn't have been so angry with MI7 when he was in London. Now he was out here, he was beginning to see things in a clearer light.

Still, he'd done the right thing. What now?

For the very short term, he was safest here in the house. Let anyone seeking him – be it Alec, Edna, Cordelia or Mitchell, or Ruby Parker herself – do the legwork. He wasn't going to them. Al-Iddrissy would be here in a few hours with his first consignment of information. He didn't want to miss it. He got up for a glass of water, lay down on his bed again, and slept.

This time, he awoke to the sound of a car horn repeatedly honking and the dogs barking. According to his watch it was three in the afternoon. He swung his feet onto the floor, stood up, pulled on a bathrobe he found hanging on the door and looked out of the window. It was al-Iddrissy and three friends from last night - the driver, the gunman and the T-shirt: he'd forgotten their actual names - in a sturdy-looking car. No convertibles in this corner of the world, not any more. They stood at the fence with the dogs baying at them.

*"Are you coming out?"* al-Iddrissy shouted, holding up a can of orange as if proposing a toast. *"Rabea's brought your gun back! It's a nice piece! And we've got information! And we're going on a trip to the mountains! How about joining us?"*

Mordred tried to remember his train of thought before he'd fallen asleep the first time – before the phone call - and the facts supporting it. Alec and Edna, that's right, and the militia map he'd ordered for half a million dinar with an equivalent sum to pay on delivery. What had he been thinking, trusting these men? They were people smugglers. However much they tried to dress themselves up as philanthropists, of course they weren't. God knows what they got up to in that warehouse when he wasn't around. And going for a car ride with them probably wasn't advisable. And shouldn't he be on his colleagues' tail?

Yet he wasn't here to play it safe.

*"Come on in, I'll get the front door!"* he yelled back.

He fed the dogs again, stroked them, played with them a little, then herded them into their kennel-compound and gestured out of the window for al-Iddrissy to let himself and his friends into the house. He hadn't properly explored the place yet, but there was a spare gun and ammunition in his bedside cabinet.

Not that he'd need it if they'd brought his back.

Which they wouldn't be doing unless they wanted to show they trusted him. So perhaps he had nothing to fear after all. But he shouldn't be too complacent. *Remember what they do for a living.*

Funny thing about males, himself included. How, often, they seemed able to build walls between incompatible behaviours, shielding each activity from interference by the others in a way that, if they encountered it in a stranger, they might even say was psychotic. Conventional affection for family and friends versus visits to prostitutes; rarefied appreciation of Mozart versus the administration of a concentration camp; systematic exploitation of migrants versus a sedate day-trip into the countryside.

He was no better. He laughed. The spy who supports animal sanctuaries.

When he'd finished getting ready, he went downstairs. His guests had switched the TV on and moved the chairs in a semicircle to face it. They got up to greet him. The driver returned his gun, loaded, and they went out to the car. No need to worry about switching anything off: the frequent power cuts were quite capable of taking care of that. He sat on the back seat between al-Iddrissy and the gunman.

They drove at high speed through Tanarej and made for the Jebel Nafusa mountains. There were no roadblocks on the way, and no one fired at them. They made small talk, mostly about local characters, events or relationships Mordred had no acquaintance with.

"That's the Hotel Mediterranean," al-Iddrissy said when they passed the only high-rise building left undamaged in the former tourist quarter. "The Americans have an underground base there. At least, that's the rumour. Explains why it hasn't gone bust. Pentagon dollars."

"Bullshit," the driver said. "People will believe anything nowadays. Like the owner's Jewish, and his daughter works for the CIA, and his son works for Mossad, and his wife doubles as Hillary Clinton in the daytime, and Angela Merkel at night. It's bollocks."

"Makes life more interesting, though," al-Iddrissy replied philosophically.

The journey seemed to take for ever, but soon the beige of the lowlands changed to green and they reached an altitude cool enough to be bearable. The driver pulled abruptly into a forest clearing by the edge of the mud track. For an uncomfortable moment, Mordred thought they might actually be about to kill him, but no. Another car pulled up, six men got out, one opened the boot, a subwoofer played Ali Farka Touré and Tinariwen at top volume; everyone took off their shirts and danced without smiling or making eye-contact. In Britain, this would have been risible: archetypal Dad Dancing. Here, it seemed somehow appropriate, but eccentric. The bare torsos were the oddest part. At least, for Libya.

Six CD tracks later, they all put their shirts silently back on and resumed their seats. The two vehicles went their separate ways, the mysterious subwoofers disappearing down the hill in the opposite direction. In Mordred's car, the driver put his foot down hard on the accelerator, the small talk resumed apparently where it had left off, and al-Iddrissy pointed out a clutch of Touareg tribesmen, way in the distance, on camels.

After about forty minutes, they came to a village. Small white houses, cuboid and two-storey, all the colour of dry clay with darkened interiors and steps up the outside. The car stopped at what looked like the only shop and Mordred's companions got out and embraced the proprietor, an elderly man in a striped long-sleeved shirt or *jalabiyyah* and a headdress. They opened the boot to reveal crate-loads of supplies: rice, tea, flour, bottles of olive oil, dried fruits, salt and pepper and spices in labelled polythene bags. The man gave them a wad of banknotes and laughed and shook their hands.

For the next hour, they drank tea, told jokes and passed a hookah round containing a mixture of cannabis, tobacco and molasses. They ate lamb and rice. Mordred was a vegetarian as a rule, but occasionally – as now - ate meat for the Queen.

The men became louder and even more garrulous. Their jokes focussed increasingly on misunderstood genitals. They slapped each other's arms, patted each other's faces, and inadvertently spat tiny fragments of food. Occasionally, they underlined some point of order by making an animal noise. Yet the only time things looked like really getting out of hand was when the driver reached across the table and attempted to pinch al-Iddrissy's cheek but ended up tugging his hair and spilling his tea.

Mordred originally had them down as widely differing in age, but now realised their behaviour bore all the hallmarks of a friendship continued since childhood: brutal directness, indifference to table manners, long periods of low-level boredom, a grudging intimacy caused by past failures to hide mortifying personal issues. On close inspection, they all looked to be about thirty-five.

After dinner, they drove back to Tanarej without speaking until they reached the town's outskirts. Al-Iddrissy leaned over to Mordred.

"We're all descended from Senussis," he said, pointing at his friends, as if there might be some confusion as to who was meant. "We sometimes drink alcohol; it's not the sin people think it is. Bloody Wahhabis are ruining Islam. Muhammad, peace and blessings be upon him, was the first Sufi, did you know that?"

"Er, no," Mordred replied, unsure which bit he was being asked about. But then, he didn't know any of it.

A minute later, al-Iddrissy was asleep. There'd been no chance to ask him about the 'information' he'd claimed to have earlier, but that would come. He'd wake him when the car stopped, presumably outside his house, as they'd discussed over dinner.

His mind felt clear, even though, after that hookah, it probably wasn't.

Edna and Alec, that's right.

It suddenly hit him. They almost certainly weren't alone. What were the chances of him just stumbling across them like that?

Obviously, he had, so the question was irrelevant. But imagine he'd stumbled across Cordelia, the agent with the novel who'd sat behind him on the bus to work every day for nearly a month. My God, how surreal *that* would have been! *I know they told you to follow me, but this is ridiculous*. Or Mitchell. Or Young Ian. Or all three. For all he knew, the whole of bloody Thames House could be here.

And Annabel. What if he got back to his house and it had been burgled? No, she was too blonde: she'd never pass muster here. But Tariq - ? No, outside his job description.

He was beginning to panic. Burglary, yes, they'd try that. No - well they would, but they'd never get past the dogs. - But they might kill them with poisoned meat. - No, no, they knew how much he loved dogs: they'd never do that to him. – Would they? They were spies: they might.

Suddenly, he wanted to tell the driver to hurry up, even though he was already going so fast they'd have no chance if an obstacle loomed out of nowhere. Anywhere else, they'd have a fleet of police cars on their tail now.

Nice to see them zoom up the hill skidding round each corner with so little road to spare they were continually in danger of rolling down a slope and into a tree. The miracle of the hookah. Made you invincible. Imagine that: Edna and Alec turning up only to find he'd been killed in a car crash. Arriving on foot with moments to spare. There they'd be, standing outside his front gates, wondering what to do about the dogs when –

The car screeched to a halt.

Good God, he was home. No sign of Alec or Edna, thank God.

Now the difficult bit. Trying to get the Libyans to come inside and tell him what they'd found in the way of information. He expected to have to shake al-Iddrissy awake, and possibly the gunman on his other side. He hadn't turned to look at him.

But he didn't have to do anything. They all got out and went to the fence, obviously waiting for him to let them in. When he unlocked the gate, they followed him without speaking. There was nothing threatening about their behaviour. They were just tired. For all he knew, they might simply be expecting beds for the night. The dogs barked, meaning they were okay, that was the main thing right now. He'd feed them in a minute. Tomorrow, he'd have to go in town, get them something more to eat.

The men went through into the living room. The TV was still on. They watched half an hour of a Turkish quiz-show. Mordred made and served tea. Afterwards, al-Iddrissy picked up the remote. He yawned and pressed 'off'.

"We've got some of the information you asked us to gather," he said.

"I was about to ask," Mordred replied. He didn't want them to get the impression he thought it secondary. He'd gone out with them on an excursion; he'd met their friends, enjoyed their hospitality, smoked their cannabis. But now, the main event. By his tone of voice, he hoped to convey the impression he didn't see it as anything other.

He led them into his kitchen and gestured for them to sit at the table. The whole house was laid out and furnished according to western models – no human-size cushions, rococo embroidery or arabesque patterns, only desks, display cabinets, sofas, wardrobes, free-standing single and double beds, all like they were fresh from *Homebase*. They each took a ladder-back chair and faced each other.

"What have you found?" Mordred said.

"Well," al-Iddrissy began. "There are about four pockets, occupying different buildings in different parts of the city. Along the coast, separated by about a mile – the length of the town seafront – you've got two. To the west, pro-government groups; mostly, from what we can discover, sympathetic to General Haftar; in the east, a Touareg militia. South-east, Zintan – but not in strength. South-west …? Well, we don't know. We spent the morning trying to find out."

"A black hole," T-shirt said. "It wasn't occupied by anyone a week ago, but now it's being policed. And not in a nice way. Islamists, probably."

"But that could mean anything," the driver said. "Shura council, Ansar al-Sharia, Daesh, Abu Salim Martyr's Brigade. I mean, it's not like they're paying subscription fees or anything. In this country, right now, 'belonging' to something's a bit like being a football fan. You support the Tehaa if you're wearing a Tehaa replica shirt and scarf."

"One thing we can say," T-shirt went on. "If what we've heard is true, the black hole's getting bigger every day."

"Like it's angling to take over the town," al-Iddrissy said. "Very bad for business."

Mordred hmm-ed. "Zintan's anti-Islamist, isn't it? And Haftar definitely is. Do they know what you know?"

"Unlikely," the driver said. "Otherwise, they'd have done something. They probably haven't been out looking. Which means they'll likely find themselves ambushed and driven out of the town. Before you ask, we can't tell them. They know us. They know what we do. They don't like us, but they leave us alone most of the time. If we went to them with a story, they wouldn't believe us."

"It all depends on how big the black hole gets," T-shirt said. "And how much it wants total control."

"Which means we'll have to leave too," al-Iddrissy said. "They won't stand for people-smuggling, even the humane sort. It's 'un-Islamic'. Even you'd be un-Islamic, Omar Ouyahia."

Mordred nodded. "When you say it's in the southwest of the town, how big an area do you mean?"

"Several blocks and growing," al-Iddrissy said. "That bit of town used to belong to the government officials. It was mostly wrecked in the revolution. No one's rebuilt it, obviously. No one's rebuilding anything now. Most of it's probably uninhabitable, and it was all looted years ago. But some of it's probably okay. It must be if someone's taken to living there."

"Could you take me to see it?" Mordred asked.

"Tomorrow," al-Iddrissy said. "Not tonight. I'm tired and no one goes out much at night now, not if they've any sense, especially somewhere like that. No, tomorrow. We'll pick you up in the morning early, while it's still cool. We'll get something to eat too. In Tanarej. Boost local business."

"Suits me," Mordred said. "Do you know where I might get hold of dog food?"

The Libyans exchanged baffled looks.

"Your dogs eat special *food?*" al-Iddrissy said. "Of their *own?*"

"It's not unusual," Mordred replied. "If they're guard dogs."

Silence.

"What about fish?" the driver suggested. "Will they eat fish?"

"We could get them a dead goat," T-shirt said. "Or a gazelle, even. Would they eat that?"

"Thanks for the suggestions," Mordred said. "I'll ask if anyone knows when we get into town."

They saw themselves out. A few moments later, he heard the car pull away. He fed the dogs and opened the kennel compound so they could patrol. It was pretty obvious where Mabel was. The only remaining question was whether to attempt her rescue alone, or try to get Edna and Alec on board.

Difficult one. He needed to think.

## Chapter 14: A Baddie Comes to Town

Johannes Mladenov was about forty, of medium height and build. He had a light-brown complexion, a well-trimmed beard and his face was midsize and unremarkable, neither intimidating nor overly genial. Only his eyes looked anything out of the ordinary, and even then, just in certain lights. They seemed to be a window to nothing. All anyone in the world knew about him for certain was that at one time he'd been an exemplary officer in Assad's Syrian Arab Army, and that, at a certain point in the conflict, he'd 'seen the error of his ways'. He renounced the Ba'athist cause and put himself out for tender to the highest bidder. Nowadays, he was, in effect, an international assassin.

He arrived in Tanarej the day after Hannah and Charlotte had gone to see Sir Malcolm Rhys-Dwyer at Horvath. He knew this was where John Mordred would be because the government that purchased his, Mladenov's, services was in contact with the men who were holding Mordred's sister, and she was here. According to Mladenov's sources, Mordred was good enough at his job to be well advanced on his quest now.

Mladenov spent his first day in Tanarej resting in an inn on the seafront. He'd paid upfront for a week's accommodation, but he didn't expect to be there that long. Phyllis Robinson was due to arrive in two days' time. He'd booked both of them into the fully-functioning high-rise Hotel Mediterranean in the former tourist part of town. Far more comfortable than his present place, but also more risky. The Americans had established a base in its cellar and, as far as he was aware, not even the Government of National Accord knew they were there. In theory, Tanarej was a relatively quiet spot from which Washington could monitor Libya's progress towards democracy – or lack of it - without domestic political interference.

But no one liked being spied on. The Americans were about to get what had been coming to them for years, since well before the revolution, before even the construction of the hotel. They didn't know it, but they were pinned in from four sides. The Touaregs and the pro-government forces, to the east and west respectively, would turn a blind eye, although they might kill one or two escapees; Zintan likewise. But the Islamists to the southwest were set to outnumber them all, and pretty soon they'd have the hotel and its environs entirely surrounded. Simply a question of bringing in more reinforcements. Not as easy as it should be, but progress was happening. Another few days.

Not that any of this mattered, except insofar as Mladenov was expected to work with them. Which by implication meant, against the Americans. A pity, since he had nothing against the United States.

Or anyone at all actually. His brief was to kill John Mordred and Phyllis Robinson, but he didn't especially relish the prospect. They were probably pleasant enough people. From what he'd heard about John Mordred, at least, he was one of the good ones. In past centuries, he might have been regarded as a divine fool, with his irrational love of animals and strange addiction to good causes.

But well, life was completely meaningless. Earthquakes, tsunamis, wars, famines, sudden reverses in good fortune hit the just and the unjust with equal severity. In such a world, Mladenov was just a conduit. He did his job well, but had he not been around, someone else would have done it perhaps even more effectively. There were only a certain number of human destinies in the world, and for each individual person, that number was fixed at one. He, Mladenov, was destined to kill John Mordred. That was the way the universe was. No one had built it like that. God was a fiction, but fate wasn't.

When he'd recovered from jet-lag, he went out into Tanarej and spent the day switching between eateries in the town centre. He ordered lemonades and teas and pittas and wore sunglasses to disguise himself from Mordred, if their paths crossed, and also to conceal the fact that he wasn't a local. In difficult times, the stranger tends fare less well. Nevertheless, he had no option but to sit alone, and this in itself made him stand out. He gradually noticed children staring at him. He'd become a curiosity. He cursed and went back to his inn, where he stayed the remainder of that day.

His plan the next morning was to keep walking. Change of clothes and new sunglasses, something a little more downmarket. He opted for the local *jalabiyyah,* kaftan, and an Arab headdress. As far as he knew, he was unrecognisable from yesterday, but there was no room for complacency. He'd make a pit-stop occasionally for refreshment, but his idea today was to keep moving and repair to base for another outfit if necessary.

At the end of eight hours wandering from one part of the town to another, always with his eyes peeled, he felt weary and dispirited. Perhaps he'd overestimated Mordred. Certainly, there was no sign of him.

On the other hand, this was a reasonably large town. Statistically, he might roam for a long time – longer than he had – and still not bump into him. Nevertheless, he could be here.

He needed to be more proactive.

Someone like John Mordred, looking for his sister, probably wouldn't potter about like an amateur detective, peering through windows, handing out leaflets and knocking on doors. No, he'd make contacts, as influential as possible, and use them to unlock the various possibilities. He'd get *them* to do the legwork.

And it would be no use him trying to co-opt the legal authorities. They'd want ID and paperwork, as they always did. No, it would have to be someone - some *group* of people - outside the law. But not too far outside. Probably not gunmen, because they could be unpredictable. They might 'rescue' his sister only to demand a new ransom. What he'd need ideally was a bunch of relatively harmless rogues.

Put like that, the solution was obvious. Tanarej, whatever else it was known for nowadays, was renowned as a hub of the people-smuggling business.

And of course, people-smugglers would be ideal. All he had to do now was find one or two and follow the trail. Shouldn't be difficult.

Four hours later, he had discovered Mordred's house. He stood in the forest, out of view of the windows, taking pictures with his phone for future reference. A low, brilliant white building, hilltop location, obviously lots of rooms, closed shutters, a high fence and patrolled by dogs. No surrounding dwellings, at least not for half a kilometre.

He immediately changed his plans. Phyllis Robinson and John Mordred needn't die together, after all. Mordred could go first. No one would know if he was killed out here, not for a day or so, anyway.

Sniper?

Superficially, that looked the obvious choice. He had a suitable rifle on standby. But as a solution, it wasn't without problems.

Firstly, this was a big house, obviously built to accommodate more than one person. Likely there were other people inside. Indeed, he'd spoken to a neighbouring farmer who said the occupier came and went "always in company". So probably more of a commune than a single resident.

Which raised the next question. How to recognise Mordred himself?

In his natural habitat he had blond hair, but he'd almost certainly have changed that. Distinguishing the probably significantly altered man through telescopic sights, on the far side of a high mesh fence, possibly with trees in the way, would likely be difficult, and the consequences of an error acute. Failure on the first shot would mean the news reaching town sooner, and possibly being on hand to greet Phyllis Robinson on her arrival. Depending on how detailed it was, there was no telling how she might react. And unpredictability was his worst enemy.

No, he needed to be cautious. No room for subtlety; an all-out assault. Poison the dogs, breach the defences, kill everyone inside, pile the corpses up somewhere out of view – including the animals' – then leave everything looking pristine, at least from outside. People close by would probably overhear shooting, but by the time they got here – assuming they dared to venture anywhere near, or could be bothered – it'd be over. As if nothing had happened.

No news to reach the town. Nothing untoward waiting to pique Phyllis Robinson.

Perfect.

He was about to leave when someone emerged from the house. The dogs barked and came running.

John Mordred. My God, *in the flesh!*

He fed the animals. Suddenly, they weren't like guard dogs any more. They seemed almost as happy to see this particular human as they were pleased by the food. He stood with his hands on his hips and watched them fill their stomachs, then played tug-of-war with them using a rope. He threw sticks for them; he tossed them balls of cloth to catch; he even allowed them into the house to explore.

Mladenov took more photos on his phone – the man this time, rather than the building - aiming and enlarging and moving left to right to vary the angle. Apart from anything else, they'd be useful when he met Phyllis Robinson; he could already envisage four or five ways how.

After about twenty minutes, Mordred went inside again, locking the dogs out. They obviously knew the show was over because they slunk off to drink from a bowl of water, and lay panting in the shade.

If there was anyone else in there – and there probably was – the chances were they thought this guy was insane. They might even surrender without a fight, just to get rid of him. Hell, they might even hand him over.

But no. That would be far too perfect a world.

Mordred spent the next morning exploring the house. So far, he'd merely used it as a place to sleep and sit. It had eight rooms including a kitchen, three bedrooms and a basement all furnished to the same bland taste.

The basement was a surprise, its entrance located behind a huge wall-tapestry with a diamond design. Perhaps this had once been the home of a Gaddafi-supporter. Quite probably, in fact. It hadn't been built recently, and anything worth owning in this country pre-2011 was then property of the regime. Its basement wasn't much of a secret hiding place, but it might lead to an emergency exit tunnel. Unlikely though, because no one really expected the Arab Spring till it hit.

The basement smelt foul, like something was buried there. He switched the light on, but couldn't see any likely culprit.

It contained a set of fridge-freezers – fifteen in all – with enough food for a six-month siege. The fridges were mostly empty, although four were stuffed with rotting food - hence the odour. Mordred bagged it and put it outside, away from the dogs. He wasn't quite sure what to do with it next. Take it into the woods and leave it for wild animals? He didn't want it beside the house too long: it would ruin his social life.

The freezers were a completely different proposition. Meat for the dogs, clearly labelled; halal chicken, lamb and veal for human consumption, frozen fruit, cooked rice, vegetables, fish, potato chips, herbs, and a variety of delicacies: suet dumplings stuffed with beef, expensive ready meals, sauces, desserts. He need never shop again, except that he was a vegetarian. Even so, he could whip something up.

The important thing right now was that he didn't have to go looking for dog food. He left a pile of lamb chunks out to defrost and found the phone Cairo had left for him as a courtesy. Time to give them an update. Least he could do, and if his initial assessment had been correct, they were working together now. Had been since his arrival.

As usual in these sorts of cases, the contact number was physically inside the phone, in blocks of three digits inscribed on the battery. He went through the mechanical moves necessary to retrieve it and keyed it in.

"John," said an urbane voice on the other end. Sounded like Mohammad Reza, the official he'd met on his arrival in Tripoli. "What can I do for you?"

"Who am I speaking to?" Mordred asked.

"You mean, which organisation, of course. Egyptian foreign intelligence. I hope your stay so far has been satisfactory. I repeat: how can I help?"

"I'm close to finding my sister," he said. It felt odd speaking to Anonymous, but there was probably no reason for concern. He'd decided to make this call – it wasn't forced - and he was almost certainly speaking to the right person. "However, from what I've discovered, there's a huge influx of Islamists arriving in the southwest of Tanarej, the former government quarter."

"On what do you base this claim?"

"I've men working for me. It's what they report."

"And have you confirmed it in person?" The voice sounded almost patronising.

"Not yet. But there's a slim possibility I might be killed in the attempt. In which case, I thought it only right, given all you've done for me, to let you know in advance that there may be a situation emerging here that it's not in Egypt's interests to countenance. I mean, before it's too late for you to do anything about it."

"That's very considerate of you, John. And I promise you, we'll get onto it right away. We'll investigate the matter from our end, and if it turns out there's anything in it, we'll be in touch speedily."

"Thank you."

"No, thank *you*, John." The line went dead.

*Would* they do anything about it? No way of knowing, although if he was right, they wanted to keep him sweet. They'd probably at least go through the motions.

The dogs began barking. A car parped its horn outside. Bloody hell, al-Iddrissy and his pals, come to take him Pedigree Chum shopping. How was he going to explain that he didn't need to go any more? Easy, on the face of it, but then they'd probably want to take him tea drinking and hookah smoking again. They were meant to be earning that extra half million dinar.

What time was it? He looked at the phone. 11.15. He went to the window.

Al-Iddrissy stood with his hands on his hips. *"Come on, Omar Ouyahia!"*

Pretty well dressed for a shopping spree, especially given the dearth of enthusiasm he'd shown yesterday.

Then the penny dropped. It was Friday. They were off to the mosque for *salat al-jummuah*. He hastily fished out a suit from the wardrobe – luckily, a good fit – and threw the lamb pieces for the dogs, and let himself out of the house. "Thanks for coming to pick me up," he said breathlessly. "I was going to order a taxi."

They all laughed.

"This isn't Algeria," al-Iddrissy said. "You've got to be careful who you get in a car with here. Especially if you live in a big house. If you want to go anywhere, Omar Ouyahia, give me a ring. That way, you'll be safe. Do you have a prayer mat?"

"I forgot to bring it."

"I've a spare in a bag in the boot. Perfectly clean. Sometimes, unless you get there early, you have to perform *salah* in the street. Quite acceptable, everyone does it. Well, not everyone, obviously. Today, I thought we'd try and get inside, listen to the *khutbah*. You should hear our mullah. He says some nice things. Inspiring things."

The mosque was a nondescript building along a narrow street. They performed *wudu* in a small fountain in a courtyard and went through into a hall as broad as it was long in which hundreds of men were already lined up facing the *qibla,* the direction of Mecca. Plaques on the wall with Arabic writing on, denoted Allah, Muhammad and the four rightly-guided Caliphs. A smell of soap and male perfume permeated the air. They performed the necessary *rakahs,* and the mullah ascended into the pulpit and spoke of compassion and the Muslim duty to look after the poor, the weak and the defenceless. The congregation was reminded of how Muhammad had stood up to the Quraysh in Mecca, and how he'd suffered persecution for righteousness's sake. In some ways, it was all very much like a Sunday church service in rural England: well-intentioned, pious, a little abstract. Out of the corner of his eye, Mordred glanced at al-Iddrissy. For some reason, he was silently weeping. Maybe he did that all the time. People-smugglers probably had a hard time reconciling the central tenets of Islam to their mode of life. They'd probably be filled with self-loathing occasionally, and they'd vow to change. Then they'd emerge into the fresh air and it'd come to nothing, just an embarrassing memory.

Afterwards, the congregation filed out in a happy mood. People exchanged greetings and embraced lengthily and went on their way. Mordred felt a hundred times better. He didn't feel he was acting the part of a Muslim; rather, in some mysterious way he'd learnt from friends of his - Yousaf Sharif and his daughter – he was one. And a Christian. And maybe nothing, and everything.

"I thoroughly enjoyed that sermon," al-Iddrissy announced out of nowhere when they were travelling back. "I've vowed to change my ways."

The driver and the gunman laughed. T-shirt didn't.

"You're always saying that," the driver said eventually. "Every time we go to the mosque. We don't actually attend every week, Omar Ouyahia," he continued quietly. "We went today because al-Iddrissy's in love with you, that's all."

Al-Iddrissy banged the back of his head with the flat of his hand, gently enough to indicate he knew it was a jest. The driver laughed again. It must have hurt a little, but he didn't swerve, but he didn't continue to rile his friend.

"I really feel we could build something great here," al-Iddrissy went on. "Something like Muhammad, peace and blessings be upon him, built in Medina. A really virtuous town. With God and Omar Ouyahia's help. According to their plan."

"I agree," T-shirt said firmly.

"I'm giving up wine," al-Iddrissy said.

"You're a couple of bloody Wahhabi, Islamic State, al-Qaeda, arse kissers!" the gunman burst out. "Listen to yourselves!"

"Remember God, Hamdo," al-Iddrissy replied, unfazed. "Remember God."

Mordred didn't know what to think about this sudden turn of events. He'd expected to hand over money, not become an inspiration.

Nevertheless, maybe he could make his idea work. It was a good one. Maybe the Egyptian government – or the Algerian, or the Tunisian, it was in all their interests – would payroll it. Hell, maybe he could even get an EU grant. Seriously. Stranger things had happened. He'd been fired from MI7, after all. He had nothing to go back to. And he'd get to look after the dogs. And these guys were good fun, and Tanarej was a bit chaotic, but he'd known worse. After he'd rescued Mabel –

He suddenly saw the Hotel Mediterranean loom out of the window. For some reason, the sight affected the pit of his stomach.

Then it hit him. My God, he'd forgotten! Of course! That's why all the Islamists were pouring in. Because they knew the Americans were here.

And the Americans probably didn't know a thing about it.

It was time to pay a visit to the Hotel Med. Today. Sooner the better. Now.

Somehow, he'd have to get rid of al-Iddrissy and his gang.

Or maybe not. It was time to start putting all the pieces of the puzzle together.

"Stop at the fruit market," he told the driver. "Let's start by feeding the hungry."

## Chapter 15: Mordred Misses Out on The American National Dish

"I'd rather they didn't see me," Mordred said when they reached the warehouse. "Remember the prophet Isa: 'When you give alms to a poor man, do it in secret and God will reward you in Paradise'."

The car pulled up. It had taken Mordred a lot of persuasion for them all to agree. According to the driver, distributing free fruit to customers undermined the essentially commercial nature of the relationship; the gunman claimed they'd expect it every day. Even T-shirt and al-Iddrissy looked uncomfortable. "They don't really expect me to be a good person," al-Iddrissy said. "It confuses them." However, he was willing to give it a try, once. "They'll be on a boat in a week," he said. "It won't matter what they think of me then."

"Like what a soft touch you are," the driver said. "What jerks we all are."

They all got out and opened the boot. Ten carrier bags full of fresh fruit: dates, grapes, oranges, watermelons, tomatoes.

"After this, I'm going to the former administrative district to take a little look at the Islamists," Mordred said.

"Well, don't expect a lift," the driver said.

"What's the matter with you today?" al-Iddrissy exclaimed, turning on him. "He *never said he wanted one*. Next time, wait till you're *asked* before you say no!"

The driver slammed the boot. "Sorry for embarrassing you, Mummy!"

Al-Iddrissy went to punch him. Rather than dodge, the driver attempted a deflection. He unbalanced his opponent, but not enough to stop him bringing his body up close ready for another shot. They grabbed each other hard, thrusting their chins into their necks for facial-protection, unclutching just long enough to attempt more punches before frantically grasping again. Their clothes tore. They grunted. They fell over. Because they were both more concerned with defence than attack, and because their eyes were scrunched shut, no blow reached its target. After a minute, they lay completely motionless.

"I'll surrender if… you will," the driver said in a gasp.

"Deal," al-Iddrissy said. *"Deal!"*

They unclutched and stood up, brushing themselves. They looked exhausted.

Mordred could see what was happening. Al-Iddrissy was the driver's best friend, and he resented Omar Ouyahia's intrusion. He was virtually a middle-aged man, but right now he looked tearful.

"Let's get that fruit upstairs and into the hands of the migrants!" T-shirt exclaimed happily.

"Go away and screw yourselves," the driver said. "It's a stupid idea. They want to go to Europe! They've paid for their passage! They don't want a *watermelon*. They'll think we're trying to fob them off, like there's bad news round the corner. *Sorry we can't take you folks, but hey, here's an orange and a bunch of grapes.* I know that's what I'd think."

"We haven't even *got* their money," al-Iddrissy said. "Not yet. It's still with the middlemen."

"It'll make them suspicious," the driver said. "A ton of fruit out of nowhere." He hissed bitterly through his teeth, a kind of contemptuous sigh. "If anyone wants me, I'll be on the beach."

He was right, of course. Looked at soberly, it was a stupid idea. Mordred had wanted to see if Alec and Edna were still there, and perhaps lie in wait and shadow them afterwards; and he thought he could do something kind for the migrants in the process. Idiotic.

"I'll go after him," he offered. Although God only knew what he'd say.

"No, let me," al-Iddrissy responded gruffly. He left Mordred alone with T-shirt and the gunman.

In the space behind the warehouse, Mordred suddenly caught sight of a bedraggled man and a woman in a burka. The size differential – in effect, the height of the woman: over six feet tall – meant it must be them. And of course, the space behind the warehouse wasn't used for anything. Mostly, it was rubble and detritus. It certainly wasn't the kind of place any respectable man would lead his wife unless something very specific and crucially important was at stake. They were on their way somewhere. God had seen the mountain of fruit, recognised the nobility of Mordred's intention, and this was his reward. All he had to do now was follow at a safe distance. He made his excuses to T-shirt and the gunman and set off.

The couple crossed the town in no hurry, yet with solid determination – they obviously knew exactly where they were headed - and without speaking. A few blocks and an acre of wasteland later they arrived at a long-abandoned-looking high-rise with a mortar hole in the side. They entered through the front door without breaking stride. Mordred waited till they were out of view. They couldn't know he was following them, otherwise they'd have confronted him by now. But he daren't cross the space in front of the building. There would be others inside, and the risk of being seen from there was too great.

But at least now he knew where they kept base. He'd return when it was dark, surprise whoever was working with them.

Next up, it was time to find the Americans.

Of course, they and the Americans would be working together. Anything else would be too coincidental. And if he was honest, a man turning up at night to a top secret overseas base in a mortar-blown high-rise would probably be shot dead well before reaching the eternal debate as to whether to press the doorbell or use the knocker. No, he'd need to approach this cautiously – via the Hotel Mediterranean.

All the way here they'd been avoiding main thoroughfares, but there was no need for that any more. Half an hour later, he reached the former tourist section of town and the hotel.

From a distance, it looked taller than it was. Six floors would hardly qualify as high-rise anywhere else, but Tanarej had the deceptive appearance of hugging the ground, as if patiently waiting for some predator to pass overhead. The hotel was a 1960s-looking stacked rectangular concrete building with identical balconies on each level and a low entrance. Al-Iddrissy had been right: there was no way something on this scale should be still in business. Ninety per cent of its rooms must be closed to customers. How to pay chefs, waiters, cleaners? Impossible. Even with a miracle, in the long run, it was probably deteriorating faster than incoming funds could save it. The idea that the Americans were holed up here, once it gained currency, would be difficult to suppress. And the CIA weren't stupid: they'd know that. Quite possibly, therefore, they'd long abandoned ship. This might yet be a ghost-hotel, because the tricky thing about rumours was how they tended to persist in despite of facts.

If this was an American base, and the US and the UK were collaborating in Tanarej, they almost certainly knew about the presence of John Mordred here. London and Langley were rarely 100% open with each other, but that would go by the board on a joint mission. They knew he wasn't going to bomb or shoot them. And they were probably monitoring all sides of the hotel by CCTV. In theory, therefore, all he had to do was hang around looking as much like John Mordred as possible. After a while, someone inside would see he was behaving suspiciously, then run an ID check, after which he'd be identified and probably welcomed inside for hot dog and a glass of Wild Turkey. Then he could ring Alec on the other side of town and do a *Guess what?* And Alec would curse and fume because, as usual, the great John Mordred was one step ahead.

It seemed an excellent plan, and for the first time since arriving here, he relaxed a little. Soon be amongst spies, snoops and eavesdroppers again. Home sweet home.

He bought an orange and sat outside the building on a bench. He peeled it. He ate it. He got up. He walked round the building.

He ascended the steps to reception, then pretended to change his mind and reversed. He bought some dates and a cup of juice. He sat down where he had before, only a little farther along. He stretched, yawned, looked directly at the hotel, showed his face to the sun at different angles, did another circuit of the hotel.

Nothing. No signs of life at all. Surely someone must have clocked him by now. Didn't they recognise Mordred the Magnificent when they saw him?

True, he'd been sacked, and technically they needn't acknowledge him. But that would be petty. At the very least, they should send someone out. *Clear off, you're behaving suspiciously and if you stay put, we'll call the fuzz.* That's what they'd do at Thames House. When you saw someone going to great lengths to make an exhibition of himself, you at least dignified him with a bucket of cold water.

He'd have concluded the hotel was closed for business and possibly abandoned, had it not been for the fact that it so obviously wasn't. The front doors were open, and reception was manned.

What could he do? Actually go inside? Approach the receptionist and ask to see the CIA? But the receptionist might not know a thing about it, and anyway, it was taking exhibitionism a step too far.

He was on the point of giving up and getting a taxi home when someone came out. A bearded man of about forty, medium height and build, dressed in local clothing.

Only he wasn't local. A variety of signals - from the way he strode, to the way he moved his arms, even the manner in which he held his head - strongly suggested he was a westerner, and, less starkly, that he was American.

Bingo.

Here it came: (1) Clear off or (2) Wild Turkey.

But it was neither. The man swept a sideward glance at Mordred – he'd obviously seen him from inside: he recognised him as having a specific purpose – but it wasn't the kind of glance

Mordred was expecting. It was fearful. When their eyes met, the fear intensified. The man stepped up his pace and headed off.

Mordred was good at reading micro-expressions. The distress he'd witnessed was genuine. After a split second's hesitation, he decided nothing would come of standing idly in front of the hotel. His best bet now was to give chase, only discreetly, keeping out of view. The next level of reaction was panic and he didn't want to inspire that.

It was rather like the Alec and Edna pursuit all over again, and for a brief period, Mordred even thought the man might be going in the same direction. But then he performed an about-turn. His expression showed he thought he might be being followed, but wasn't sure. After about five minutes, it became clear he was walking randomly. He didn't do any shopping, he didn't alter pace, he didn't look to either side except to change direction.

Probably, he was some low-level guy; a trainee or a technician. He'd come outside for a breath of air, and now he was being followed. Rotten luck – or rather, pretty fortunate, because of all the people who could shadow you, those who simply wanted to shake your hand were always best.

Eventually, he ended up in a narrow lane between two rows of houses. Because it was relatively deserted, it suddenly became clear Mordred wasn't the only one following him. Two young men in black *thawbs* zeroed in on him. They carried guns on their backs, but they didn't look like they thought they'd need them. They drew knives from somewhere within their garments.

Mordred ran forward. He grabbed the left arm of the nearest man and swung him into and then over the other. He retained his grip and turned with increasing speed through two complete revolutions like he was throwing an Olympic hammer. The man started to leave the ground and his arm dislocated. The shock of what was happening probably meant he didn't feel anything - yet. When Mordred let go, he almost flew into the wall. His head was the last thing to collide with the perpendicular, and the whiplash felled him.

The other man was clambering to his feet. Mordred was dizzy and slightly drained but the knowledge that he hadn't far to go filled him with a second shot of adrenalin. He dodged round the back of his opponent and lifted him up by the top of his trousers. The man's front half plummeted. He was concentrating on clinging to his weapon at all costs, and his remaining hand wasn't enough to stop his forehead smacking the ground. The knife entered his belly by his own hand. Probably not deep enough to kill him, but once he saw the blood, his face filled with terror and he panicked. He got up, staggered out of the alleyway and ran.

As usual when he'd won a fight, it took Mordred a second to realise it was over, then he felt like laughing and performing a cartwheel.

However, the American had a gun trained on him.

"Well, that's nice," Mordred said in English.

"What just happened?" the American replied. He seemed genuinely uncertain.

"Well, those men came at you with knives. I did two moves I've never tried before – they're actually banned in the work gym – and now here we are, with you saying thanks for saving my life. But in a peculiar way."

"You're – you're *English?"*

It sounded like the cue for a witticism, but it'd probably fall flat. "Yep."

"I don't just mean, 'speak English'. I mean, actually English."

"The country that invented Toad in the Hole and Nigel Farage."

The man lowered his gun and offered a handshake. "Thank God. I'm Jack Talleyrand, by the way. Who were those two men?"

"I didn't catch their names. Normally, when man A saves man B from being killed by man C, it's more likely that C and B will know each other than that A and C will."

"Why were you following me, just out of interest?"

"I'm John Mordred, formerly of MI7. You're with the Americans. I was hoping to introduce myself and get an invite to the Hotel Mediterranean."

"Why? What do you think's in there?"

"A CIA sub-station."

Talleyrand laughed. "You'd be surprised how often I've heard that. It's a long discredited theory. I've actually had locals in to look around. A while ago, I admit, but nothing's changed."

"So what is it?"

"You'll never believe me."

"As you Americans often say: try me."

The man chuckled. "Tell you what: why don't I show you? Come on."

Mordred was surprised how quickly he found himself in front of the hotel again. They'd been walking in random directions, but never straying too far, it seemed, from their point of origin. They walked up the steps to the entrance, then past the reception area without slowing. The man on duty nodded a cautious greeting, but didn't smile. They went up four carpeted steps and through double doors, then along a corridor. They stopped halfway along and Talleyrand opened a door on his left. They went down a flight of stone stairs into a huge low-ceilinged hall about the size of a gym, but narrower.

The lighting was subdued, but sufficient to show two rows of about thirty occupied beds, one against each wall.

A hospital.

## Chapter 16: Not Quite Seattle Grace

There was very little electrical equipment, and in some ways it looked more like a scene from the early 20th than the 21st century. Cots plus bodies plus blankets, about sixty beds in all, arranged in two close-set rows, one on each side with a wide central aisle. The floor, the walls and the low ceiling were hard stone. There were no skylights, only neon strip-bulbs dangling from the ceiling, and not enough of those for full visibility. It was cool, but not cold. Two men and three women patrolled without looking at each other, only stopping occasionally to examine notes on clipboards attached to bedframes. They spoke to the patients just long enough to elicit rudimentary information. All the men in the beds – there were no women – looked sub-Saharan; the five orderlies looked European. A CCTV monitor next to where Mordred and his companion stood gave a live view of the building's entrance. Presumably, why, earlier, Talleyrand had emerged from the hotel looking askance at Mordred.

"We're members of *Tobias*," Talleyrand said. "A Christian charity based in Fivepointville, Pennsylvania. Two Americans, an Icelander, an Italian, a German, three Brits."

Mordred didn't know what to say. Weren't there other charities that did this sort of thing? Why not join them?

"I know what you're thinking," Talleyrand said. "The fact is, we do the work others won't. Tanarej is considered too dangerous for any official NGOs."

"As was almost proved twenty minutes ago."

"I haven't been on the receiving end of anything like that before. Like I say, we've quashed the rumours that there's a CIA substation here. No one in Tanarej believes that now."

"What about people from outside the town?"

"I don't think they know enough about this place. What I mean is, to care whether somewhere's got an enemy base, you've usually got to care about that somewhere. No one cares about Tanarej. Ergo no one cares about its alleged facilities."

It was the worst logic Mordred had ever heard. Still, probably best to be diplomatic. "I wouldn't be so sure," he said.

"If we weren't here, no one would help these people. Christ didn't flinch when he knew his life was about to end, and neither must we."

"There must be others in this town who would assist wounded civilians. Human nature's usually pretty generous, up to a point. Don't endanger yourselves by underestimating it."

"Believe me, if I thought that was the case, I wouldn't be here."

"Maybe explain why you think it isn't."

Talleyrand sighed. "Obviously, with a civil war going on, innocent people get shot by accident. Or sometimes they get kidnapped and injured when their families can't or won't pay the ransom. It pains me to say it, but there's still a fair degree of racism in this country. Men and women come across the Sahara from places like Mali, Niger, Eritrea, Ethiopia, Sudan, and when they get here they're treated like fourth or fifth class citizens because they're black. When they're caught in the crossfire of some local militia squabble, they tend not to cope very well afterwards. We patch them up. We've even been known to work with the local people-smugglers to get them on boats. MSF wouldn't do that. I'm not putting MSF down, either, just stating a fact."

"Why the secrecy, though?"

"Because: racism. We treat these people better than a lot of people think they deserve. Look, maybe the local population *would* help them in ideal circumstances. But there's a civil war going on. People can barely hold their own kith and kin together. They don't want the added burden of an uninvited guest. A lot of Libyans think exactly the same way about immigrants that a lot of Americans and Europeans do: if we make things unpleasant for them when they arrive, maybe they'll stop coming."

"'Do not mistreat or oppress foreigners in any way'," a young woman with blonde hair said, as she walked past. "'Remember, you were once foreigners in the land of Egypt'. Exodus 22 verse 21." She disappeared up the stairway.

"Well, thank you for showing me around," Mordred said. "I'd better be on my way now."

Two and two making four suggested that the Islamists in the southwest of the town were massing ranks for what they thought would be a glorious assault on the CIA. What would actually transpire was the demolition of a hospital with everyone inside. And that, on *top* of the Mabel situation.

Apart from anything else, the problem was far worse than he'd thought. Had this place housed the American security services, he'd have been able to count on reinforcements. And not just any: those of the greatest military power the world had ever seen. Now he had nothing. From hero to zero, as they probably said in Fivepointville, Pennsylvania. In record time, as they probably added if they wanted to be cruel. Zilch, as someone would have called from the back of the crowd, just to ensure he got the message.

"I should really repay your kindness," Talleyrand said. "You saved my life. How about a drink?"

"What of?"

"What would you like?"

"Wild Turkey?"

Talleyrand chuckled. "We've got pineapple juice," he offered, as if the two drinks were interchangeable. "Or pure water from Gadaffi's great underground river."

"No, sorry, I only drink Wild Turkey. I'd better be on my way now."

"You seem pretty eager to leave. You won't tell anyone what we're doing here, will you?"

"I'm English. Why would I?"

"I mean, don't let it slip after a few bourbons."

"I'm unlikely to be doing much alcohol round here."

Talleyrand chuckled again. "You'd be surprised."

"If even *you* haven't got any, and you're a United States Christian, it's unlikely I'll pick up a bottle in the local *souk*."

"Probably. But then how do you survive, if Wild Turkey's all you drink?"

"Let's not argue about Wild Turkey." One of the long list of sentences that, had he been approached about it before birth, he'd have sworn he'd never utter. "I'm sure you've a lot of work to do. Look after yourself, and be careful next time you leave the building. Someone's obviously got it in for you."

"Oh, I'm sure they were just opportunists. They've learned their lesson."

Mordred stopped himself on the verge of saying, 'I wouldn't be so sure' again. The conversation had already gone on too long and he had errands to run. They shook hands a second time and Mordred exited via the stairs they'd come down several minutes earlier. He tried not to break into a run; it didn't seem dignified.

The Egyptians should be his first port of call, but they were already supposedly looking into the Islamist situation. Whether it would renew their sense of urgency to know an attack on a hospital was imminent, he didn't know. He could already imagine one possible reaction: *First, he tells us there's a build-up of Islamists we know nothing about, then he tells us they're about to attack an underground hospital we've never heard of. What's his hidden agenda, and what sort of fools does he take us for?* By the time they realised, it'd be too late.

According to what al-Iddrissy had told him, there were at least three other groups in town he might collaborate with. To the west, pro-government groups; in the east, a Touareg militia; in the south-east, Zintan. They might conceivably be persuaded to work together. Just for one job. But he'd need a middleman to help arrange it. Then he'd have to go and see Alec and Edna, maybe eat a slice or two of humble pie, whatever it took. He could always spit it out if they wouldn't phone the SAS and tell them to get out here pronto, a group of evangelical Christian medics was about to be annihilated. The SAS liked that sort of thing, after all. They liked goodies to be goodies and baddies baddies. And they were probably in Sirte with the Americans. They and the SEALS or Delta Force or whatever could fly in together. Only take about twenty minutes.

He was fantasising. Concentrate on the task in hand.

He crossed the short distance to the town centre and found the square he'd come to when he'd first arrived here, a few days ago. *La Fiodora*. He hoped to God Nasser Ragai, the supposed PFG lieutenant he'd conversed with, really was the proprietor here. If not, he was in trouble.

He'd have to be, wouldn't he? That was his wife – Abrar? – surely? She'd appeared without a hijab and said Enjoy in English. She wouldn't have been that informal in the presence of two men neither of whom was her husband.

But that wasn't a certainty. Beware of rationalising from stereotypes. He knew nothing at all about Abrar, or Nasser Ragai, or even the PFG, really, if he was honest. For the first time, he felt like what he'd probably been all along: a bumbling, absurdly over-confident ex-pat who was about to get his come-uppance. Seemed such a long time ago he'd trounced those two villains in the alleyway. Now he was about to get a taste of his own medicine.

The man behind the counter wasn't Nasser Ragai. He was someone Mordred had never seen before. About fifty, tall, with long limbs and a side-parting. More like an academic than a militiaman, although the two occupations weren't mutually exclusive any more.

As previously, Mordred was the only person in the shop. The thin man looked at him like he couldn't believe he had a customer.

"Can I help you, sir?" he asked. Something in the way he said it suggested he'd once dealt with tourists, but it was centuries ago.

"I'm looking for Nasser Ragai," Mordred said.

He deflated and adopted an air of genuine perplexity. "Who?"

"Nasser Ragai."

"I'm afraid I don't know anyone by that name. Do you want to order anything?"

Mordred sighed. Everything in this man's face said he was lying. But you didn't need a degree in micro-expressions to see that. Reason alone said that Nasser Ragai had exclusive use of the premises last time he'd been here, and without the knowledge of the actual owner, that was implausible. Time to sweat it out. Stay put until something happened.

"What have you got to drink?" Mordred said.

"Tea. That's all."

"With sugar?"

"No. No sugar."

At that moment, the 'something' that Mordred thought he'd have to wait at least an hour for, happened. Abrar walked out from behind a curtain concealing the shop's rear. She glanced at Mordred, then her expression filled with apprehension. She turned on her heel and disappeared the way she'd come.

It would be discourteous to say anything. She knew he'd recognised her. As The Manual of Effective Spycraft said: never go point-scoring with the natives. Be nice.

He smiled. "Thank you. Without sugar will be fine."

Since they were the only people in the shop, it was natural for Mordred to begin a conversation. His host didn't like it - he'd probably have preferred to leave Mordred alone and go after Abrar until the shop was empty again - but he had to stay put because he was the host. That was a serious obligation in the Arab world. At first, Mordred could see he loathed it. Possibly, he expected more questions about Nasser Ragai, but Mordred avoided the subject entirely. Instead, he talked about his impressions of the town, encouraged the proprietor to share, and sprinkled his observations with quotes from the Qur'an. After half an hour, the proprietor introduced himself by name: Moatassem al-Arab. He came from behind the counter, sat opposite Mordred and they were friends. Mordred was on his third sugarless tea.

Then the proprietor unexpectedly discovered some sugar, and poured them both another cup, and this time it was on the house. They drank so much they had to keep going to the toilet. Because the door was more like a gate ending halfway up the frame, you could hear everything in the café. So Mordred heard Abrar emerge, frantically whisper, then run away again. Once or twice, he saw her peeking at him from behind the curtain. He pretended not to notice.

After an hour and a half's conversation about matters congenial to both parties and entirely unconnected with Mordred's ostensible reason for being here, his host started to show signs of guilt. Again, Mordred ignored it. They were talking about Gaddafi. The proprietor confided that he missed him.

"We've had more people killed in Libya than in thirty-four years of the *Jamahiriya* combined," he said. "We always had money and electricity and everything was cheap. Yes, people were arrested and tortured, but then, look at *now!* And Gaddafi was Libyan. Bloody Daesh are getting the shit kicked out of them in Syria so they come here and start trying to drag us fourteen centuries into the past! The seventh century! When tents were the pinnacle of technology!"

"No one wants to go backwards," Mordred agreed.

"I'll tell you what the Arab world needs now. Twenty or thirty Atatürks. I'd like to see Erdogan go three rounds with Mustafa Kemal, I tell you. He'd kick fatty's arse. He'd kick all their podgy arses, all the pasty, old pious hypocrites. He'd bring us into the 21st century so we can start giving America and Britain and France a run for their money. That's what your David Camerons and your Francoise Hollandes really fear, Omar Ouyahia. They fear it far more than ISIS."

Odd how tea and conversation, after a while, became just like beer and conversation: you relaxed and said things that might get you into trouble if you said them on Facebook. It was probably time to go. If someone overheard, there might be trouble.

Mind you, a lot of people felt the same way, from what he'd picked up. Just not the trigger-happy people, and that's always who you had to beware of most. *Careless talk costs lives*. Always true in wartime.

"I'd better be going," he said. "Thank you, Moatassem, for the tea and the conversation. And of course, the hospitality."

The guilt on the proprietor's face intensified. He put his hand over Mordred's.

"Omar Ouyahia," he said in a hushed tone. "When you first came in here, as I remember, you asked for a certain *Nasser Ragai*. May I enquire as to why you wanted to speak to him?"

"Can I speak confidentially?"

The proprietor laughed. "We've being doing so all along! Honestly, the things I've got off my chest today! Things I can't usually speak of with anyone else except my wife! You've no idea what a tonic you've been. But it was all hush-hush, obviously. You know that. Now it's your turn to confide in me. And I'll do what I can to help you."

"As part of my stay here, I'm trying to turn Tanarej into a better place."

"I've heard that. A lot of people have."

"Today, chance and rumour took me to the Hotel Mediterranean where the CIA were supposedly holed up."

The proprietor laughed. "I could have saved you a journey! There hasn't been any such thing there since 2012. I admit, it's odd how the hotel's still in business. It should have closed down long ago. But" – he shrugged – "there are possible explanations for that. Perfectly innocent, rational ones."

"However, there is *something* there. An underground hospital."

The proprietor leaned forward. "A *hospital?* Are you sure?"

"I saw it with my own eyes. It's run by a Christian charity, fronted by Americans."

"*The* Americans?"

"No, just Americans. Ordinary people like you and me. Do-gooders from Pennsylvania, to be precise. They've got about sixty beds, full of sub-Saharans. You wouldn't set up an operation on that sort of scale if it was a front for something else."

"Immigrants?"

"The organisers say someone has to care for them. And they're right."

The proprietor drew his eyebrows together and nodded, as if something important had just occurred to him after a long period of forgetfulness. "Of course. Amazing how you tend to lose sight of basic moral truths when there's a war on. You're quite right, Omar Ouyahia. Only… I don't see what this has to do with your 'Nasser Ragai'."

"Let me tell you about my other discovery then. There's a build-up of Islamists in the town's southwest. The former government section."

"What do you mean, 'build up'?"

"They're coming in from outside town. I don't know exactly where, but they're not local. I think the idea that there's a CIA base in the Hotel Mediterranean has reached them through a process of Chinese Whispers – information serially transmitted through many intermediaries becoming increasingly distorted in transit," he added, quickly realising 'Chinese Whispers' would make no sense, "and it's somehow changed from dead news to supposedly alive news. They're going to launch an attack on a hospital."

"Oh my days. When?"

"I wish I knew. Soon, I would imagine. When they've enough men."

"And that'll be the pretext to a takeover of the town. *You were sitting on a hornet's nest, you idiots. We saved you*. That's what they'll say. And of course, once they've assumed control, they've got a base to attack Tripoli."

"I hadn't really thought about that, but you're right."

"What will you do now?"

"I'm not sure I have much choice. Go home and pack my bags. I'm the sort of man Islamists love to kill, unfortunately. My house overlooks the town, so they'll probably want it for a base. And once they find out I've been to the Hotel Mediterranean – someone will have seen me go in: as you say, I'm fast becoming a local curiosity – they'll need to keep me quiet."

"What about fighting back?"

Mordred smiled. "One man versus an army?"

"I'll stand by you, Omar Ouyahia. And I have friends."

Mordred patted his arm. "We don't even know how many of them there are. If they're coming in clandestinely and looking to make this a base to attack Tripoli, you can be sure they won't want heavy casualties. No, they'll wait till there's enough of them to mount a relatively bloodless coup."

"Bloodless for them, not for us. Then we've got to act as quickly as possible! The longer we wait, the stronger they get!"

Mordred smiled sadly. "Don't throw your lives away. Harsh regimes come and go. You're probably better off keeping your head down. As for me, I'd better get packing."

The proprietor looked about to argue but thought better of it. He sighed. "Good luck, Omar Ouyahia. I wish you could stay."

"Me too. But as Allah wills it."

They completed their farewells with a prolonged handshake and a hug and Mordred set off on foot for home. He decided not to go and see Alec and Edna. Not yet. If his calculations were correct, Nasser Ragai would be waiting for him when he got back.

## Chapter 17: Dead Dog Time

It wasn't Mladenov's preference, but he was outvoted on the way over. The problem with killing guard dogs was knowing what to do next. If the owner was in the house, he'd realise he was under attack as soon the firing began. You couldn't kill dogs from a distance without firing. The occupant might then lie low for a while then come at you, all guns blazing, the moment you stepped on the premises - which of course you'd have to eventually. Alternatively, he might not even be in. If he came back home and saw the corpses of his four animals in the front garden, he'd probably double-back for reinforcements. Either way, you ran a strong risk of forfeiting at least the advantage of surprise.

But although these men were tough, they were afraid of dogs. They regarded them as alien and unclean, and exaggerated their power to kill. Their continued existence would demoralise them.

In the practical sense, killing guard dogs was always simple: under threat, loyalty meant they came running to each other's aid, and stupidity meant they presented an easy target. There were four when Mladenov arrived, in full daylight, with seventeen hardened fighters from Misrata; ten seconds later, there were none. No one emerged from the building to see what was going on, but that didn't necessarily mean anything. Hurling a grenade was out of the question. Only if Mordred was inside was it the ideal tactic; if he was out, it was the opposite.

Mladenov was here mainly in an observer's capacity; in fighter's garb, so was expected to follow orders. He wanted to make sure Mordred died. Though he couldn't say it, he didn't quite trust these men to tell the truth. When it came to recounting their exploits, they habitually turned defeats into victories. Eventually, they came to believe their own fabrications, and their tales actually did become inspiring morale-boosters, even to themselves. He needed to see what transpired with his own eyes.

"Spread out, surround the building and wait," the leader commanded. Said Mohammad was fifty-seven with a grey beard, a hard-lined face and small eyes. There were three generations of jihadis here today, and he was the sole representative of the oldest, those who'd fought the Russians in Afghanistan. The remaining sixteen were split between those who'd fought the Americans and British in Iraq and Afghanistan, and those who'd stood up to Assad in Syria. They didn't always get on, but mostly they deferred to age, experience and assertive ideology. Said had all three. Like his men, and Mladenov, he was a foreigner here.

The men did as he commanded. They thinned out amongst the trees till they were alone, then they got down on their haunches, propped their guns at their sides and waited. They could sit like this for hours, virtually motionless. They found it easy because, on the whole, they didn't have a thought in their heads.

Mladenov stayed with Said Mohammad. In many ways, the grizzled old mujahid was ideal for this job. It was in his personal interests to see Mordred die. He was, after all, newly married to his sister.

An hour after Mordred's visit, Moatassem Al-Arab found Nasser Ragai outside an inn more or less adjacent to his own tea and snacks bar. Al-Arab was out of breath. He pulled out a chair opposite the PFG lieutenant and sat down. There were three other tables, all vacant. Ragai had what looked like a glass of fruit juice in front of him.

"I've been looking all over town for you," Al-Arab said. "Why do you have your phone switched off?"

Ragai laughed. "I get into the habit of switching my mobile off. It's a requirement of dealing with highly flammable liquids. Relax, Moatassem. What's the matter with you?"

The shop owner came out – a small man with large glasses - wiping his hands on a cloth. Al-Arab ordered an orange juice he could hardly afford. Every *dirham* counted nowadays. "I've just been talking to Omar Ouyahia Abu Farafisa," he said as the shopkeeper disappeared back inside.

"The Algerian? Was he looking for me?"

The way Ragai said 'Algerian' sounded for some reason like he didn't believe it. But that couldn't be right.

"I didn't tell him where to find you," Al-Arab said.

"Why not?"

"You told me not to. Besides, I didn't know where you were! I've just spent the last hour looking for you!"

"Calm down. Here, put your money away. Let me." Al-Arab's orange juice arrived. Ragai paid for it. "What did the Algerian want?"

"He's leaving," Al-Arab said.

"Already?" He laughed. "I thought he had big plans to 'Islamify' the people-smuggling business! Impressive man on the surface. I quite liked him, as a matter of fact. And I've been hearing good things about him in town. Shame he turned out to be a quitter, but there we are. You don't expect me to run after him, I hope? Not that it would do any good. He's his own man."

Again, the odd note of scepticism in his friend's voice. Al-Arab made a concerted effort to ignore it. "Aren't you going to ask why he's leaving?" he asked.

"Let me guess. No one in Tanarej shares his idealism."

"A bit more than that. He's afraid of being strung up from a balcony."

"I thought he had bodyguards."

"Apparently not. At least, I don't think so. He says there's an ocean of Islamists sweeping quietly into Tanarej with a view to taking it over. And he thinks their first act will be to kill him."

Ragai almost choked on his drink. He looked at his friend as if he was mad. "What made him say that?"

"He thinks - "

"He must *know!* He wouldn't be leaving if he wasn't sure!"

"He says - "

"Where?" Ragai demanded. "Where are these guys? I haven't seen them!"

"Southwest, in the old administration district."

Ragai put his thumb on his cheek for a quick philosophical ponder. "I mean, there are Islamists and there are Islamists, good and bad, like all things. But if these guys are *massing*..."

"That's roughly what he said," Al-Arab said.

"And you don't think he's actually got a bodyguard? Hell, they could be after him now. Where is he?"

"He went home. His house. On the hill."

"Walking?" Ragai asked.

"I believe so."

"I need to get on to those no-good pals of his: Al-Iddrissy and his crew. They'll know if there's any truth in it. Meanwhile, I'll see if I can catch up with him on his way home, give him a bit of cover, at least till he leaves town. Leave it with me, Moatassem. You did right to come and find me. Absolutely the right thing." He downed his juice, picked up his rifle and left his friend alone.

Ten minutes later, sweating heavily, he ascended a staircase in a two-floor office-block two streets back from the seafront. He went into a small room with a desk, a chair, two shelves and a window looking onto the street. He closed the door impatiently behind him, rummaged around in the desk drawer and took out a mobile phone. He pressed 'call' and waited.

"Mr Ragai?" said a voice on the other end. Faint touch of an English accent, nothing more.

"Is Alec Cunningham there?" Ragai said. "I have very important information for him regarding his former colleague, John Mordred."

"I'll put you through," the voice said calmly.

Thirty minutes later, Nasser Ragai and Edna Watson stood at the base of the hill leading up to Mordred's house. Edna was dressed in men's desert-army fatigues and a camouflage cap. They observed the summit through two pairs of binoculars, passing laconic comments back and forth. Then they got in a jeep and set off at speed for the eastern rear of the encirclement. Ragai's troops – mainly reinforcements summoned from Jathran's battalions in the east and the pro-government forces west of the town - were approaching at a run from all sides to ambush the ambushers. It was likely to be messy. Only maybe less so if someone could stop Mordred on his way up. However, he'd yet to make an appearance.

One kilometre from Mordred's house, and the same distance from Edna and Nasser Ragai, Alec Cunningham waited alone in an armour-reinforced saloon car with blackened windows. He too wore camouflage. He expected the signal to drive up to the house any time now. If the guys lying in wait for him were anything like competent, they wouldn't try to kill him before he'd removed the padlock. Ragai's men would have to be a split second ahead of that and fully accurate and fully apprised of the threat. A big ask, but that's why he was in camouflage in a reinforced car.

Where the bloody hell was Mordred? Typical of him to complicate matters. Even without trying he could put a spanner in the works. It was amazing.

Ragai drove Edna to the summit of an adjacent hill, about a mile distant from Mordred's house and on a slighter higher elevation, enabling a better view of the soon-to-be killing field. They got out and resumed binocular gazing.

There was a faint crackle from the radio transmitter attached to Ragai's belt. He picked up and spoke. Edna's Arabic was good; she'd trained fairly intensively since joining MI7 just over a year ago, but Arabic plus interference defeated her.

"We think we've identified the whole crew," Ragai told her a moment later. "Sixteen in all. Time to send Mr Cunningham in, if he's prepared. If we wait any longer, John Mordred may arrive."

Edna unhooked her own transmitter. "Alec? Are you ready? Over."

"Standing by; over."

"You have clearance to approach. Good luck. Over and out."

Ragai was already watching. She looked through the binoculars again. There were so many things that could go wrong here. Alec could easily die.

Maybe best not to be so pessimistic, though. They didn't know he knew about them, so they wouldn't be expecting him to dive behind the car even before he'd undone the padlock. They certainly wouldn't think he knew their positions, or that he was a better shot than most of them, or that he'd have a better rifle and one or two other weapons to hand.

Nevertheless, still one versus sixteen. Hardly encouraging odds. And John hadn't even appeared yet. When he did, they might even find themselves facing a hostage situation. Where the hell was he?

Still, better late than early. At least, in this situation.

The saloon car suddenly appeared coming up the hill in no apparent hurry. It stopped leisurely in front of the gate. Alec got out and made a big show of speaking to some non-existent occupants on the back seats, then he went to undo the padlock.

There was a loud barked command through Ragai's transmitter, and a collective crack of gunfire, like an execution squad from a distance. Then shouting. Tentative whoops of what sounded like triumph.

Then complete quiet.

Edna looked through the binoculars again. Two of Ragai's men were running through the undergrowth to shake hands with Alec. She could tell from his body-language that he wasn't sure it was time to start celebrating yet, but a few more moments of quiet seemed to persuade him. He undid the padlock, pushed opened the gate with two of Ragai's men helping, got back in the car and drove up to Mordred's front door.

"Time for us to get over there," Ragai said.

Although Mordred's house was on a hilltop it was screened on nearly all sides by forest. Said Mohammad's men came as close as possible without breaking cover, but knew they were hypothetically vulnerable to an attack from the rear. Yet any farther back, the trees would have blocked their sight-line.

In reality, since no one could suspect their presence, all that mattered was the *kafir*'s house was surrounded. Said Mohammad instructed his second-in-command to storm the building and kill its occupants the moment Mordred made an appearance, then he found a little niche in the forest – two trees had grown together, and a shepherd had constructed a makeshift shelter – to sit with the other *kafir*. Here they could savour the victory Allah grants his followers and eat pitta with slices of fresh mutton and herbs. And smoke cigarettes, which, contrary to the teachings of the false believers, was condemned neither in the Qur'an nor the Sunnah.

They didn't speak, because ambushes forbade it. Said Mohammad was eager to see the corpse of his brother-in-law, because men who want revenge are always the most dangerous; and Mladenov wanted the same thing, but for different, more clinical, reasons. They'd speak afterwards.

They both saw the car appear on the road up to the house. In no hurry at all, which was excellent. They sat up, their throats dry, spines tingling. The driver got out, spoke to someone on the back seat. He went up to the gate, again casually. Any second now the mujahideen would be forcing the front door.

And then it came. The volley they'd been expecting. They jumped slightly, even so. A chunk of meat fell out of Said Muhammad's pitta. He picked it up and thrust it in his mouth, then craned his head forward for a better look.

For a few seconds, he didn't know what had happened. There were no holes in the car, not one.

Next he saw the driver was alive and apparently unharmed.

Then men whooped and emerged from the forest.

Not his men.

They'd been ambushed. The very possibility he'd completely discounted!

For the first time in a long while, he felt afraid. He and the *kafir* had to get out of here. They had to ditch their guns so they'd look like peasants. They had to walk without hurrying and look humbly at the ground. If they met anyone, they had to keep going.

He relayed all this to Mladenov.

"If we're stopped, we'll be searched," he explained when Mladenov expressed scepticism about disarming. "If they find us with guns, we'll be arrested. With a fancy pistol like yours, we'll probably be disembowelled. We're more plausible together, but do as I say, or I'll leave you to find your own way back, and I might not be so hospitable next time we meet. This is your fault."

"Mine? How can it possibly be mine?"

"Because it's not mine, and that only leaves one alternative!"

They got up and trudged through the woods. Whoever had set the ambush would be almost as hampered as they were in terms of the outer perimeter of their positioning. Too far away and the forest would form too thick a barrier. No, they must have crept up silently and waited to pounce. Even the car was probably bogus.

After about five hundred yards, they left the shelter of the trees and took to the road. They were clear now.

This 'John Mordred' was obviously good at his job. Even Mladenov had spoken of him with respect.

Perhaps it was time to let his sister go.

But that wouldn't placate him. It'd increase his confidence because it'd look like a sign of weakness.

"Why did Allah allow that?" Mladenov said quietly.

It came out of the blue. "What?" Said Mohammad said.

"I asked, 'Why did Allah allow that?' It's a simple question. You're supposed to be his foot soldiers."

"It is not for a *kafir* to know the answer to such questions!" Said Mohammad replied, trying to keep his voice down but too furious.

"There *isn't* an answer, that's why. All you Islamists, you're all losing, all over the world. You're even blowing *each other* up."

"I won't discuss such things with you!"

"Because you're stupid, that's why. Because you can't. You're a moron. Has it ever occurred to you that maybe Allah wants you to be peaceful for a change?"

"I'll have a gun in my hand pretty soon, and when I do - "

"I'm sick of your lies. You and people like you. You'll be telling this as if it was a great victory in a few days' time, and all the time, *you can't even see the obvious!"*

Said Mohammad noticed that the baton of rage had passed from him to Mladenov. His anger turned to apprehension then fear. He'd left his rifle behind in the woods. He was defenceless.

Suddenly, Mladenov struck him on the head with what felt like a rock. The blow was so heavy he almost lost consciousness. He sank to his knees. Blood trickled down his face. He'd been in dire straits before and come through, so –

But Mladenov had kept his gun. He took two steps backwards and aimed it at Said Mohammad's head.

"I'll plant a sign in your corpse saying, 'Great victory won here'," he said. "Just so the vultures don't get the wrong idea."

"No! Please!" Said Mohammad raised his hands. "Please, my friend. Please! *Please!"*

Just then, a man emerged at great speed from the woods and knocked Mladenov flying.

After leaving the tea shop, Mordred walked around town for thirty minutes to give Moatassem al-Arab time to go and find Nasser Ragai, He sat on the beach and watched a woman and her husband and two toddlers playing in the water like the town had no troubles. He took a walk to where Alec and Edna were, just for a look and to be near his friends for a change. It felt odd them being in there, him being here, and unable to communicate. Why were they in Tanarej? For Mabel? For him? Because of the Islamists? Sooner or later, he'd have to call on them. But then, what if they were here to abduct him, orders of Ruby Parker? Do what they'd failed to do in London?

But no, he didn't think they were like that.

He was becoming depressed now. Time to set off for home. On foot, so he could scan the approach more effectively. Ragai might be waiting for him when he got back, but so might al-Iddrissy. So might anyone. He'd blabbed his mouth off in the tea-shop, now he needed to be cautious. Probably call in at the hospital first.

He went back to The Hotel Mediterranean and walked straight past reception and downstairs into the hospital without stopping. Talleyrand was waiting for him.

"Don't think much of your security," Mordred told him.

"The only reason I'm not holding a gun is because I saw it was you," Talleyrand said, pointing to the CCTV screen. "What can I do for you?"

"Do you have a pair of binoculars I could borrow? Only I'm going home and I think someone might be waiting for me."

Talleyrand found a small pair in a room behind the hospital and Mordred bought a cooked flatbread and set off for home. At the bottom of the hill, he looked through the binoculars. The house itself was concealed by trees, but you could see nearby portions of the road. And yes, even in that small space. Armed men, waiting for him.

Ragai, presumably. Well, he wasn't going to be bullied into divulging what he knew. If the PFG lieutenant was that eager to speak to him, he'd need to be a bit more subtle. He went into the woods at the side of the road, sat down, ate his flatbread, and reclined. Within ten minutes, he was asleep.

He dreamt of Mabel again and awoke some time later to the sound of two men arguing. A theological dispute, by the sounds of it, although he didn't catch the detail. He looked out from between the trees while taking care to remain hidden. Two of them, one young, one old. Father and son possibly.

He suddenly saw something he wasn't expecting. The young man turned on the old and whipped his head with a rock, knocking him to his knees. He then drew a gun. The old man cried and begged for mercy.

Mordred sprang to his feet, rushed out and knocked the attacker over before he could pull the trigger. Whoever he was, he hardly had time to realise what was happening before Mordred punched him unconscious.

Mordred picked up the gun and thrust it into his pocket. He turned to the old man. "Are you okay?"

"Thank you, sir," the old man said.

"Come to my house. It's just up the road. I'll put a bandage over that wound."

The man stood up and wiped his head with his sleeve as if the injury was nothing. "Allah saves," he said.

He walked away like he was in a dream.

No point in going after him. You couldn't right the wrongs of the entire world, and at least he'd been grateful.

The young guy could just lie there and get sunburn. Discover his expensive revolver was gone when he woke up. That'd teach him.

Right now, it was time to go home. If Ragai was going to interrogate him at gunpoint, so be it. Time was of the essence. He'd find a way to get through to him.

He retrieved his binoculars and set off up the hill.

The journey was longer than he expected and, given what awaited him, possibly not worth the effort. He was about to double-back and go back into town when a jeep rounded the corner and pulled to a halt just in front of him. He had to look twice at the driver.

Edna Watson?

"Hi, John," she said, as casually as if this was the staff canteen. "Nice to see you again."

## Chapter 18: Alec Cunningham Again

Edna and Mordred got out of the jeep in front of the house and went straight through to the living room. Alec was sitting on a sofa with Nasser Ragai and two young militiamen. They'd reserved an empty armchair for him. Two PFG soldiers lolled on a carpet in the corner. A small pile of chicken bones and an empty drink can stood on the floor in between them.

"Well, look what the cat's dragged in," Alec said in Arabic.

Everyone chuckled. Nasser and his two men stood up, stretch and left.

"Welcome to my humble abode," Mordred said. "Feel free to sit down. And help yourself to food and drink."

"You do realise I just almost got killed saving you from certain death?" Alec said.

"Edna told me. Thanks." He sat down on the armchair. "Why are you here?"

"Rescuing you. I've just said."

"I meant, generally. In Tanarej."

"We're here to liberate your sister, dummy. Although we do know there are Islamists here too, in increasing numbers. And a hospital that they're planning to attack. So we're also here to prevent that."

Mordred grinned. "When did you find out about the Islamists?"

Alec looked hard at him.

"Just now," Mordred said. "Nasser told you. And Nasser found out from Moatassem, whom I told about two hours ago."

"You think you're so bloody clever, don't you? You're like the insufferable little swot in primary school who always has the right answer to every bloody question."

"I didn't mean it like that."

Alec scoffed bitterly. "Of course not, no."

"What I meant was, it's no good trying to hide it: you're only really here to rescue Mabel. Which means you're here for me. And for that, I'm unbelievably grateful. I take it Ruby Parker's had a change of heart."

"About five minutes after you slipped through the net."

"You're the 'special one'," Edna said with a grin. "A kind of MI7 José Mourinho."

"The mind boggles," Alec remarked.

"Well, I'm glad she's changed her mind," Mordred said, "because when I get home, I'm going to beg for my job back. Obviously, I'll have to eat humble pie and start again as a junior agent, or maybe a typist or a lavatory attendant, work my way up and so on, but I'm not ready to retire yet."

"Can we talk about something other than you?" Alec said. "Incidentally, we've known you were here – I mean, in this location - for some time. Nasser recognised your photo."

"Don't you want to know where I got my lovely big house from?" Mordred replied.

"I think I can guess."

"The Egyptian government," Mordred said.

Alec shook his head. "Traitor."

"They've treated me very nicely. Better than the Queen did, with her fickle ways."

"Don't blame the Queen."

"The big question is, who else is with you and Edna in that blown-out high-rise on the other side of town?"

"How did you know about that?" Alec said

"I followed you, obviously. Who's over there?"

Alec ground his teeth. "Young Ian and Tariq. We need Tariq to conduct surveillance. He confirmed the existence of the hospital you mentioned. Hacked their network."

"No Annabel or Phyllis?"

"Annabel's in London. Phyllis left the service."

"She… ?"

"Left MI7, yes. I don't know what you did to that girl, but she was miserable for the four weeks leading up to her departure."

"Bloody hell. I may *not* go back and work there then."

"Listen to fickle you. Just like the Queen. Allegedly. Incidentally, you do know your sisters are worried sick about you?"

"What do you mean?"

"Apparently, you arranged to meet them in Selfridges for *breakfast?* Then you ran away from Charlotte, *the fat one?* And you ditched your phone in the *bin?* And you'd had your hair shaved and probably had *chemo?"*

"Charlotte: 'the fat one', like I wouldn't know who you meant otherwise. Actually, she's not fat. Not really. A bit. Just at the moment, not usually."

"Anyway, last time we heard, they hired Horvath to find you."

*"Horvath?"*

"'The best', as Hannah, the lanky one, put it."

Mordred laughed. "Well, that's the end of that. I'll never be found."

"Anyway, what are we going to do about these Islamists?"

"My main objective has to be to find Mabel. Then stop the hospital being attacked - "

"Which means we've got to take out the Islamists," Alec said. "Attack being the best form of defence. They're not going to kill her unless they think we're trying to rescue her. Quite the contrary. They might even shield her. She's an asset."

"Which means ideally the people attacking them need to be local," Mordred said. "PFG and pro-government. The city of Zintan's not far off either: I'm sure they'd be willing to send a few brigades, maybe mount an attack from the rear. I believe they've a limited presence in Tanarej already. In any case, it's not for us to say. I'll explain the situation to Nasser and make a few recommendations, although I'm hardly qualified to advise someone with the expertise he probably has."

"So what now?" Alec said. "What about your baby sister? I suppose you've got a 'plan'? You usually have."

"No plan at all, unfortunately. All I know is roughly where she is."

Edna stuck her hand up. "Ideally, we'd need someone with inside knowledge of the Islamists' base. Unfortunately, none of the guys positioned to attack this place survived, or we could have interrogated him. However, we could kidnap someone."

"From the other side of town?" Alec said.

"Why not?" she asked.

"You might start getting suspicious if one of your fighters disappears," Alec said. "Like someone's preparing to attack and they've kidnapped a man to get intel."

"Come on," Mordred said: "they must have desertions all the time. It's probably normal."

"Granted," Alec said. "But if I was in command, I'd know which of my men was inclined to abscond. If I was any good, I'd know most probably aren't. Statistically, if we kidnap a random man – which we'd have to, since we don't know anything about the situation in there – we'll probably end up with one of the less likely ones. And if we don't, what's the chance of their information being any good? Ideally, we need a senior figure, but we're unlikely to get one of those by chance."

Edna nodded. "We'd have to watch the place for a long time to identify possible targets, and we probably don't have that luxury. Bad idea."

"Even if we did get a senior commander," Mordred said, "he probably wouldn't talk."

"You'd *make* him," Alec said. "This is your sister we're talking about. Look," he went on in a more sombre tone, without waiting for Mordred's response, "I hate to say this, but rescuing Mabel may need to go on ice for a while. It was different when she was just being held by a small coterie of fanatics. Right now, she's somewhere in the centre of a vast anthill, and if *you* haven't a plan, *I* certainly haven't. In sum, none of us has the foggiest idea how to get to her. Short of some senior commander falling wondrously into our hands and being miraculously willing to supply accurate information – don't forget that, even under torture, he could happily feed us complete crap, knowing we can only check its validity by going in, thereby getting ourselves killed – we're up Excrement Creek without a paddle."

"So what are you suggesting, Alec?" Edna asked.

"It's not a suggestion," he said. "If I'm right, and I am, we haven't any choice. We wait till Nasser and his men – with whatever allies they can muster – have scattered the anthill then we gather information about Mabel from the survivors on both sides. We should get a pretty good picture. At that point, her captors should be demoralised, bedraggled and on the run. We can meet them on our own terms."

"Assuming she survives the firefight," Mordred said.

"As Alec said," Edna put in, "she's an asset. They'll probably go overboard to keep her out of harm's way."

Alec sighed tetchily. "It's time I said something."

"That'll make a change," Mordred said.

"I'm serious."

"You mean, to me," Mordred said.

Alec seemed to gather himself. "It is possible they'll keep her out of harm's way, but that assumes a very naïve view of the situation."

"I think I can see what's coming," Edna said. "We discussed this at Thames House."

Mordred could feel the subtext. It came from both of them. *Brace yourself.*

"It's unlikely Mabel's being held entirely against her will," Alec said. "Especially after this length of time. Uncooperative hostages are a drain on resources, morale and goodwill. Unless there's hope of a significant payback, they're a dead weight, and you're better off killing them."

"You're saying you think she might be dead?" Mordred asked.

"Worse than that," Alec replied.

He gave a laugh of shock. "What the hell could be worse than her being dead?"

"Psychologically, she'll want to stay alive. She'll behave in such a way as to maximise her chances. That means going through the motions of being happy to be there. Add Stockholm Syndrome into the mix, and it's quite likely she's not so much a captive as a wife."

Mordred felt the word like a blow. "It wouldn't happen that quickly," he said.

"I'm not helping my case by pointing all this out," Alec went on. "A moment ago, I said we should wait till the anthill's scattered. Before that, I said they'd shield her. But we might very well find she's in their front line. By choice. Even if not at the start, then at the end, when they're routed."

"She's a bloody doctor – nurse. Was on her way to becoming a doctor. She's an intelligent woman."

"She's an idealist," Alec said. "And she's chosen to exercise her idealism on the borderline of life and death. Exactly the same territory as religion. And she lost the man she loved, from what I heard. And let's face it, she can't be *that* savvy – not at the moment – if she set off for Libya at the invitation of some woman she's never met before, one even her deceased lover didn't know that well."

Mordred drew a deep breath. "And you discussed all this at Thames House, did you?"

"I'm not saying it's a fact. I'm saying it's a possibility. You need to be aware that the touching reunion you're expecting may not happen. Instead, she may shoot you."

"You said they wouldn't hold on to an uncooperative hostage unless there was a chance of a 'significant payback'. But that's exactly what we've agreed. Money, in the first instance, then guns."

"Except they probably think they can have their cake and eat it."

Mordred got up, although he had no idea why standing was preferable to sitting. "I suppose I should have thought of all this before," he said. "I don't know why I didn't. It's a mystery." He went behind his armchair, put both hands on the headrest and looked at the ceiling.

Edna went to get up. "We're here to help," she said.

Alec held up his palm to her. "Give him a minute," he said quietly.

Mordred walked into the kitchen and looked through the window into the distance. If Mabel *was* the wife of someone, she was probably still alive, that was the important thing. She'd be traumatised, but then that would be true anyway, whatever the details of her predicament. *She'd be alive.*

Alec was right. They needed a senior commander if they were going to unlock the ant's nest. If they waited till Ragai went in, if she really was a mentally compromised collaborator, she might well be killed in the melee.

Where could they get a senior commander from? They couldn't. Not at this late stage.

Maybe if he prayed to God? It had worked before. He wasn't much of a one for organised religion, but there was definitely something to be said for it. *God, please give me a senior commander* probably wouldn't work. Not enough detail. He found himself saying it anyway. *From the other side. In that block on the other side of town. Where the Islamists are.* What on earth was he doing? Looking for an excuse to blame God when it all went wrong? End up one of those bitter atheists? *Listen, God, go back through my memory banks. Please. There's a picture of the place I mean in there. You'll know it when you see it. Or go to Walid al-Iddrissy and search his brain. I wouldn't trouble you, Lord, only it's Mabel.* He was going mad, mad, maddy, mad.

What about those two men he'd met on the road earlier? The shepherd and his son? And why was he thinking about them?

The son, in particular.

Because *he was going to pieces*, that's why! He needed to stop thinking about the million different bits of the picture that Alec had just smashed in front of him, and start thinking about how to manage the immediate future: the next few minutes, hours, days. He made four mundane decisions to help him look like he was managing and returned to the living room.

"What are you going to do now?" Alec asked him. "Any thoughts?"

"I can't continue to stay here," he replied. "It's no longer secure. I'm going to move into the hospital. Return the binoculars I borrowed, keep an eye on the CCTV and mount a proper armed guard, as discreet as possible. I'll need you to help me, take it in turns to keep watch on the hotel entrance. Obviously, I'll have to take the dogs with me. I'm thinking I could train them to guard the medics."

Edna and Alec looked at each other.

"I'm afraid there's some more bad news," Alec said.

## Chapter 19: A Decent Burial

When Mladenov regained consciousness, his first fully-fledged thought was that he had to get away. However, a whole host of feelings, impressions and sensations preceded this, mostly intense. First, amazement that he was still alive; then horror that it had been *John Mordred* who felled him; then the sinking feeling that Said Mohammad had escaped, so next time they met, the boot would be on the other foot. There were probably soldiers out looking for him this very minute – *Wanted, dead or alive, the kafir coward, Johannes Mladenov* - depending on how much time had elapsed ...

By now, he was walking. Obviously, through the forest was his only option; along the road would be insane. He couldn't have been unconscious long. The soldiers up at Mordred's house wouldn't remain for any length of time, not now they'd done what they came for. None could have driven past yet, otherwise they'd have picked him up. The chances of them being as careless as Mordred were slim indeed.

If not much time had elapsed, he might still be able to catch Said Mohammad, finish what he'd started. He didn't have his gun any more, no, but after what he'd done to the old fraud's right temple, he'd still have the advantage. Another well-directed rock should do it.

But no, he wasn't thinking. He didn't even know in which direction Said Mohammad had gone. He might have collapsed and died by now. That would be best, yes. In the woods. And get eaten by whatever wild creatures inhabited this part of the countryside. Army ants. Oh, sweet justice.

But wait a minute! Maybe Mordred had taken him back up to his house. *Come with me, old man, I'll patch you up*. No, it's fine, your sister's waiting for me in bed. *No, I insist, let me help*. No, really, I'd rather screw your sister. *Come on, I'll make you some tea and fix you up with a bandage.* Oh, okay then, I suppose I can do both.

They were probably sitting up there now, drinking British coffee and eating *magrood*. Picture-perfect brothers-in-law.

But no, Said Mohammad was far too much of a coward to pull off something like that.

Mladenov shook his head. He needed to stop speculating and start planning. Looked at objectively, he was in trouble. He'd be back in Tanarej soon and he needed to arrive there with a plan, put it into action, and clear the hell out before the Islamists found him.

First up, they didn't know where he was staying, he was pretty certain of that. Providing he wasn't recognised at any point in town, if he got back to his lodgings, he'd be safe for the foreseeable. He could clean himself up, get a new disguise, and put things in place for tomorrow morning.

Which was when Phyllis Robinson arrived.

The way he understood his contract, he was working for two connected parties. The government in Khartoum and Horvath in London. His brief was to kill John Mordred and Phyllis Robinson, but there was also the delicate matter of stopping anyone finding out who was funding the Islamists, and that they were trying to draw Mordred.

What he needed to do next was kill Phyllis Robinson and flatten The Hotel Mediterranean. And of course, he needed to do both at the same time, in one brilliant display of fireworks. Make an unmissable show of it; that way his employers would be suitably impressed, and he'd have made a significant return on what they'd invested in him. They could probably warn Said Mohammad off.

In fact, they would. Obviously they would. It'd be like the old 'half now, half when the job's complete' scenario. You don't kill your employee when he's only done fifty per cent of what you've paid him for. If you're going to do it at all, you wait till the mission's fully accomplished. But if he does the first part superlatively, then you simply don't. Ever. Eliminating Phyllis Robinson and The Hotel Mediterranean in one consummate gesture would convince them he was a man to be reckoned with. They'd definitely tell Said Mohammad to bury the hatchet.

Mordred would be easy to draw once Phyllis Robinson was dead. He'd come running distraught, and he could be picked off from a rooftop. That simple.

Then, before Mladenov left Tanarej for good, he'd see to Said Mohammad. No loose ends.

Tomorrow morning. That's when it would begin. The first half – if you could call it that: more like two-thirds – accomplished and out of the way. And the remaining third in the afternoon.

In twenty-four hours he'd be out of here for good.

"Do what you've got to do here," Alec told Mordred when their conversation ended. "You won't be coming back. That's not me giving you an order, although I suppose I'm morally entitled to do that, since I'm prioritising your safety. It's just a fact. Edna and I will wait."

Mordred rose from the armchair he'd slumped back into only a short time beforehand and looked around himself. Nice house while it had lasted. Hidden in plain sight, always the best form of concealment. But now the cat was out of the bag, and Alec was right. Once he left – probably in less than an hour - coming back wasn't an option. Given the comprehensive nature of their defeat, it was unlikely the militants would send fresh men up here, but rocket propelled grenades and mortar bombs would work just as well, if not better. And that was only a matter of time.

"Let us know if you need any help with anything, John," Edna said.

"You need to hurry," Alec said. "They'll start shelling the place once they realise you're still alive."

"I thought you killed everyone," Mordred said. "Who's going to tell?" He realised as soon as the words were out of his mouth that it was a stupid thing to say. He was so wound up about Mabel he wasn't thinking.

"We only killed the ones we saw," Alec said gently. "If we're sensible, we assume there were others who somehow slipped through the net."

Alec didn't labour it, thank God. Could those two he'd met on the road coming down have been fleeing combatants? The elder didn't have a gun. But the younger? He took the revolver out of his pocket and looked at it, the first time he'd done so.

"Where the hell did you get that?" Alec asked with something like a surprised laugh. "A prezzie from the Egyptian government?"

He told the story of the two men. He knew it would make him look moronic but he was past caring. To make things easier for Alec – he fully expected him to fly off the handle – he made the obvious explicit. They could have been enemy personnel in full retreat.

To his surprise, Alec simply shrugged. "We all make mistakes. Don't worry about it. You've enough on your plate."

"You say you think you've seen the younger one somewhere?" Edna asked. "Could it have been in town?"

"I don't think so," Mordred replied.

"I was in a seminar at Thames House last week," she went on. "The guy leading it – some kind of Lampeter don - said a trained intelligence officer should be able to distinguish, in his or her own mind, two categories of face-recognition: firstly, the common or garden he-looks-like-Jack-Whitehall; secondly, the highly unusual he-looks-like-someone-I-saw-in-a-classified-document."

"Edna's right," Alec said, as if it needed his approval.

"It's a good point," Mordred said. He'd had that same lecture, years ago. He'd completely forgotten it. "It was the second. I'm sure I've seen him in London. In the castle!"

"'The castle'?" Edna said.

"John's obviously feeling better," Alec said. "His old pretentious self. Franz Kafka, probably the dullest book of all time."

"I still don't know who he was," Mordred said.

"I want you to think about it until you do, then," Alec said. "It's imperative we find out."

Mordred took a breath and exhaled hard. "It doesn't make sense. He'd have to be some kind of high-level international troublemaker, probably a gun-for-hire. What would he be doing here? And why would he be accompanied by, or feel the need to accompany, sixteen perfectly competent riflemen?"

"What else have you got to think about?" Alec said. "Sorry, I didn't mean that in the wrong way. I meant, this could be an important lead. Don't throw it up on supposedly 'logical' grounds."

They didn't say any more for a while. Mordred used the phone the Egyptians had given him to call Cairo. It seemed only polite to tell them their house had nearly come under heavy attack and it'd probably be reduced to rubble within a day or so, and that all their dogs were dead. And he also wanted to ask how far they'd got investigating the Islamists.

"We're still looking into it," the voice on the other end replied tetchily.

He got the impression they didn't care much about him or the house or the dogs any more. Somewhere between his arrival in Tripoli and today, they'd lost interest. Maybe they'd discovered he'd linked up with Alec and Edna, which meant he wouldn't be coming to work for the General Intelligence Directorate. Maybe that young man he'd punched unconscious was working for them. Maybe they'd used him to infiltrate the Islamists. Mordred coming at him out of the woods when he was about to kill a fleeing fighter would have cheesed them off, to say the least.

But he was letting his thoughts run away with him again. Pure silly speculation. He put the phone in his pocket for safe keeping, then went outside into the garden to take a last look. When he saw the corpses of his four dogs, almost piled up on each other where they'd rushed in to help each other out, he almost cried.

*

Half an hour later, Alec came out to see him. It was getting dark now. There were no lights on in the house, because they didn't want to draw attention. The sun had yet to disappear below the horizon, but once it did, all the light would drain away as quickly as if someone had pulled out a bathplug.

"What are you doing?" Alec asked.

"What does it look like?" Mordred replied. He wiped the sweat from his face and kept digging.

"For the dogs?"

"I get that you think it's stupid. They belonged to the Egyptian government so I've just been on the phone to Cairo. No one there gave a toss. They're just stupid, dispensable animals, as far as they're concerned."

"Welcome to my world. You do realise we've got other things to do? It's getting dark, by the way."

"Why don't you give me a hand, if you're in such a hurry?"

Edna appeared with two more spades. They dug a trench big enough for the corpses to lie in full-length, side-by-side without looking crammed. Mordred could hear the voices of the sixteen dead fighters in the trees just beyond the compound. 'Those are just animals. We deserve your first consideration. Bury us, not them!' They could all go to hell.

But they were probably there already. If the universe was like they thought, if there really was an Allah and he really had built a *Jannah* and a *Jahannam* to separate the good from the evil, they almost certainly were there, yes. No wonder he couldn't hear them.

When the digging was finished, he remembered something. "You go down into the town," he told Edna and Alec. "They'll probably start shelling this place soon. I'll follow in a minute."

"You're almost done," Edna said. "This is all slightly insane, I know, but with respect, I'm staying."

"I've reversed my opinion," Alec said. "I'm pretty sure they won't start 'shelling the place' after all. "If you're right, they're trying to sneak *en masse* into the town. They sent fighters up here because they thought they could kill you discreetly. A mortar attack signals to every militia in a fifty mile radius that there's a newbie in town. They're not going to want that. And Nasser's got the roads up here covered. They'd have to come through the woods if they're that intent on a second attempt, but my guess is they'll leave you till later. They probably think you've gone, anyway. They'll have made the mistaken assumption that you're sane."

Edna passed him the corpses of the four dogs. He laid them gently to rest, all in the same position, as if they were sleeping. They silently filled the grave in. Afterwards, he made four crosses and hammered them in. He stood back to examine it and laughed at his own idiocy, then filled with emotion.

"Everything's so bloody *shit!"* he said furiously. It was true. Mabel was probably dead; the dogs certainly were; he'd never see Phyllis again; he had no job, and he was angry enough to get two machine guns somewhere in town tomorrow and go over to where he knew those bastards had been keeping her and shoot them, and keep shooting them in their groins, hearts, heads, stomachs chests legs backs till they were all gone or he was shot dead in turn.

Edna put her arms round him and wiped his tears like he was a child. Good thing she was tall enough. Alec slapped him affectionately on the back.

"We all have days like this, John," he said.

Ten minutes later, they were walking down the hill. Alec had decided to take a route through the woods, but since he was Alec, he had a state-of-the-art compass and four or five other gadgets whose sum effect meant anyone stupid enough to intercept them would be in far greater danger than they were. Him being Alec also meant he had to mentally organise people and events in his professional vicinity to make them more manageable, and give orders to ensure that outcomes he deemed ideal actually happened. Needless to say, he'd once been in the army.

"The first thing we have to do when we reach that hospital is evacuate everyone," he whispered. "Find somewhere safe and make sure they all relocate there."

"They won't go," Mordred said.

Alec chuckled. "Once we persuade them they're likely to go down with all hands if they stay put, I think you'll find they change their minds."

"I think you'll find they won't," Mordred replied.

"Are you being facetious? If so, why?"

"You don't understand the first thing about them. Firstly, they're looking after people they rightly or wrongly believe are the victims of prejudice. That's partly why they're physically underground, and secretive with it. Whatever other location you find for them is never going to satisfy their requirement for confidentiality, even assuming you could discover an acceptable-in-every-other-regard, ready-made hospital ward somewhere for them in this town, which you almost certainly can't. If they believe it's not in their patients' interests to move, neither will they."

"It's certainly not in anyone's interests for them to get massacred."

"I'm with John on this," Edna interjected. "There is an alternative. We simply post guards at the hospital."

"Even assuming we had enough men," Alec said calmly, "and we were army generals rather than intelligence officers, the Islamists probably won't mount an 1815-style infantry attack. Rather, they'll bombard the place from half a mile away. No one inside will stand a chance, including us if we set up shop there. Look, they'll be bombing it because they think the CIA are inside. They've got no beef with medics. Uprooting everyone isn't ideal, but it's better than the alternative. It'll save lives. That's what they're supposed to be about, isn't it?"

It wasn't bad logic, but it wasn't clear how Talleyrand and his colleagues would take it. It had the effect of reducing Mordred and Edna to silence for the moment.

The next morning, they went to The Hotel Mediterranean. Mordred introduced Alec and Edna to Talleyrand, and Alec outlined his argument to the American roughly as he'd introduced it on the trek through the woods some twelve hours earlier.

"Out of the question," Talleyrand said when he'd finished speaking. "We're staying here. This place is built to withstand a blast. It's designed like an air-raid shelter."

Alec smiled. "You talk as if those two statements are equivalent."

"What do you mean?"

"An air-raid shelter's nothing. It simply protects the occupant from flying debris. My father had one in his garden in World War Two. It was made out of turf and corrugated iron. It wasn't a bomb-proof underground bunker."

"Where are you going to move us to?"

"We don't know yet. Right now, we simply need your consent to move *in principle*."

"There isn't anywhere."

"How do you know that?"

"I've looked. I've been here for well over a year. How long have you been here?"

Alec drew a sharp breath.

"A few days," Mordred answered for him. "Sorry to embarrass you, Alec, but there's no room here for vanity."

"The alternative is that everyone in this building dies," Alec said, unruffled. "Which is inconsistent with the Hippocratic oath."

"I hear you loud and clear," Talleyrand said. "But some of the patients can't move, and others won't. They feel safe here. They might not even hear us if we say there's going to be a mortar strike. Others will choose to risk the consequences. They've been through a lot. Some of them actually believe God's with them; that he'll save them from anything."

Alec sighed.

"I'll tell you what I'll do," Talleyrand said. "I'll call a meeting of the team. I'll tell them what you've told me, and that anyone who wants to leave is free to do so. I'll make the same offer to the patients. But if anyone wants to stay, I won't throw them out. I can't. I've got to stay here with them. It's my duty."

"That CCTV," Edna said, "how closely is it monitored?"

"Not as closely as it ought to be," Talleyrand replied, obviously relieved by the change in tack. "The receptionist watches it, but he's got other duties – not many, I admit, but a few; and we doctors watch it when we can. But sad to say, there are periods when there are no eyeballs on it at all."

"Well, that's one thing we can do," she replied. "If there's going to be an assault, it may well start with a suicide bomber. It's not impossible. If we can stop them getting through, it'd be a start."

"Even with a mortar campaign," Mordred chipped in, "they'll probably send scouts in to do a recce. A few familiar faces, acting suspiciously - "

"Describes half the population of Tanarej," Talleyrand interjected. "Fine. Watch the CCTV, if that's what you want. Apologies, I don't mean to sound rude, just: it's very busy here. Thank you. As I say, I'll put your proposals to the entire hospital community. Quite a lot of people may choose to leave, but I'm pretty sure not everyone. I appreciate your concern, but right now, I'd better get back to work. Nice to meet you, Edna, Alec. Good to see you again, John."

## Chapter 20: Mladenov's Golden Hello

The day after she signed up for Horvath, Phyllis embarked from Sicily in a large speedboat with a two-man crew, all leased by the company specifically for her. She stayed on deck with a pistol in her handbag most of the way – a lone woman on a dubious mission backed by a shady company might expect trouble at some point - but the pilot and his assistant gave her no cause for concern. Two-thirds of the way across the Mediterranean, she transferred to a fishing boat requisitioned by her Syrian colleague, 'Johannes Mladenov'. (She guessed that wasn't his real name.) Four men in charge this time. Again, no conversation, no hassle, nothing to break the monotony but an Arabic novel and the occasional cruise ship on the horizon.

She'd stepped onto the Italian boat in a long summer dress, linen blazer and yachting shoes; twenty-four hours later, as they were coming into port, she changed into a long gown, a *jilbab* or over-garment, and a *hijab*, all in beige. A three-day journey, all told.

She wondered why Johannes had chosen Tanarej for their first meeting. From what she'd heard, it was a relatively quiet spot, not really the kind of place you'd bring a kidnap victim. You'd want to be among like-minded militants, surely, somewhere with lots of concealment options. Tripoli, Benghazi or Misrata would suit better than an obscure fishing-town.

But maybe that was all wrong. Perhaps the quietest, smallest place would give the best cover after all. No one knew anything much about Libya any more. Down was up and right was left.

As her boat came into the harbour, she wondered whether Johannes would be there to meet her. She couldn't see anyone obviously waiting on the quayside.

She hoped he hadn't brought her to Tanarej *because* it was quiet. Sometimes these guys fancied themselves as Romeos. They thought they'd begin by wining and dining you, and that would lead to romance, and that would lead to the sorts of things spies were supposed to get up to when they weren't being shot at or Kung Fu-ing enemy agents. She'd bloody kill him if he turned out to be that sort of pathetic dud. She wasn't here for a holiday, and certainly not a tryst. She wanted to find John, either knock some sense into him or help him do what he obviously felt he had to, and get back home in double-quick time.

There were lots of ways a male colleague could turn out to be a disaster, though, and the Lothario option was just one. He could also be (and this was much more common) the *I'm a man, and you're just a little lady* type. Settings 1 to 10 on the macho poseur scale. Sometimes, he could be overly deferential, but that was usually okay, because, providing it wasn't inverted conceit, it was repairable. He could be vain, awkward or resentful around women, or just a bully. He could also be useless in the conventional manner of both sexes.

But there were good men. John, obviously; also Young Ian, and at least thirty others in her circle. They weren't that rare.

And actually there were plenty of crappy women, come to think of it. They also fell into categories.

She needed to stop thinking and just judge 'Johannes' as she found him. In a minute.

She was nervous, that was why her brain was working overtime. Calm down.

The problem was, he made a difference: if he was okay, they'd stand a better chance of finding John; otherwise, a lesser. Maybe a much lesser.

So she had to be prepared to ditch him if he didn't measure up. Her Arabic was easily good enough to allow her to make headway alone, and, although the absence of a male companion would definitely prove an obstacle in places, it wasn't an insuperable one. She'd proved it before, in Morocco.

Although that had just been a holiday. And Morocco wasn't a war zone.

Shit, shit, shit. So much riding on this. She couldn't believe the last four days, what she'd committed herself to. Like a nightmare. And she might be dead tomorrow.

For the time being, yes, she'd keep an open mind.

The sound of the boat's engines dropped a semitone. Ropes were thrown and the harbour edged up to the boat with a gentle bump. Suddenly, they could have been in Cornwall or Devon: seagulls, sunshine, ship's masts, bleached and coloured houses, the smell of fish. A ramp was laid to shore. Phyllis picked up her travelling bag: she re-located lightly but efficiently – soap, towel, toothbrush, four changes of underwear, basic first aid requirements, a blanket, socks; and - when she knew she wasn't going through passport control, as now - a gun, knife, and an essential toolkit for burglaries. She expected everything else to be there when she arrived, and she wasn't usually disappointed. It would be Horvath's second test – after Johannes.

She suddenly spotted a man looking at her. It had to be him: no other man would look that glaringly at a woman – although she was alone, and it was just possible he was some kind of religious nut-job. About forty, otherwise unremarkable. Beard a bit too well trimmed for a pious zealot. His mouth broke into a smile and she realised he wasn't looking disapprovingly at her, after all. There was something odd about his eyes, though. A kind of void that made him look unpleasant, when he probably wasn't.

He was holding a trunk. Quite heavy by the looks of it, and reassuringly large.

"Miss Robinson," he said. "I'm your opposite number from Horvath."

He made no attempt to keep his voice down, but he wasn't being reckless. Pointless switching to whisper-mode for 'Horvath'. It meant as much here as 'Jabberwocky' or 'Bandersnatch'. They didn't shake hands. Men and women never did here.

A few people looked at her in a *What's a white woman doing in town?* way. Whether Mabel Mordred was in Tanarej or not, kidnaps weren't unheard-of in any part of Libya now. Maybe it was paranoia, but she sensed herself being sized up as a potential victim. Not that these men specifically would do it, but that, regrettably – so she imagined them thinking - they knew others who might.

"I've booked a taxi," he said. "Someone I know can be trusted, don't worry."

He led her over to a white saloon car and opened the door to the back seat. She got in and watched him lug the trunk over to the boot and swing it in with difficulty. It must be even heavier than it looked. The car actually drooped slightly when it was loaded. The driver slammed the lid shut and got into his seat. Johannes climbed in next to Phyllis. He was sweating heavily.

"We'll speak English," he told her as the car pulled out onto the road. "The guy in the front doesn't speak a word of it, and there's really no need for excessive caution."

His last seven words triggered a mental tube-light fashioned into 'dud'. She asked, as if she didn't know, "What do you mean?"

"I mean, we're done."

"You'll have to be more specific," she replied coldly.

"I've found him. John Mordred."

She stopped looking at the road and turned to face him. Her impulse to elbow him in the eye disappeared. "Sorry, say that again. Without the name, please."

"I've found the guy we're supposed to be looking for. We're going to pay him a visit this afternoon. I can book us a boat out of here *for good* for tomorrow evening, if you like. Back in Italy for next weekend. How does that sound?"

"Highly suspicious, if I'm honest. Are you sure?"

He took his phone out, switched it on, and showed her the photos he'd taken of Mordred with his dogs. Her face changed from scepticism to incredulity.

"My God," she said. "When were these taken?"

"Yesterday. By me of course."

"Where is he?" She realised as soon as the words were out of her mouth it wasn't the kind of thing to ask in a taxi, whatever the linguistic capabilities of the driver. "Sorry, tell me later."

"Local," he replied diplomatically. "As I say, we'll check into the hotel first. You settle in, have a shower, a nap, relax a little. We'll meet for lunch in the restaurant at noon, and get a car out to his place this afternoon. Assuming he's in, we'll take it from there. Otherwise, we'll wait."

"Why not go now? Right away?"

He smiled. "We can do that if you want. I just thought you'd like to prepare yourself mentally first – I understand it's a while since you last met. That you'd want to unpack a little, eat, that sort of thing."

"Why is he here – in Tanarej? Do you know?"

"I understand he's looking for his sister. Which I guess means there must be some connection between that and the locality."

"Would you – ? I mean, you're obviously pretty good at locating people - "

"I can't tell you how I did it, if that's what you're going to ask." He broadcast a genial smile clearly intended to obviate offence. "The private security business is rather different from its government equivalent. At least, in that respect. Once we share our little trade secrets, we're likely to find ourselves out of business."

"You misread me. My question was going to be, would you help the two of us find his sister?"

"Of course. I do believe Horvath expects it. And it's all money in the bank to me."

She was starting to warm to Horvath now. Perhaps it wasn't such a bad firm after all.

They drew up in front of The Hotel Mediterranean. Judging by its exterior, and from what she'd already seen in the rest of Tanarej, possibly one of the most prestigious resorts in town. She was impressed. Another point to Horvath. Johannes got out, paid the driver and called a huge man over. The man had obviously been waiting because the instructions he received were minimal. His job was to take the suitcase inside.

As they climbed the steps to the hotel entrance, she got the impression Johannes was becoming increasingly nervous. He lowered his head unnaturally, and seemed eager to get their keys quickly at reception. From what Phyllis saw of the guest book across the counter, virtually no one else was staying here. The receptionist was on the phone when they got in, but he quickly hung up and handed a pair of keys over.

They went upstairs to the first floor and entered a room at the front of the hotel. It was furnished in the European style, only with marble floors. A large wardrobe, a dressing table, a double bed, *en suite* bathroom and a balcony almost directly above the entrance.

"It's lovely," she said.

"Relax and settle in," Johannes said, apparently more at ease now.

The factotum porter set the suitcase on the floor next to her bed and withdrew with a tip. She put her travel bag on the bed.

"Don't forget," Johannes said. "Lunch is at noon. I'll see you then."

He withdrew without turning his back on her, like he was a courtier. She hadn't noticed till now, but there was something about him. A niggling little – what? Somehow, he was just *too ingratiating*.

Which wasn't fair. It said more about her, clearly. She sat on the bed and pulled her shoes off.

She was quite curious to see what was in the suitcase. What sort of things did a man like him think to buy someone like her? Maybe Horvath had given him a list. She hoped it was practical stuff.

She got down on her knees and tried to undo the catches. It was locked.

Bloody hell, he'd taken the key with him. Still, simple matter to ring down to reception, find out what room he was in.

No phone. Obviously not as prestigious a joint as it looked. She'd just have to pay him a personal visit then.

She tried the door handle.

Then again.

Locked? Why would it be? It'd have to be from the outside.

She suddenly had a long, horrible sinking feeling. Her travel bag. There was a crowbar in there; a small one, but it'd do.

Within a few seconds, she'd prised the suitcase lid open. It took her a moment to adjust to what she saw inside. No clothes, no toiletries, no shoes, snacks, cosmetics.

She was looking at a bomb. A huge one.

Just then, something happened that almost caused her to faint. Afterwards, she recounted it as one of the two or three genuine *just when you think you've seen everything* moments of her life. Probably the biggest.

John Mordred came out of the bathroom dressed like a local. He looked at the suitcase, then at her. He didn't smile. Instead, he went straight out to the balcony, looked down and threw himself off.

Five minutes earlier, Mordred and Alec had been sitting in front of the monitor covering the hotel entrance when a taxi pulled up. It was too far away for either of them to distinguish faces, but even so, they both sat up.

"Bloody hell," Alec said in a bored tone. "Don't tell me we've got a paying guest here. Miracles never cease."

"Look at the size of that suitcase!" Mordred said.

"They're obviously planning on staying a while."

"Rather suspicious, don't you think? I'm serious. No one's moving into Tanarej right now."

"I take it you've never heard of the noble profession of journalism," Alec said. "What happens is, you want some sort of prize, but you don't want to risk getting your legs blown off somewhere like Benghazi or Sirte. What you do is choose the quietest place on the map, put up there for a week, hardly ever leave the hotel, then hawk your 'stories' to gullible editors. You can prove you've been to Libya, most editors don't know their arses from their elbows as far as this part of the world's - "

"Hang on," Mordred said, leaning forward.

"What?"

"My God, that guy. That guy there – not the big one: him: *him, the smaller one!"*

"What?"

"He's the one I saw yesterday! Coming down the hill! With the gun! He's trying to hide his face, but it's *him!"*

Alec put his face next to the monitor. "Bloody hell. I don't believe it. That woman with him. That's Phyllis! It's bloody *Phyllis!"*

"Who *is* that guy, and why's he with *her?"*

"Get on the phone to reception, find out what room she's in. Get into there somehow, eavesdrop like crazy, find out what the hell's going on. I'll go out front and grab him if that's what's necessary. Take your phone. Call me as soon as you find out *anything at all."*

Mordred waited in the *en suite* till he was certain Phyllis's beau had gone. He heard her behaving with increasing panic. When he emerged, he saw what she was doing, and it was as if his brain sped up and the world slowed down. Whatever he did now, there wouldn't be any second chances. For some reason, she was locked in the room with a colossal bomb, easily capable, from the look of it, of taking building and basement comprehensively down in a single blast.

In the device's centre was a mobile phone. The bomber would wait till he was a safe distance away – probably quite a long way, given the size of the thing, then call the bomb phone, an electronic circuit would close, and that would be that.

No time for explanations. He walked onto the balcony just in time to see Phyllis's mysterious companion emerge from the entrance.

There was suddenly an even better solution than ringing Alec. Alec might get confused; in the panic, they both might.

It had worked in London. It would work here.

A fraction's miscalculation, he'd break his spine on impact with the ground, he knew that.

He jumped. In a sitting position.

And didn't miscalculate. Right on target. Whoever the man was, Mordred heard his neck snap first of all – slow-mo still - and he seemed to concertina to earth under 84 kilogrammes of human falling at a rate of 9.8 metres per second squared. His mobile phone, which he'd been holding ready to detonate, dropped from his grasp and slid uselessly across the pavement, where Alec picked it up.

"Good call," Alec said.

He'd probably been waiting a lifetime for a witticism like that, and Mordred had handed it to him on a plate. Still, he was alive. They both were.

Swings and roundabouts.

Then Talleyrand was there alongside them, bending down, accompanied by a colleague. Mordred rolled off his victim and got uncertainly to his feet, as the medics took a pulse and looked for other life-signs.

"We need to get him inside," Talleyrand said. "Quickly, before the local police get here. He's alive. Get something hard to carry him on," he told his colleague. But someone had anticipated him. A stretcher was already on its way.

They moved him carefully inside. Phyllis emerged from the front of the building just in time to meet them coming in. She held a crowbar.

"What kind of a weird hotel is this?" she said. She looked like she was in shock.

One way or another, they all were.

## Chapter 21: The Peanuts Episode

The medics carried Mladenov down into their underground ward and transferred him to a vacant bed. They administered life-support then examined him, exchanging brief, muted comments in sombre tones. After five minutes, Talleyrand ordered a neck brace, and announced the diagnosis to the room: cervical fracture: in layman's terms, a broken neck. Only further investigation would reveal whether it was a minor compression or a more complex breakage. And that was only his most serious injury. Either way, the patient wouldn't be going anywhere for at least six weeks. Any ethical problems with interrogating him when he regained consciousness were nullified by the fact that he'd tried to destroy the hospital now saving him. He'd taken a heavy blow and there were broken bones in his chest, feet and lower legs as well as his neck, so it wasn't impossible he'd sink into a coma, but they'd do everything they could to prevent it. Comas here were unmanageable. In the end, you usually said farewell to the sanctity of life, someone else needs the bed. You uttered a prayer, unmoored them from support and quietly let them go.

Alec set to work recovering stills of Mladenov from the CCTV, ready to send over to Tariq. It was a fiddly process. Everything in The Hotel Mediterranean was antiquated. They even used VCRs instead of DVDs or condensed computer files. In the end, he decided it was quickest just to replay the tape and take photos of the monitor with his phone. He sent them to Tariq in a batch, and Tariq despatched them to London for analysis. Thirty minutes later, the results came through. The bomber's real name was Nizar Mayyaleh, a Syrian ex-army officer wanted in four separate countries for the murder of state officials. A rare prize, because he obviously touted for business... somewhere. The question was how, where, and to which intermediaries of which governments?

But then Phyllis's story entered the mix, its nub being that Nizar Mayyaleh was Horvath's man. And Mordred's, that he'd seen him coming down the hill after a failed Islamist assault on his house. Suddenly a new level of complexity appeared. The chances of revealing the bigger picture on a range of important issues seemed to alter slightly – whether for better or worse, hardly anyone knew.

By this stage, the international communications network looked set to overload with the sheer volume of conversation. As fast as facts went from The Hotel Mediterranean to London, updates to previous facts arrived from the same destination, all routed through Tariq. Then Tripoli got involved, then Washington, Paris, Berlin. For a brief period of about twenty minutes, Mayyaleh was by far the most interesting figure in the entire Arab world, partly because virtually nothing was known about him. Yet he'd assassinated politicians, mingled freely with *mujahideen*, and planted an explosive device large enough to send Big Ben into outer space. Whatever the truth about him, it looked set to be astonishing.

The overriding specific question quickly became, how had Horvath come across him, and who else was he working for? Since he was a professional without an ounce of idealism, he couldn't possibly have planted the bomb on his own initiative. And it seemed unlikely even Horvath would go that far.

Back in London, Malcolm Rhys-Dwyer and Paul Ayton were brought in to – in the official parlance - 'help the police with their enquiries'. Their story was, they'd picked up Mladenov's name from an online register of recruitables maintained by Syllon, a privately-owned industrial espionage firm in Pittsburgh, USA. Neither man had any idea Mladenov was really Nizar Mayyaleh; it wasn't a name that would have meant anything to them anyway. In the time-honoured fashion, Horvath's computers were seized for analysis. On the other side of the North Atlantic, Syllon denied everything. They'd never heard of Horvath or Mladenov or Mayyaleh. Meanwhile, computer forensics searched in vain for any connection between the two companies.

The various interlinked questions were considered so important that two United States army interrogators were reassigned from special-forces duty in Sirte. Joined by a medic and enough equipment to keep the 'human intelligence source' alive, they travelled by helicopter to Tripoli, then transferred to two second-hand cars and a van for the journey to Tanarej. They wore Arab clothing. Within a day of their arrival, they'd revived Mayyaleh sufficiently for him to answer questions. Eight hours after he was told he would never walk again, he accepted US witness protection in the form of an S-5 Visa designed for overseas informants. In return, closely attended by American and British observers including Alec and Edna, he revealed everything.

John Mordred and Phyllis Robinson sat fully clothed, side by side, up against the headboard on the bed in her room. They shared shelled peanuts from a cup and watched an Arab TV show on a videotape. Downstairs, Alec and Edna were still sitting in with the prisoner.

Whether because of the shock of nearly getting blown to pieces, or awkwardness at being thrown together too brutally, or the oddness of finding themselves in an unfamiliar and potentially lethal location, all their conversation so far had focussed on relatively unadventurous and impersonal matters. Him: *How did you get here?* Her: *How did you know about the bomb?* Him: *What were your first impressions of Mladenov?* Her: *Is this really a hotel?*

"I love you," he said, suddenly, as he put the cup of peanuts to one side.

"Well, the feeling's mutual," she said levelly, after a pause. "Although I suppose you already know that."

"How would I?"

She sat up a little more and turned to him. "Oh, well, let's see." She sounded annoyed. "I'm here. End of clarification."

"You might like me, but not necessarily love me."

"You're a moron. You actually don't deserve someone as considerate and loyal as me, but there we are. Where are the peanuts?"

"I put them down so I could talk to you."

Her mouth popped open. "Did I *say* you could put them down?"

"Er, no."

She got up, walked round the other side of the bed, and grabbed the cup, spilling half of them on the floor. "Well, then, *don't bloody put them down! I was still eating them!* And what's the matter with you anyway? Are you *actually saying* we can't talk to each other with a few snacks in our mouths? Who the hell do you think you *are?* Just because *YOU* can't bloody speak with peanuts, it doesn't mean *I* can't! It's not like we even have to *face each other while we're speaking!* We could speak *facing forward! Why bloody NOT, eh?* We don't actually have to look in each other's mouths while we talk! *For God's SAKE, John!"*

He stood up to apologise. She threw the peanuts at him and punched him hard in the face. Next thing he knew, he'd landed on his back by the balcony.

Her face filled with horror. She chuckled manically, then resumed her former expression, rushed over, fell to her knees and clasped him in an embrace.

"Oh my God, I'm sorry!" she said. "I'm sorry! *I'm sorry!"*

"I guess that wasn't entirely about the peanuts."

She laughed and cried at the same time. "Shit, we are *so* not suited! What the hell would Gandhi say? I'm sorry, John. Oh, God, I'm really sorry. I've never done anything like that before. I'm really, really, really sorry. I love you. You can't even begin to imagine how much. Oh my God, I'm *so* sorry."

He put his arms round her. She was squeezing all the air out of him, but that was okay. More than that. It was quite nice.

At that moment, the door opened and Alec came in. He regarded them with composure. "I don't know what's just happened here," he said, "but to be fair, John, you probably deserve it."

It was the kind of thing teenagers called 'spooky', only a hundred times more so. *God, please give me a senior commander* had worked. Mayyaleh not only knew all the major locations and numbers of Islamists in the former government quarter, but he knew exactly where Mabel was being kept and how she was faring. She was on the fourth floor of a former administrative block called '6 October Plaza', a room numbered '16' on the east side. She was apparently in good health, although taciturn. She was the fourth, and 'favourite', wife of the brigade leader whose life Mordred had inadvertently saved on the hillside just yesterday. To Mayyaleh's knowledge, she was allowed all the usual freedoms of a wife, and never kept in restraints.

After Alec told him all this, Mordred went to sit on the bed with Phyllis. No more freezing her out, and the news wasn't that bad. In some ways, it was the least worst outcome of all. To begin with, she was alive; secondly, she was a man's 'favourite' wife, which meant he'd probably take at least elementary precautions to protect her in a battle; thirdly, Mordred had saved the life of her 'husband'. Had he allowed Mayyaleh to murder the old man, Mabel would simply have been married off to another fighter – that was how these gangs worked – and her predicament possibly exacerbated.

After sitting in on his second interview with Mayyaleh, Alec came up to Phyllis's room with news. By now, this floor was everyone's base. There were no other guests in the hotel, not even journalists. As Mordred had suspected ever since learning about the hospital downstairs, the entire building was sustained as a sophisticated piece of camouflage by charitable donations originating in Fivepointville, Pennsylvania.

"Looks like the powers-that-be are finally beginning to take you seriously," Alec said. "Although that probably has more to do with Mayyaleh than you."

"It was me that captured him," Mordred replied.

Alec smiled. "It's no thanks to you he's talking. You almost smashed him to smithereens."

"Stop being a smartarse," Phyllis told him. "Everyone knows that John saved my life, probably yours, and definitely everyone's downstairs. The Islamists would have put out the complete obliteration of this building as a heroic assault on a CIA base, and Mayyaleh would have got away scot free. Yes, John nearly killed him, but I'd like to have seen *your* solution. Just because you're in on the interrogation, doesn't give you the right to come over all morally superior. You're lucky to be here at all, and you owe it all to my boyfriend."

"So you're back on again?" Alec said. "Sorry, that's not an appropriate question. What I mean is, I apologise. You're quite right, Phyllis. 'It's no thanks to you' was just a throwaway comment. I didn't mean it, John, honestly."

Mordred laughed. "It's fine." He turned to Phyllis. "It's just the way Alec and I are. I'd be uncomfortable if he started being nice. I'd think he knew something I didn't, like I've been sacked or infected with a deadly virus."

"You *have* been sacked," Alec said.

"I resigned."

"There have been big developments in London apparently," Alec said. "Turns out there's an actual government that's been aiding the Islamists."

"Which?" Phyllis asked.

"I'm not allowed to say," Alec replied.

"Qatar?" she persisted. "Saudi Arabia? I bet they've a hand in there somewhere."

Alec smiled. "I'm sorry to stand on ceremony, but you don't officially belong to MI7 any more. It's irrelevant anyway. In its infinite wisdom, the British government has decided that trading relations with that country's allies are too important to sever. The fact that Country X has been supporting terrorists who kidnapped one British citizen and tried to lure another to his death isn't sufficient justification for losing billions in arms deals. In any case, X denies all knowledge of the kidnap. 'Had we but known', etcetera."

"What do you mean, 'tried to lure another to his death'?" Mordred asked.

"From what Mayyaleh's told us," Alec said, "they knew all along that you were a British intelligence agent. Just *how* they could have known is a complete mystery, and must remain so for all time, although if you were to ask me, I'd say there was a simple enough solution. Country X was working closely enough with the Islamists to realise that two Mordreds – it's an unusual name, after all - might well be related, and it had the technological capability to match the data on Mabel's phone to its own intelligence data. But then, I'm an old cynic. I don't suppose that *can* be the solution, because the FCO completely rules it out."

"The utter bastards," Phyllis said.

"The great news is," Alec went on, "Ruby Parker's incandescent with rage. She's ready to re-employ both of you *post haste.* Just to thumb her nose at the lily livers in Whitehall, you understand, not because either of you is actually any good... Which was another joke, by the way."

"It was *really* funny," Phyllis said. "Well done."

"So they didn't want money or arms after all?" Mordred said.

Alec grinned. "Now *that's* funny. No, they simply wanted to put a bullet through your skull. They knew you would come out here sooner or later. When Mayyaleh told them how close you were, I gather they were rather taken aback. That's when they planned the ambush on your house. But luckily, Edna and I had arrived by then."

"And Nasser Ragai," Mordred said. "Who'd probably have saved me without either of you."

"But never let the truth stand in the way of a good story," Phyllis put in.

Alec shrugged. "Anyway, so eager is Country X to avoid upsetting the British government any more, and so shocked and betrayed do they feel at the realisation that the people they're sponsoring are actually holding a British citizen captive that they're pulling out all the stops to get her free. As in, 'Sorry guys, but if you don't release her, we'll have no option but to withdraw your funding, and we might even pay someone to attack you'."

"How's that going down?" Phyllis asked.

"Not terribly well," Alec said. "They don't need earthly help. They've got Allah."

Mordred sighed. "I think someone should just hang out a banner where they can all see it, saying, 'Sorry, Allah just doesn't like you that much'. I mean, he probably doesn't."

Alec looked puzzled for a moment, then recovered. "Yes, I see. On the highly controversial premise that he actually exists."

"I mean, it's not like they keep winning," Mordred said. "Look at those guys who attacked my house."

"Allah liked them so much, he took them all home to live with him," Alec said.

"So what now?" Phyllis cut in. "I mean, sorry to interrupt Philosophy Club, but I'd quite like to rescue John's sister and get back to Blighty."

Alec laughed. He loved the word Blighty. They all did. "We've entered the endgame," he said. "Yesterday, Unity Government forces routed two groups of Islamist fighters on their way here. Those inside Tanarej are now completely surrounded, and considerably outnumbered. There won't be any more relief columns."

"Again: so what now?" Phyllis said.

"So long as they're holding a British citizen," Alec told her, "we've got to maintain the siege. Some time today, we'll deliver surrender terms which they'll immediately reject. Ultimately, they'll try to break out using women and children as human shields. There will be a conventional firefight, lots of people will get killed and we'll 'win' in the most limited sense of the term possible. It'll be messy, in other words. Right now, the army's priority is to stop the media getting wind."

"They won't use Mabel as a shield, though, surely?" Phyllis said. "Not in the first instance. She's their trump card. They'll at least keep her back till the game looks lost. I admit - sorry, John, it's true - she's of no more intrinsic worth than any other woman or child in there, but that's what they'll be thinking. That we care more about westerners."

"By and large, we do," Alec said. "So what?"

"Obviously, it makes us just like them," she said.

"Wrong," Alec replied. "Because we're not using women and children to hide behind. As for using her as a kind of 'trump' shield – I think that's what you're really getting at here - they'll know that once they start firing at us, we'll only back down if she's physically in the way. But she's only five and a half feet tall and one foot wide. Her use in that sense is likely to be pretty restricted."

"It sounds like everyone's reconciled to her death," Mordred said.

"It would be foolish if we hadn't considered every conceivable outcome," Alec replied.

"And the deaths of countless others," Phyllis said.

Alec threw his hands up. "We can't *make* them back down! And we can't just let them take over the town! Every time these bloody Islamists occupy a place it's exactly the same: they flog 'immodest' women in the streets, hang liberals from lampposts, force Jews, Yazidis, Druze, Agnostics to convert, ban everything in sight, torture, enslave, liquidate, and generally behave like out-and-out Nazi thugs. We're not going to fire the first shot, I've told you that; but if they start trying to break out, they have to be stopped. And putting some bloody peacenik in front of them with a megaphone and a sunflower just won't work. Think Hitler; think the Jews – whom these guys probably loathe, incidentally: they all do: all Islamists. Would you be so squeamish then?"

"I think we should try talking to them," Mordred said.

Alec went out onto the balcony and rested his hands on the rail. "That's what I love about talking to you. Seeing water glide off a duck's back."

Mordred smiled.

"Well, thankfully," Alec continued, "- and I only say that because I quite like you: I'd like to see you reach your thirty-second birthday - you're wasting your time on this occasion. You're just a civilian now, remember? You've no jurisdiction in this situation, no leverage, not one ounce of influence. Why do you think you and Phyllis have been confined to this room? You're well and truly, one hundred per cent out of the loop."

"Who would I need to speak to?" Mordred asked.

Alec laughed. "You mean in an ideal world? Well, the siege is being coordinated by Major-General Sir Edward Masters, CBE, and Lieutenant-General Hank Dobbs of the US army. Good luck finding them. Even I don't know where they are, and I'm on the inside. And if by some fluke you do locate them, good luck getting them to take the slightest notice of you. In fact, best of luck in persuading them not to arrest you and throw you on the nearest plane, just for your own safety. That is, if they don't regard you as a harmless gnat, best ignored. Good luck with all of that, John. You may need it."

Mordred reached calmly into his bedside drawer, took out the phone from the house on the hill and pressed call.

"Hello?" said an encouragingly friendly voice at the other end. "Mr Mordred. How can I help?"

"I'd very much like to speak to Mr Mohammad Reza," he said. "As soon as possible. Tell him it's urgent."

"Hold the line, sir."

Alec frowned and came back into the room. "What are you doing? What's going on? Who are you speaking to?"

Mordred put his index finger to his lips. "Ssh! This is important."

## Chapter 22: Basement Pow Wow

Two hours after his conversation with Alec, a taxi arrived outside The Hotel Mediterranean. Mordred and Phyllis got in the back. Alec sat shotgun in the front. The driver didn't speak, but Mordred picked up from subtle expressions of his body-language that he was American and probably more west than east coast.

"I know you feel you've got to do this," Phyllis told him. "And I understand. We've both had dangerous jobs all the time we've known each other, and that's probably not going to stop anytime soon. But please be careful."

"Relax," Alec put in from the front. "He'll almost certainly get the big red light."

"I won't," Mordred said. "I mean: I *will* be careful. I won't get the big red light."

Their driver grinned.

"What's so funny, Sergeant?" Alec asked.

"Just 'the big red light'," the driver replied. "Ignore me."

"You mean, as in red light *district?"* Phyllis asked him incredulously.

"As I said, ma'am, ignore me. Sorry. Long time since I was on leave."

Mordred laughed. Not at the gaffe, but its attempted defence. In some parallel universe, this guy and he were best friends.

The car drove to parts of the town that looked like they'd long been forsaken to make way for the *jinns* that were supposed to inhabit the desert across the Arab world. There was an almost exotic eeriness to the vacant office-blocks, shuttered shops and empty thoroughfares. Walls were chipped where bullets had gone in. Whole sides of buildings had been blasted away. Something awful had happened here, sometime recently, but there was no one left to tell the detail. Only ghosts.

They stopped at the end of a street of single-storey commercial properties with flat roofs. Ahead of them stood seven or eight floor high-rises, all in close proximity and surrounded by what, from the look of it, had once been parkland, but which was now a wasteland strewn with every conceivable kind of junk: abandoned cars, huge chunks of cinder block, coils of wire including the barbed variety, mattresses, household detritus. And pitted with holes of varying sizes and probably depths.

The high-rises were presumably where the Islamists were. He couldn't see an ISIS flag anywhere, but he'd given up thinking these guys were Daesh a while ago. It didn't quite fit the bill somehow. And of course no foreign government would subsidise ISIS. ISIS was all too obviously a rival state with global territorial ambitions.

But that didn't mean they weren't incipiently ISIS.

Even if that were the case, though, *no flag* must mean they weren't ready to commit. Which must in turn mean that they still needed whatever government was behind them. And if that government really was trying to lever Mabel's freedom, there might be a chance.

The driver got out and ran round to open Phyllis's door. The two men let themselves out. A Private stood at the open door of a metal security-screened former shop. He came forward, greeted them and saluted. They accompanied him into the shop. In a former confectionary salesroom, Nasser Ragai was waiting with Mohammad Reza and Nouri Said Younis. They all looked incredibly relieved to see Mordred. They embraced him. Mordred introduced Phyllis and Alec.

The Private seemed eager to move them on. He led them downstairs into a basement room with a central square table, seats, maps on the wall, and a group of about thirty senior ranking army officials, mostly Libyan, but four Egyptians, six Brits and five Americans, all in combat gear. Handshakes were exchanged, although the NATO versions were a lot frostier than the North African, and seemed a grudging concession to politeness, or the first move in a drawn-out encounter whose chief object was to sway the locals and humour Mr John Mordred before denying all his requests.

Everyone sat down at the table. Even though it was square, it was obvious who Major-General Sir Edward Masters and Lieutenant-General Hank Dobbs were. Their juniors regarded them with a deference as subtle as it was probably habitual, and this created the impression that they exuded authority. Of course, it was a foregone conclusion that one or the other would speak first: probably Dobbs since he was the highest equivalent rank in the room. He leaned forward.

"So Mr Mordred," he said. "Talk us through this 'plan' of yours."

"It's perfectly simple," Mordred said, noting the cynical tone and deciding not to put too many of his pieces into play until it changed. "I simply cross no man's land waving a white flag, then I talk to the militants."

Dobbs grinned. "Approved! Meeting adjourned."

Everyone laughed.

"Perhaps you could give us a little more detail, John," Masters said tetchily. "What makes you think, for example, you won't end up like poor Terry Waite? You probably don't remember him, but I've met him several times. The Archbishop's envoy to Lebanon. Went over there to secure the release of four hostages. Got kidnapped himself. 1987. Didn't get out till 1991. What makes you think you can pull off what he couldn't?"

"Because we're sure as hell gonna be *pissed off* if they get another human shield to play around with," Dobbs said.

"How many women and children do you think there are in there?" Mordred asked. "If you've got close to three hundred fighters, say, that probably means three hundred women, and even more children. Don't forget, they were planning to take this town over. That means settling down here, so they won't have left their families elsewhere. So while 'one more human shield' might seem like a clincher in a discussion like this, you're actually talking about increasing the strength of that shield by probably less than a fifth of one percent."

"Jesus," Dobbs said. "Haven't you heard that they prefer westerners?"

"If you've ordered a media blackout, there's no reason you should be deterred from using full force just because I'm over there," Mordred replied. "I give you full permission to do whatever you think necessary."

Dobbs scowled. "Gee, that's awful kind of you."

"What do you actually want?" Mordred replied.

Dobbs drew himself up. "Honestly? *Honestly?* I want you to get the hell out of here, Son, and leave this situation to people who know a little more about it than you do."

"You mean, the Libyans?" Mohammad Reza interjected calmly.

Dobbs let out a loud groan. He let his palms flop loudly on the table.

Masters smiled. "Hank's frustrated because we're trying to help you, Mohammad. Since 2011, all we've heard is how Britain and France and the United States started something in Libya but declined to get involved in the aftermath. Well here we are, back helping."

"No one's saying *push off back home,*" Mordred said. "It's about facilitating. There's very good evidence to suggest the Islamists out there aren't ISIS, which means they're almost certainly Libyan. You may not agree with them; they may not be good for the health of the country. But killing them isn't the answer. Not if there's an alternative. Look, put it another way. There are probably people in our own countries we don't agree with. We may even think they're harmful cranks. But they're still our countrymen. We don't want them massacred. That's how the Libyans at this table probably feel about the people across that wasteland."

"The trouble is," an officer said – British – "if we allow them to leave, they'll just cause trouble elsewhere. We're laying up problems for ourselves."

"What are you thinking of offering them, Son?" Dobbs asked Mordred. "I mean, just out of interest."

"An honourable withdrawal under cover of nightfall," Mordred said.

There was a kind of muted gasp of horror.

"We should *at least* ask them to surrender their firearms," someone said.

"They'll see that as a humiliation," Nasser Ragai said. "And besides, there are so many weapons around in this country at the moment, it'll be five minutes before they pick up new ones. No, if you really want to stop *these particular people* causing trouble elsewhere, you've probably got to kill them. And given that you're both civilised representatives of civilised countries, it's impossible you would decide to do that in advance. If it happened at all, it would be uninvited."

"And obviously it would entrench bitterness in this country," Mohammad Reza said. "Drawing the dividing lines a little more firmly in the sand."

"Forgive my French," Dobbs said, "and nothing personal: but that's bleeding-heart liberal bullshit. It's exactly the sort of thing that makes matters worse."

"We Brits and Americans aren't the only people in the country trying to eliminate Islamism with force," a junior British officer added. "Look at Haftar and Zintan. And the government itself of course. We've got to support them. How will they feel if they know we've deliberately let an entire enemy army slip through our fingers?"

"They haven't actually done anything yet," Mordred said. "Even that bomb in the hotel was more Mayyaleh than - "

"We know what they were *going* to do," Dobbs said. "And don't forget, they came up to your house to kill you."

"You can't condemn an entire community because it contains a few murderers," Mordred replied. "Besides which, the culprits are dead now."

"So we've got to wait for them to kill before we start wiping the floor with them?" someone said.

There was silence for a moment. Half the room thought it was a good question; the other thought it outrageous.

"So you want to kill them all before they've actually fired a shot?" said Mohammad Reza.

"That's not what I said," the same person retorted irritably.

Mordred leaned forward. "If we allow them to leave with their weapons, with honour, with their families, they'll see it as an act of generosity. They probably know we can whip them. We'll be sowing a seed. Possibly."

"And if it works," Nasser Ragai said, "lives on both sides will be saved. Not just Libyan lives, but the lives of British and American soldiers. It's in everyone's interest."

"These are Islamists," Alec said. "As I told you back in the hotel, John, they're the enemy of everything good: democracy, women's rights, Jews and Christians, you name it. I'm for giving them the hardest *possible* time consistent with getting your sister back."

To a man, the British and the Americans uttered a low 'hear, hear'.

Suddenly, it was as if a fissure had appeared in the table. Alec, NATO and a few Libyans and Egyptians on one side; Mordred, the remaining Libyans and Egyptians and possibly Phyllis on the other. He didn't know what she thought; she hadn't spoken yet, but she squeezed his hand under the table. He knew he had to respond immediately if he was to stand the least chance of salvaging his hopes.

"They're Islamists now," he said, "but at bottom, they're Muslims. The trouble is, whenever anyone talks about Islam as an intolerant faith, they're buying into the fabrications of the extremists. They're agreeing the hating version of Islam is the right one, the only one. But it isn't. It's the wrong one. The right one is Rumi, Nizamuddin Auliya, Rabia Basri, *The Conference of the Birds*, Mustafa Aykol. The men in those government buildings may be Islamists, but Islamism isn't the essence of them. The essence of them is *Islam*. And that's a different matter. That's what they can go back to."

No one spoke.

"I haven't the faintest idea what you're talking about, Son," Dobbs said.

Everyone on Alec's side of the fissure laughed again. But the fissure itself was looking a little less threatening now.

"We're grateful for your help, General," Mohammad Reza said irritably, "but the fact is, we'll have to manage this country long after you've gone. You can help us by taking our advice. Our strong counsel now is that you listen to Mr Mordred. I don't say this lightly. I have great admiration for him, and I certainly don't want to lose him, but he has a plan to avoid bloodshed, and he's been so expert in navigating the various pitfalls of this country up to now that I genuinely think he may have a chance here. As I say, it's the lives of your soldiers too."

"Can you even speak Arabic?" Masters asked.

"He was recruited to MI7 chiefly for his linguistic skills," Phyllis said. "He's probably better than any Brit or American in the entire country."

Dobbs turned to Mohammad Reza. "You spoke of Mr Mordred expertly 'navigating the various pitfalls of this country'. I admit, I'm beginning to be *ever so slightly* persuaded by this crazy plan – which I never thought I would be. Could I ask for a brief adjournment? I'd like to consult with my colleagues, here and abroad, about Mr Mordred's intelligence service record." He turned to Mordred. "If it transpires you're as good as your friends think, maybe I'll give you the all-clear. But at your own risk. If you get captured, don't expect any preferential treatment. Once we start firing – if that's what it comes to – you're on your own."

"I give you full permission to do whatever you think necessary," Mordred said. "If you want me to put that in writing, I'd be happy to oblige."

Mordred, Phyllis and the Libyans went upstairs into the shop where they sat and drank army tea. After twenty minutes, Alec came upstairs looking grim.

"You're cleared to go," he told Mordred. "But Major-General Sir Edward Masters would like to see you alone for a moment. One British citizen to another, that's all."

"Whereabouts?"

"Downstairs. First left. Apparently it used to be a cleaners' cupboard." He grinned. "Should bring back memories."

"I never did apologise for that," Mordred said.

Silence.

They grinned at each other. Alec slapped him on the arm. He went downstairs.

First left actually was a cupboard, although probably more storage than cleaning. It was roomy for a start. Whatever had once been kept here had now all gone, possibly looted. Masters stood by the wall looking agitated. Mordred closed the door.

"I feel it's my duty to tell you this," Masters said, "Although I'm pretty sure it'll make no difference whatsoever. You're being used. You're allowing the Libyans and the Egyptians to sacrifice you for ends that are wholly theirs and none of yours. There's still time to get out if you change your mind, as I would strongly advise you to do. You're taking a risk that not *one* of them would take in a million years, and they're putting you forward because you're a westerner. Ultimately, they don't care about you at all. You're a very talented intelligence officer, from what I've heard, and Britain can scarcely afford to lose you. Once you're gone – once *any* of you are gone - other countries get a tiny bit stronger. And that may be another of their motives. Think, John, please. You've let yourself get carried away. Just *think*."

"My sister's in there," Mordred said. "I don't like to sound like I'm some kind of macho man, but I'm getting exactly what I came out here for."

"There are other ways of retrieving her."

"We've already tried shock and awe. Last time, remember? It didn't work. The difference is, we only *think* my plan won't succeed; whereas we *know* the alternative won't."

"I wasn't involved in that."

"Neither was I. Look, none of us in that room was being altruistic. Maybe you're right: perhaps they are using me. But I'm being selfish too. I'm exploiting them to get what I've wanted for a long time. We're all being mercenary, and we're all entirely happy. How often does that happen?"

Masters sighed. The fight seemed to go out of him, but in a genial way. "If you need anything at all, or if you change your mind, just say. You're going to need a hell of a lot of luck over there. Don't take anything for granted, and don't overestimate their willingness to reason."

Mordred shook his hand. "Absolutely not."

## Chapter 23: Phone Call x 2, Local Rate

Thirty minutes after his conversation with Major-General Masters, Mordred sat on the bed in his room in The Hotel Mediterranean. It was early evening. On the dressing table, the kettle had just boiled. Alec made tea for himself, Edna and Phyllis. The women sat on armchairs in a kind of limbo. What now?

"Are you sure you don't want any, John?" Alec said as he poured boiling water into the cups. He took a flask from his pocket and put a shot of vodka in each.

"Not for me," Mordred replied. "You realise you could get arrested for that? Just out of interest?"

"We're here to help," Alec replied. "Not for a holiday. And we're not harming anyone."

"Make mine a double," Phyllis said miserably. "I can't believe you're even contemplating this, John. I feel quite angry again, now I've thought it through properly. Masters's comment about Terry Waite probably wasn't too wide of the mark. It hadn't struck me like that before. It could be years before we see you again."

"I don't think it'll come to that," Mordred said. "Terry Waite didn't have a sister living in-house. They're not going to want to put up with that for four years."

"Doesn't mean they won't kill you," Alec said. "They can keep her entirely out of the way. She need never know it's even happened. No complications there."

"I'm their ticket out of here," Mordred said. "I doubt they'll be that defiant."

"It's more a question of them realising that," Edna said.

"Or caring," Phyllis added. "Which of course they will, but they'll feel it's 'unmanly' to show it. So they'll go to the opposite extreme."

"You mean, shoot me," Mordred said. "Nice that everyone's being so upbeat."

"Just say if you want to back out," Phyllis told him.

Alec handed a cup each to the women and sat next to Mordred. "Am I allowed to ask who you were on your phone to earlier? It didn't sound like London."

"Annabel sends her love, by the way," Phyllis interposed. "And says, 'don't do it'. Her actual words."

"I was speaking to a man I met when I first came here," Mordred said. "Former people-smuggler by the name of Walid al-Iddrissy. I just wanted to say sorry for deceiving him. I pretended to be an Algerian with ideals. Even I really liked me."

"You rang him to *apologise?*" Alec said. He paused to process the idea. "You actually worked a local to get valuable information, then afterwards you rang him to *say sorry* for the deception?"

"He was okay with it. He said it'd have been different if it hadn't been my sister I'd been trying to help, but he'd have done the same in my position. He's with Nasser Ragai now."

"God help us," Alec said. "Talk about re-defining 'intelligence'."

Phyllis chuckled darkly. "Every cloud has a silver lining. At least the former people-smuggler's happy." She raised her tea-vodka concoction. "Cheers."

Alec sighed. "Let's get back to the matter in hand. The question is, John, how do you intend to make first contact? That may prove a major logistical problem in itself."

Mordred smiled. He reached into the bedside drawer and took out a mobile. He pressed call and put it on speakerphone. Edna, Phyllis and Alec exchanged mystified, slightly alarmed looks.

"Er, what are you doing, John?" Alec said as they listened to the ringtone.

"Hello?" a suspicious voice on the other end came. "John Mordred?"

"The same."

"What – what do you want?"

"Look, whoever you are, let's stop pretending now. You never wanted money and guns. You wanted to lure me over here so you could kill me. Not that you personally wanted me dead, only the government that's sponsoring you. Well, it's changed its tune now. It very definitely wants me to live, and it'll be very, very sorry if anything happens to suggest that's not your number one preference too."

"What are you calling me for? Do you want to speak to your sister again?" The tone was sardonic.

"You must know we've surrounded the buildings where you're holed up. A lot of people on my side of the blockade want to see you defeated, and they don't care how. A battle to the death's okay with them. If the press was here, our military commanders might worry about collateral damage in the form of women and children, but it isn't. So there'll be no one to feel sorry for you when it's all over. Or ever remember you even existed. Have you ever read *Black Hawk Down?*"

"I don't know what you mean. A book?"

"The true story of an American military disaster. October 3, 1993. Two helicopters crashed right in the centre of enemy territory in Mogadishu. The US was on the back foot from start to finish. But do you know how many fatalities it suffered? Eighteen. Against over five hundred for the Somalis – on a conservative estimate. One part of what made the difference was body-armour and state-of-the-art machine guns capable of punching holes in concrete and tearing fully-grown trees to ribbons. The point is, the Americans have weapons you haven't even seen in your worst nightmares. *I* haven't even seen them, and I have nightmares all the time."

"You cannot frighten us. If we die, we go to paradise to be with God." Islamism's number one cliché.

"Why did the first Muslims lose the Battle of Uhud?" Mordred asked. "According to Muhammad, peace and blessings be upon him, it was because God was displeased with them."

There was a long period of silence. Maybe 'pbuh' had caught them off-guard. For a moment, Mordred thought he'd lost the connection. Then he heard a muffled discussion in the background. It sounded energetic.

"What do you actually want?" the voice said breathlessly, at last. "What are you calling for?"

"I want to meet face-to-face. I want to come to you and I want you to guarantee my safety in and out."

"To what purpose?"

"To negotiate a peace agreement that will allow you to preserve your honour."

"We won't surrender."

"I didn't mention surrender."

"You want your sister back."

"I don't think that's too much to ask. If someone kidnapped your sister and married her off to a British soldier, wouldn't you?"

"What if she doesn't want to come?"

"I admit that's not impossible. But it is highly implausible, given how much time has elapsed between the committed MSF medic and the dutiful jihadi wife. Either way, I need to speak to her on my side of the blockade."

"You mentioned a face-to-face meeting?"

"With assurances."

"When you hear the muezzin call *Salat al-Fajr*, wait thirty minutes and then come across to the main building facing Commerce Street. Alone and unarmed. We'll be waiting to receive you."

The line went dead.

"Give me that," Alec said, swiping the phone and walking across the room.

"What the hell are you doing?" Mordred said.

But Alec had already pressed Last Recall.

"Who is this?" demanded the voice on the other end of the line. "I've already given you a time and - "

"Listen to me," Alec said indignantly. "John wants to play this nicely. He wants to meet you halfway, which is a hell of a lot more than you probably deserve, given you've already tried to kill him at least twice. Now I'm a friend of his, and I just heard him ask for assurances, and I didn't hear you give any. So let me ask: are you willing to give me your word that you'll give him safe passage in and out? I need you to say it."

"You're trying to tell me you've been - "

"Before you get on your high horse about me listening in, we all know you had guys doing exactly the same at your end. Now say the words, or it's off."

Muffled discussion at the other end. No one sounded enraged however. Going by the tone – the words were indecipherable - they grudgingly conceded Alec was being reasonable.

After nearly a minute: "We vow not to harm John in his coming in or his going out."

"Thank you," Alec said. He hung up and tossed the phone onto the bed. "I think it was really important for me to say 'thank you' there. Don't you, John?"

Mordred laughed. They'd just done good cop/ bad cop. Perhaps useful for the Islamists to know there were more hawks than doves out here.

"I agree," he said. "Good manners never hurt anyone."

## Chapter 24: Into the Hornets' Nest

From the top of one of the buildings, somewhere out of view, the muezzin called the *Adhan*. *Salat al-Fajr,* the first prayer of the day.

Thirty minutes to zero.

Eighteen people sat in silence in the shop where the basement conference had occurred a day beforehand. Apart from Mordred and his three MI7 colleagues, seven were Libyan NCOs in fatigues, the others a mixture of British and American officers. Alec looked at the floor. Phyllis sat with her elbows on her knees and her head in her hands. Edna had her fingers interlaced in her lap. She looked around the room a few times and once accidentally caught Mordred's eye. She shot him a sad smile.

They were all in thrall, in different ways, to the clock on the wall. For long periods, its ticking was the only sound, then a plane would pass overhead or a car would arrive in the street, followed by a just-out-of-earshot conversation, or someone in the room would sigh or suppress a nervous yawn. Outside was equally quiet. All around the former government blocks, three thousand guns of varying power were directed towards the militants.

At seven-thirty, it was as if something in the air fractured. A split second later, Mordred stood up. Everyone around him followed suit, but without enthusiasm. As far as he could tell, they thought he was going to his death or worse. No one shook his hand: it might look too much like goodbye. Five minutes later, as he passed the front line and walked into the no man's land between the two camps, he received a few pats on the arm and one or two encouraging comments, but nothing too wholehearted. He checked the phone in his pocket.

This was the first test: whether someone on the other side would take a pot-shot at him. It would only take one – whoever it was wouldn't even need to be acting on orders – and all hell would fly loose. Mordred would probably die where he stood.

But the stillness endured.

He worked his way round the junk to get to his destination. A mess like this probably gave the besieged time and space. In an all-out assault, it would work like a series of barricades. So probably put here by the regime back in 2011. And how weird to be thinking that – *how, historically, did all this waste accumulate?* – when he really ought to be scared witless. But there it was. Feelings almost never obeyed scripts.

As he got closer to his goal – a five-storey concrete building painted white and mauve – he scanned the entrance for greeters. There weren't any. The doors themselves had once been two single panes of glass, but all that remained were the shattered vestiges, and an eerily vacant reception area beyond. It was like being in a science-fiction film.

He climbed the four steps to the threshold and walked across it. He stopped at reception and since there was a bell, he rang it. More like a ghost story now. Or like someone undead would pop out of nowhere and grab him. For the first time, he felt scared, and for the second time, an incongruous reflection: *you only feel scared because of the horror movie likeness*.

Five bearded men in long robes and heavy boots appeared from the stairwell. They all looked to be in their mid-forties. Because Mordred's Arabic was honed, he understood when they asked him to stand up against the reception desk with his palms flat and his feet apart. They gestured, and one of them began miming it, but he cut in.

"That's okay, I speak Arabic."

He did as they asked without quibbling. They frisked him, removed the phone from his pocket and agreed amongst themselves that, apart from the mobile, he was clean.

"What's this for?" one of them asked.

"I'm here to try and negotiate some kind of peace deal," Mordred replied. "I hope what I have to offer will be acceptable, but if it isn't – if you want more – I may have to get back to someone over there to okay it. Saves me running backwards and forwards and you having to wait."

They made no reply. They didn't give him the phone back, but nor did they indicate they were confiscating it. Obviously, they weren't the negotiators. They were simply armed escorts. Armed for their safety, not his.

"Follow me," the talkative one said.

They went upstairs all the way to the top floor. They walked along a concrete floor past a series of what had once been offices until they came to a fire door at the end of the landing. Two men entered before Mordred and held the door for him. The others followed behind. It hadn't occurred to him until now, but no one had made the slightest attempt to tie him up. Surely good news.

The floor space was big enough for about twenty desks within an open-plan system, and that was obviously how it had once been laid out. Since then, much of the furniture had been chopped up and apparently - judging by the holes cut carefully into the carpet and the ingrained black soot circles - used for firewood. The remainder had been moved to the edges of the room to create an open space.

There were exactly seventeen people in the room, just like in the shop on the other side of the divide, less than an hour ago. This time, they were all men. They were seated on the floor in a horseshoe, with two elderly looking men inside it but towards the rear. They all had rifles slung over their backs like fashion accessories. They looked at Mordred in silence without smiling.

No Mabel.

A place had obviously been reserved for him in the gap between the two ends of the horseshoe. His escorts bade him sit on the floor facing everyone. As he did, he noticed a tea set between him and the two men directly opposite him, with tea already in glasses. There were also four plates of food. Everything had been laid out on a rug like a picnic.

One of the escorts brought a glass for Mordred, then offered him a pastry from a plate. He took one. He thanked his hosts and ate and drank. They did likewise. Still no one spoke.

Possible it was all drugged, or even poisoned, but he didn't think so. What would be the point? If they wanted to kill him silently, so no one on the other side of the barricades heard, they could as easily garrotte him. Anyway, to refuse it would be rude. It'd be a very bad start indeed.

As would being poisoned.

He ate a fried pasty with a spicy filling, a bit like a samosa, and drank his tea. A man came over with a teapot and gave him a refill. He said thank you. Another pasty was offered. He took it and ate, more slowly this time because he wasn't sure how long this would go on. It was a bit like being back at al-Iddrissy's again, that first night when they'd all sat watching Bollywood movies. He'd been plied with drinks then too.

And that had turned out more than okay.

*His last meal before the electric chair* suddenly flashed through his mind.

But no. The executioners didn't eat with the victims.

Although maybe they did here.

He was getting unnerved. It was the silence. He put his tea, and the plate with his half-eaten second pasty, gently on the floor in front of him. He smiled at the two elderly men opposite him and thanked them again for their hospitality. Hopefully, they'd take this as a signal to begin proceedings. He wasn't sure how much longer he could keep the eating and drinking in silence up.

"Can I now ask what you're authorised to offer us?" the old man on the left asked. Everyone in the room leaned forward just an inch as if they might miss something crucial if they didn't focus.

"Of course," Mordred replied, with relief.

"You spoke on the phone about allowing us to withdraw with honour, and you made it clear you weren't talking about our surrender. But that still leaves a lot of possibilities."

"Probably neither side – mine or yours – minds bloodshed. Well, we *mind* it, obviously, but we accept it's a concomitant of war. But neither of us wants a bloodbath. I'm pretty sure you have women and children in here."

"Including your sister."

Provocation? He ignored it. "I've persuaded the top military commanders on my side that the best chance of preventing unnecessary deaths is for us to allow you all to depart, with all your possessions, including your weapons, unmolested. Obviously, that leaves you free to fight another day, but maybe it won't come to that."

"Why wouldn't it?"

"Because maybe peace will intervene. This isn't Syria. You may not like the government in Tripoli, but it's not barrel-bombing you, and it's not averse to compromise. There's no reason for either side to get entrenched."

"What do you expect us to do once we've left?"

"In the short term, your friendly government has agreed to lay on a convoy under United Nations jurisdiction. It will take you to a camp near Murzuq in the south, from which you'll be allowed to leave at your own discretion. Or you'll be able to stay there a while. It's up to you."

"This camp will be safe? The Americans and the British won't bomb it?"

"No."

"And they won't attack us as we try to leave?"

"Only if it looks like you're on the march somewhere specific with hostile intentions. If you were to come back to Tanarej, for example, to make another takeover bid, you'd be fair game. Obviously, we can't make any deal in which you're immune to all further attack regardless of what you do."

"But otherwise? If we were to leave in small groups, for example, for different cities?"

"You'd be free to proceed. Even if you all converged on the same city, providing there was no concrete reason to think you were planning something destructive."

The men all turned to each other. For a moment, they didn't speak. The right-hand elderly man whispered something in the left's ear, solemn nods were exchanged. It was obvious a more fundamental discussion had already taken place sometime earlier, probably last night. They all knew what the alternative was, but Phyllis might be right: they might still prefer the foolhardy option, just to look manly.

"We accept your offer," the left said.

"Thank you," Mordred said. Bloody hell, whoa.

He almost asked about Mabel, but manners were everything here. He bit his tongue.

Still no one spoke.

"I would like to explain about your sister," the elderly man on the left said quietly.

Mordred felt his stomach sink. *Explain?* Bad news? "What do you mean?" he asked.

"Your sister was lured to Libya by Daesh," the man continued. "I don't know the course of events for certain, but according to what she told us, they intended to mutilate her then kill her on video. She escaped and we picked her up. We thought she was an American spy. After all, why else would Daesh broadcast her slaughter to the world? We were kinder. We gave her the choice to join us. Said Mohammad married her, which was the only way she could be incorporated into the group. We don't have solitary women here. A woman is a wife or a mother, an aunt, a cousin, a daughter or a sister. The last are all blood relations. Said Mohammad already has three wives and it was thought they could help your sister adjust to her new situation with us. Meanwhile, we asked Khartoum to help us identify her, so we might know what we were dealing with. The Sudanese took her phone apart and discovered she was the sister of famous British secret agent, John Mordred. Everything after that was Khartoum. We simply did its bidding. Now it has had… second thoughts, we are happy to release her."

*So she's still alive?* wasn't polite. Thank God, thank God.

"Where is she?" he asked.

"Downstairs."

"When can I see her?"

"You and she are free to leave."

Things were moving fast, almost too fast, and all in the right direction. He could hardly keep up. "You don't want to keep us as a guarantee of your safe passage?" It seemed absurd to mention it – might give them ideas – only it was obvious they must have considered it already.

For the first time, the elderly man almost smiled. "The British and American and the Sudanese governments have already agreed to observe the ceasefire. Several foreign ambassadors in Washington have apparently witnessed the terms. The compact simply awaits our approval, and we simply needed you personally to confirm the terms."

"Why me?"

"Because of all men on the other side, you're the only one we really trust." It was said without any attempt to make it sound like a compliment, rather as one might say, 'You've got a crumb on your lip'.

"Thank you," Mordred replied.

"Not all 'Islamists' are the same," the elderly man said, obviously the peroration. "If they were, why would we always argue? We differ in the details, but, with the exception of Daesh - a foreign novelty, and nothing to do with Libya, and may God obliterate it forever - we all want what's best for our country. What we already have works. So it has for fourteen centuries. And when something has succeeded that long, change is not good. We don't want to be like Britain or France or the United States. We dislike everything we've heard about your way of life – although it may be right for you - and we don't want it imposed on us. We want what our fathers had, and theirs before them. And we will keep fighting for it."

There were lots of dubious assumptions in there, but once again, etiquette was master: a set of unspoken expectations and taboos as rigorous and rarefied as those of ancient Japan. The correct response here was a kind of stylised expression of humility.

"I'll pass the message on," Mordred said. "Thank you again for your kindness."

They all stood up. Handshakes and embraces were exchanged – again, all purely ritualistic, nothing sentimental at all. The men who had brought Mordred in escorted him out of the room and downstairs again.

In the former reception area, a small woman in a chador and plimsolls stood waiting alone by the desk. Somehow, he recognised her immediately, although she had her back to him. She trembled like a baby bird. God knows what she thought was about to happen. This was probably the first time she'd been alone since she'd entered the country.

She was apparently alerted by the sound of footsteps and turned to look at him. It seemed to take her a moment to comprehend what she was seeing. Her mouth and eyes and nostrils seemed to flare in the same gesture.

*"John?"* She laughed humourlessly and squinted, as if trying to make sense of a dream she was in. "John, what are you doing here?"

He didn't like to embrace her – even touch her, yet. Not until she accepted he was really present. God help them both, she might be confused enough to insist on staying here.

"I've come to pick you up," he said. "Give me your hand."

She ignored the request. "Why? Where are we going?"

"Home."

She chuckled. "But you can't." Her face changed and she looked distraught. "They'll kill you."

"Give me your hand, Mabel. Please."

The utterance of her name seemed to add a new level of persuasion. Suddenly, he had three-quarters of her. He realised with a slight sickly feeling that up till now, it had been fifty-fifty at best. She slipped her fingers weakly between his. He tightened his hold slightly. Not enough to alarm her, but he didn't want any backsliding.

"Trust me," he said. "Just do one thing for me, that's all I ask. Just come with me now."

"Why?" she asked again. The same question. "Where are we going?"

He led her slowly towards the exit. The key now was to keep talking. Apparently, words gave him a reality his physical presence alone couldn't supply. As he led her through the front door, he told her about the Esk Valley railway trip they'd been on when she was ten and he was nineteen, and Whitby, and how she'd gone back four years later in her brief Goth phase, and how he had to tag along because she wasn't old enough to go on her own; and how he'd been both cool, because relatively young, and uncool, because he didn't get corsets and long black dresses and wouldn't let her out at night unaccompanied. And how Hannah had bought her *Operation* when she'd been accepted into university for a medical degree, and the whole family had played it at Christmas. And the time when …

He barely knew what he was saying, except that he flooded with emotion like he was telling himself. As for Mabel, it all seemed to go completely over her head. They crossed the wasteland like they both were in a trance. She kept stopping to look at him.

After what seemed like centuries, they reached the other side and another world. Hands reached out and pulled them in and he could feel the joy, not just his, and the relief, and even the love, and – thank you, God: I mean it, *this isn't just a turn of phrase!* – it was finally over. It was finally over.

## Chapter 25: Job Application Ref. 835

According to what Mordred heard later, the Islamists exited Tanarej entirely according to plan and then melted back into Libya. His concern now was solely with Mabel. The British army laid a plane on at Mitiga Airport to take them back to Britain. She'd hardly spoken since being rescued. She slept nearly all the time.

On the flight to London, she sat next to him and they held hands. He talked to her again about the past: family get-togethers, childhood games, shared holidays, years-ago walks in the countryside, campfires, fairground rides, mutual secrets they'd once considered fundamental. She listened carefully – she didn't seem to be in a trance any more – but without contributing much in return. Yet she was getting better; at least, she was obviously trying. Occasionally, she'd say 'I remember that' or 'yes, I enjoyed that' or 'you're right'.

As he'd half-expected since his first Libyan conversation with Alec, she was pregnant. Tests carried out in consultation with the Bouchet family doctor in Paris confirmed it wasn't Jean-Marc's. She didn't know whose it was. Daesh had gang-raped her. Or it could be Said Mohammad's. She was eight weeks gone, easily within the conventional limits for an abortion; she need only say the word.

But she didn't.

When their plane landed in London, it was raining. Just as he'd been told in Libya, there were two cars waiting on the runway to separate them for a few hours. One contained two of Mabel's MSF colleagues; the other, three unnamed intelligence officers. He had an appointment at Thames House.

It took them two hours to get there. An accident on the M4 meant a major traffic jam between Harlington and Brentford. They'd done him the courtesy of providing broadsheets on the back seat, but his three minders obviously weren't allowed to speak to him. He wiled his time away – or tried to – with *The Times* crossword. He noticed no one had thought to supply a copy of *Private Eye*. Obviously, he hadn't been entirely forgiven. If at all. They might be bringing him back for the MI7 equivalent of a cashiering.

The car pulled up on the double red lines outside Thames House and the four passengers went inside in a group. The chief minder signed Mordred in at reception and he and his two colleagues accompanied him upstairs and along five corridors. No one coming in the opposite direction spoke to him, although mostly they were people he'd worked alongside for years. They looked at the floor, or deliberately past him. He didn't bother saying hello. Who cared what they thought? The whole of London was the same. Full of people who'd blank you as soon as pick up a free newspaper. On the bus, on the tube, in shops, in parks, on the street. Ironically, people who actually thought they were cosmopolitan and compassionate because they didn't want Brexit.

To be fair, though, they must have been told he was *persona non grata*. They were nice people really. They wouldn't be acting this way if they hadn't been ordered to. Suddenly, he felt sorry for them. And London. He loved it really.

He loved everything and everyone actually. Now he'd got Mabel back, he was ready to forgive his enemies, pray for his persecutors and grab Ruby Parker and toss her in the air till she giggled with delight and the kingdom of God arrived on a pink and golden pony.

They went straight to her office. One of the men knocked, 'enter' was said, and they opened the door for him. They didn't follow him. One of them closed the door behind him.

Just as last time they met, Ruby Parker didn't dignify his entry by standing. She pretended to be doing paperwork, presumably to emphasise his humiliation.

"I'm back," he said quietly.

She looked at him. "Sit down."

He lowered himself onto the naughty chair, sat up straight and folded his hands in his lap.

"I'm just looking through your job application," she said. "*Foreign Language Analyst Reference 835*. It was faxed through this morning. I take it this *is* your doing? Not Alec's?"

"No, although he's kindly agreed to provide a reference. As has Annabel Gould."

She sighed. "How do you think you'd have fared in Libya had Fenella Decristoforo-Salvaterra not realised the danger you were in and taken steps to counter it?"

*I guess we'll never know* wouldn't work. She wasn't asking a question, not even a rhetorical one. The required response was a stylised expression of humility. Nothing new under the sun.

Sod it. "I guess we'll never know," he said.

She smiled thinly. "Well, as it happens, I've good news for you. You're hired."

"Whoa." He was genuinely surprised. "That's great."

"Oh, it gets better. I'm giving you your old job back. I'm not an egoist, and I wasn't trying to stop you going to Libya for the sake of it. I did it because I thought you were in danger of being killed. But that didn't happen. Technically, I was wrong and you were right, but luckily, you're not the kind of person who cares about scoring points. And thankfully, neither am I."

"But what about me disobeying orders?"

She hooted. "I've just offered you a job! Are you trying to talk me out of it?"

"No, but - "

"For the record, you didn't. You only left when your notice ran out, at which point you were a free agent. I don't have the authority to order ordinary citizens about. To be perfectly frank with you, I do feel I ought to give you some sort of ticking off, but I just can't find an impregnable enough angle."

"When can I start?"

"First of all, you probably need to take some time off to be with your sister."

"I just don't want you changing your mind, that's all. Sorry, I know that's a stupid thing to say, but second chances don't come along every day."

"I'll ask Felicity to bring the paperwork through for you to sign." She took a deep breath. "Look, I know this sounds like a terrible cliché, but we just can't afford to lose you."

He laughed. "Great."

"There is one other matter. It's mainly why I arranged for you to be picked up from the airport and brought straight to my office."

"Oh?"

"It's: how are you intending to explain all this to your sisters, Hannah and Charlotte? They've been very worried about you."

He'd forgotten he had at least one reason to be depressed. He leaned back. "It's a complicated one. I must admit, I was thinking of telling them the truth, only leaving out the fact that I was once employed by MI7. They'll never believe that last bit."

She pushed a grey document folder across the desk. "We've already put you a story together. Read this and learn it. You'll all be summoned for a meeting at the Foreign and Commonwealth Office tomorrow morning at ten. By 'all', I mean you, Charlotte, Hannah and Mabel."

"And the reason for that's explained … in here?"

"I'll give you the potted version now. Out of nowhere, Mabel's kidnappers contacted you by phone asking for a ransom. You found out from MSF that she'd gone to Libya on a wild goose chase. Years ago, you'd been on a backpacking jaunt, and that was one of the places you visited. - We know that's true, incidentally: it's in your CV. - In any case, you thought you could combine your expert grasp of Arabic with your admittedly superficial knowledge of the country, and launch an amateur rescue bid. When you got there, you discovered someone you'd met whilst backpacking was amongst the kidnappers. You'd drawn all your money out of your bank account and changed it to US dollars, and this man ensured a smooth transaction: cash for captive. With

Mabel back, you made contact with the British army in Sirte, who flew you home."

"Sounds reasonably hole-free. Why do we all have to go to the FCO?"

"You've got a special audience with the Principal Private Secretary to the Secretary of State for Foreign and Commonwealth Affairs."

"'The secretary to the secretary'?"

"I didn't invent the job title. It goes back to 1822."

"A meeting for what purpose?"

"Isn't it obvious? You're going to be told – entirely for the benefit of your sisters – that you did an excellent job extracting your sister, but that HM government wants to discourage gung-ho attempts by unqualified private citizens to resolve hostage-situations abroad. Therefore, you won't be getting any state recognition, and the media will be kept entirely in the dark about your achievement. The FCO would appreciate your understanding and full cooperation. Well done, thank you and goodbye."

"Ruthless but apparently reasonable."

"If Hannah and Charlotte look like demurring – unlikely, but we've got to consider every eventuality - we expect you to come in on the side of the FCO. You don't want any publicity, you certainly don't want Mabel pestered by newspaper editors, and so on. I'm sure it won't come to that. They're both highly intelligent women."

"What about Phyllis?"

"What do you mean?"

"Can she have her job back?"

"I can't think of any reason to say no. But we must let her decide. For all we know, she might find she likes the freedom of being on the outside."

"I bloody hope not. What about Horvath? I assume you'll be taking a drill to the root now?"

"Good God, no. It's an idiot-magnet. Every dangerous moron who wants an iff-y job doing in London makes a bee-line for it. We'd make life ten times more difficult for ourselves if we liquidated it. No, we'll let Paul Ayton and Malcolm Rhys-Dwyer off with a slap on the wrists, and hope they don't decide to chuck it all in and take up orchid growing."

"What a loss to the nation that would be."

"And entirely uncompensated-for by any gain to the RHS."

It was the first time he'd ever heard her crack anything approaching a joke. As witticisms went, it wasn't great, but it was a start.

Perhaps in the wrong direction. He didn't know what a joke-cracking Ruby Parker would look like. Probably difficult to work with. Like him.

"You're free to go now," she said. "There's a car waiting for you outside. It'll take you straight to Mabel. You've a month off work. Learn the fine detail of the story in that folder and call your older sisters. I'm pretty sure they'll be amazed. The FCO will contact you all before the end of the day."

On his way out, everyone smiled and said hello. He wondered how news of his rehabilitation had travelled so fast.

Then he realised: he was no longer accompanied by minders.

Obvious, really. And slightly depressing.

## Chapter 26: The Traditional Epiloguey Thing

The baby – a boy - would never find out exactly where he'd come from, nor would his adoptive parents. Not even Mabel knew the complete truth, although she knew enough. Judith and Esther were her revenge – 'better than an abortion' - although, as payback went, it looked, to others, thin fare. A middle-aged lesbian couple, married in 2015, who subscribed to all the classical liberal values: pacifism, universal human rights, multiculturalism, feminism, gay pride. They and Mabel made no arrangements to stay in touch, and it was tacitly understood this signified a concrete undertaking in favour of the opposite.

Throughout the time she was pregnant and being looked after at home, she maintained she'd seen such horror in Syria and elsewhere that she didn't feel entitled to dwell on her own. It paled in comparison.

Of course, this wouldn't do. She suffered nightmares, sleeplessness, suicidal moods, clinical depression, episodes of self-harming, on top of all the bodily trauma of pregnancy. Eventually, after much heated discussion, she agreed to attend a support group for rape victims. Then Hannah had a seemingly trivial insight. Her family was too old for her to properly identify with. Julia, the second youngest, was seven years older than her. She needed the company of people of her own age. University friends, MSF colleagues.

This proved to be another milestone on her road to partial recovery. The next was the birth. The social worker had arranged for the baby to go straight from the delivery room to his adopters. Mabel came home, rested for two days, then took her already-packed bags and spent the next fortnight on retreat in Holy Cross Abbey in Pembrokeshire. She walked in the countryside, sat alone, attended prayers, read devotional works, conversed with Cistercian nuns. Her family half-expected she'd do something awful to herself, but it was agreed they couldn't watch over her forever. To go on retreat was her decision. They had to accept it and leave her alone.

Mordred had returned to work by this time and moved back into his old flat. He rang home every night for news, but there wasn't any. Which was good in a way: the nuns knew something of her situation, and said they'd keep an eye on her.

One night at seven o'clock, just before the end of the two weeks in retreat, there was a knock at his front door. Phyllis and he were sitting on his sofa sharing freshly cooked pasta from a pan.

"Are you expecting someone?" she asked.

He got up and looked through the spyhole. Then opened the door. Hannah, Mabel and Charlotte. What the - ?

*"Surprise!"* they all said. They wore their usual clothes: Hannah the neo-hippy, Charlotte the zip-up plus slacks combo, Mabel a peasant-style smock and woollen tights. Only, all with overcoats.

"Is Phyll in?" Hannah asked.

"Can we come inside?" Charlotte asked, as if there was a real possibility they might be turned away.

As usual, Mordred had no idea how they'd got past the outer gate. This place was supposed to be secure. But who cared? Mabel was here, and apparently okay. Yet he could tell from their voices something was wrong.

Phyllis and Hannah exchanged hugs, then Phyllis and Charlotte, then he introduced Mabel to Phyllis and they shook hands. They all came in and sat down.

"Anyone fancy a cup of mushroom soup?" he asked.

"Real?" Hannah said.

"Er, no," he replied.

"We're all meeting at Indridason's in forty minutes," Charlotte said. "It's a vegetarian restaurant in Piccadilly. You've got to come."

"Who's 'we'?" Mordred asked.

"Us three, you two, hubbies, kids, Julia and Knut, and Mum and Dad. It's a last farewell meal. Mabel's flying out to Italy tomorrow. She's going back to MSF."

The cue for a deathly silence. It was clear Hannah and Charlotte had been shouldering the information uncomfortably for some time before they got here, and now they stood back to let it spread its horrible tentacles out.

"Are you sure that's a good idea?" Mordred asked.

Mabel looked at him. There was a new assurance in her expression, something he hadn't seen for nearly a year.

"I'm absolutely convinced it's the only way I'm going to get over this," she said. "Don't get me wrong, I'm most of the way there now. I'm not going to be postnatally depressed, I'm pretty sure of that, and I need to go back to doing what I'm good at; what gives my life purpose. Thank you for coming to get me, John, you were amazing. You still are. And I'm not going away for ever, obviously. This time, I'll be coming home under my own steam. In about six months."

He beamed. Mature, well thought-through, perfect. "Bloody hell, that's great."

"You don't think it's a bit early?" Hannah said in a superficially breezy tone that left him in no doubt she was expressing the official family line and he was expected to toe it, or else.

"Nope," he said.

She looked incredulous for a moment, as if she couldn't believe he was so stupid. Then she laughed. For some reason, it had taken just one word to demolish her conviction. She got up, put her hand on her chin and seemed to look inside herself. Her face filled with emotion. She fanned herself.

"I can't get over thinking of you as a little kiddie," she told Mabel. "I'm sorry. You're an intelligent adult. Obviously, you are."

"That's okay," Mabel replied. "I can't get over thinking of you three as pensioners."

They laughed, more with relief that she'd tried to introduce humour than because what she'd said was funny. It wasn't... particularly. Yet it wasn't forced either. It came freely and spontaneously, as if somehow integral. She was finally starting to be okay.

It proved to be a turning point. Twenty minutes later, they all set off through the frosty night air for Piccadilly. The husbands – Tim and Seth – and their two infants, plus Julia and Knut, and both parents were there already. They ate and drank and caught up on work, relationships, holidays, life. Phyllis discussed Netflix and summer holidays with Hannah. Mordred sat with Julia and Knut and talked Norwegian. No one argued about Brexit or even recalled it existed.

Afterwards, they stayed at a hotel in five separate rooms Hannah had booked for their 'last night together', as if it was the end of the world. They wandered in and out of each other's till two o'clock in the morning, drinking, pranking, baby-amusing, gossiping, swapping jokes, playing cards, and – since it was the low season and the rooms and floors on all sides were unoccupied - singing karaoke.

It *wasn't* the end of the world, not at all. When they finally turned in to sleep, they all agreed Hannah had been premature.

In a universe of second chances, it was just another beginning.

## Acknowledgements

I used several sources to write this book. Not all of them influenced it because they confirmed things I already knew. Those listed below had a significant impact on its shape, and in some cases, even preconditioned its coming into being at all.

The description of the *Médecins Sans Frontières* ship in chapter one is taken from Patrick Kingsley's excellent *The New Odyssey: The Story of Europe's Refugee Crisis* (Faber & Faber 2016), specifically – for those who are interested - pages 137-152. The character of Walid al-Iddrissy is also very loosely based on "Hajj", a Libyan people-smuggler who appears on page 57 onwards of Kingsley's book. Tanarej is a fictionalised counterpart of Zuwara – roughly what and how I imagine such a town *could be* based on Mr Kingsley's rudimentary descriptions. For the purposes of this novel, an imperfect approximation was all I needed.

Robert F Worth's *A Rage For Order: The Middle East in Turmoil From Tahrir Square to ISIS* (Picador 2016) was helpful in envisaging the internal situation in Libya in the aftermath of the Arab Spring, but also in drawing connections to developments in Syria and neighbouring Egypt. Wolfgang Bauer's *Crossing The Sea With Syrians on the Exodus to Europe* (And Other Stories, 2016) showed, in concrete terms, how Egypt has recently become much more inhospitable to Syrians, meaning that the majority of migrants reaching Libya in 2016 are from countries like Eritrea, Mali and Niger, rather than the middle east, a matter also explored by Kingsley. This is, of course, why Mordred is going the "wrong way" in the first paragraph of chapter one: he is following the newest main migrant-route. Mabel is still involved with the old one.

Oxford University post-doctoral researcher Brian Quinn's 2015 paper, 'Debunking three dangerous myths about the conflict in Libya', helped me avoid some of the more telling clichés about the country. I was particularly struck by the memorable claim of an anonymous 'Misratan commander' concerning Libya's

Islamists: "Some of the groups are more conservative but they believe in democracy, which is all that matters to me. Besides, I would say most are less religiously conservative than the Republicans in the US Congress".

Paolo Sensini's *Sowing Chaos: Libya in the Wake of Humanitarian Intervention* (Clarity Press, 2016) gave valuable background on the history of Libya pre-2011, although it also defends the highly controversial thesis that Gaddafi was, throughout his tenure, a popular leader in Libya, only unseated by NATO because he represented a threat to Western – particularly US - hegemony. The book contains a glowing preface by former US Congresswoman, Cynthia McKinney. I do not know enough to say definitively whether Sensini's thesis is false, but Robert F Worth's first-hand account, in the text mentioned above, of meeting former torturers, seeing former torture chambers and hearing tales of persecution first-hand from Gaddafi-era Libyan denizens makes me suspicious, to say the least. Interested readers can make their own judgements, in which McKinney's *The Illegal War on Libya* (Clarity Press 2012) should probably also be called to the witness stand.

By far the most useful research document for *Libya Story* was a 2016 paper published online by The European Council on Foreign Relations entitled, 'A Quick Guide to Libya's Main Players' and almost entirely penned by the Tripoli-based journalist and analyst, Mary Fitzgerald. This is an outstanding and highly up-to-date overview of the entire situation in Libya, and, for brevity and clarity, probably cannot be bettered. This paper discusses the fact, employed in my novel, that "The relationship between Tobruk and Egypt is not just defined by significant arms deliveries but also by a shared political project: eradicating political Islam and enhancing the autonomy of eastern Libya … Having Cyrenaica – the eastern region of Libya – under the role of a leader that is friendly to Egypt – Haftar for instance – would create a buffer zone with ISIS and a territorial hinterland for any opposition to the regime in Cairo." The paper also notes that Egypt has put out two statements that contradict this position.

As regards the last section of the novel, *Private Eye* magazine has published a number of reports this year detailing the extent of British and American special forces involvement in Libya and elsewhere in the region. In the public interest, and because *Private Eye*'s website is so limited – it contains no records of its weekly journalism - the author has published copies of those reports on facebook.com/talesofmi7.

JW October 2016

# Books by James Ward

**General Fiction**

*The House of Charles Swinter*
*The Weird Problem of Good*
*The Bright Fish*
*Hannah and Soraya's Fully Magic Generation-Y *Snowflake* Road Trip across America*

**The Original Tales of MI7**

*Our Woman in Jamaica*
*The Kramski Case*
*The Girl from Kandahar*
*The Vengeance of San Gennaro*

**The John Mordred Tales of MI7 books**

*The Eastern Ukraine Question*
*The Social Magus*
*Encounter with ISIS*
*World War O*
*The New Europeans*
*Libya Story*
*Little War in London*
*The Square Mile Murder*
*The Ultimate Londoner*
*Death in a Half Foreign Country*
*The BBC Hunters*
*The Seductive Scent of Empire*
*Humankind 2.0*
*Ruby Parker's Last Orders*

**Poetry**

*The Latest Noel*
*Metals of the Future*

**Short Stories**

*An Evening at the Beach*
*Wadhurst Ghost Stories*

**Philosophy**

*21st Century Philosophy*
*A New Theory of Justice and Other Essays*

www.ingramcontent.com/pod-product-compliance
Ingram Content Group UK Ltd.
Pitfield, Milton Keynes, MK11 3LW, UK
UKHW041953190726
13854UKWH00005B/1937